SECOND CHANCE

BY
DEREK MUSE

This book is dedicated to my wife and best friend Emily, who's countless hours of listening, encouraging, and helping with editing have made this book so much more than it ever would have been.

CHAPTER 1

A SUDDEN NOISE THAT sounded like distant rifle shots resounded like a thousand-gun salute in Austin's head. Those loud crackling sounds were followed immediately by the deafening reverberations of huge chunks of ice grinding and splintering as they tumbled down the frozen incline just behind Austin. The exaggerated interpretation of the sudden auditory input was understandable because Austin's mind was numb from the compounded effects of the freezing temperature, acute mountain sickness, exhaustion, and lack of oxygen from breathing thin air. Austin froze, sure that the tumultuous cascade of ice that he could only hear, but not see, would at any moment sweep him off his feet and down the mountain to his death.

However, as the seconds ticked by and the sound of the tumbling and sliding ice came to a stop, Austin thanked his lucky stars that he was still alive. He licked his cracked and bleeding lips nervously as he turned behind him to see how close the avalanche had come. The ice fall was nowhere to be seen. It had seemed so close. What did he expect? He and his buddies were hiking to the summit of Mount Rainier, Washington, in near white-out conditions. The current conditions were so extreme that an appearance by the Abominable Snowman wouldn't have surprised him one bit at the moment.

Austin and his two buddies were about an hour above the Emmons glacier on the Muir-Deception Cleaver route to the summit of Mount Rainier. This section of the trail was supposed to have been less dangerous part of the route. They had already passed the much more dangerous Disappointment Cleaver, where more than one climber over the years had come to their untimely end in rockslides and avalanches.

A strong tug on the rope that attached him at the waist to the closest of his two rope mates yanked him out of his reverie and refocused his attention on the barely discernable tracks ahead. The discomfort of the jerk on the rope reminded him of the painfully obvious: He was holding his two fellow climbers back. As exhausted, cold, and scared as he was, he knew he couldn't continue the attempt to reach the summit. Half of the 10,000 climbers that attempted the summit of Mount Rainier each year didn't succeed, and now he was going to be one of them. He should have felt embarrassed that his hiking buddies were going to have to leave him behind, but he was too weak to care. They were going to have to stuff him into his sleeping bag and then stake him to the snow on a less steep part of the trail. There he would wait until another party that was returning from the summit could help him back down.

The first half of summer had been full of excitement and anticipation for Austin as he and his two climbing partners, Nick and Seth, had planned and trained to summit Mount Rainier in September. Even though they were first-timers, they had done their homework by reading a number of climber's accounts of successful and failed attempts to summit Mount Rainier. They had trimmed their packs to fifty-pounds each, leaving plenty of room for water.

Two days ago, the trio had risen early and had hopped into Seth's SUV. They had spent that day at Camp Muir, the base camp for their route. Retiring early, they had gotten three hours of sleep and then had awakened and left for the summit at 1:00 a.m. Even though it had been dark, with the aid of a moonlit sky and with their head lamps, they had made excellent progress. But, by midday, the wind had picked up, and the snow squalls had started. Their rate of ascent had slowed to a snail's pace. The cold, wind, and elevation had taken their toll, especially on Austin. He was five years older than the other two men, and he was also thirty pounds overweight. He really shouldn't have come on the hike.

A dark shape appeared directly ahead of him in the snow. As it drew closer, he recognized that it was Nick. Nick came close and yelled in his ear above the roar of the wind, "Are you okay?"

Austin wanted so badly to say that he wasn't okay, but something inside just wouldn't let him admit defeat to his friend. Trying to hide his shortness of breath and exhaustion, he said, "This is really hard. But, if I rest for a bit, I think I can do it."

Just then, as if the gods of the mountain had decided to reward him for all his heroic efforts, the snow thinned a little, and the wind slacked up. Seth's snow-frosted shape slowly came into view from farther up the mountain.

Seth was carefully working his way back down the trail toward them. As soon as Seth was within earshot, he yelled, "Are you guys okay?"

"We're okay," Nick said.

The snow continued to let up even more, and glimpses of the summit began to appear behind Seth in the distance. Nick said, "Look behind you. You can see the summit. I had no idea that we were so close."

The three men turned their gaze to the summit as the snow stopped falling, the wind died to a whisper, and the sun shone faintly through the thinning clouds. Mount Rainier's summit glistened gloriously in the light of day, just a few hundred yards away.

With renewed vigor, the men trudged through the glistening white, powdery snow for the next twenty minutes, unable to stop with their goal so tantalizingly near. Finally, out of breath and nearing exhaustion, they reached the summit. Without a word, Austin flopped onto his back on the snow at the lip of the crater. Nick crashed down beside him but stayed seated.

Remaining on his feet, Seth scanned the horizon and then said, "Look, guys, we're above the clouds." Panting even from the effort of speaking, he stopped to catch his breath. "You can see all the way to Mount Baker."

Standing up to take a look, Nick said, "That's really cool."

"Hey, do you guys feel that?" Austin exclaimed from where he lay on the snow.

"What?" Seth asked.

"There it is again," Austin said. "I swear this mountain is moving, like we're having an earthquake."

"I don't feel anything," Nick said. "Austin, quit lying there and come and check out how high we are above—"

Some small rocks from the top of the crater suddenly broke loose. They rolled and slid down the steep slope of ice that led into the crater, coming to rest near the center.

"See? The mountain is moving," Austin said.

"Okay," Seth said. "I do feel some shaking now that my legs aren't so numb from the climb." He paused for a moment and then continued, "And now… it's gone. We just experienced a little earthquake. It's no big deal."

"How do you know it's no big deal?" Nick asked.

"Because I know," Seth said. "Earthquakes happen up here all the time, but nothing ever comes of them." Seth pointed to another section of the wall of the crater that was directly across from where they were standing and continued, "The real top of Mount Rainier is on top of that little section of the wall of the crater. It is 14,410 feet above sea level. Since I might never be back, I want to be able to say that I really made it to the top of Mount Rainer." As he spoke,

Seth had already started to walk across the snow-filled crater toward his goal. "You guys coming?" he called back over his shoulder.

"I'm there, dude," Nick said as he followed Seth.

"I'm coming, too," Austin said as he forced his tired body back into a vertical position. No way was he going to be outdone by the others.

Halfway across the expanse of snow and ice that filled the crater on top of Mount Rainier, the mountain began shaking more intensely. The ice and snow in the crater cracked and splintered all around the three men. The previously flat surface of the snow field rapidly became marred by yawning crevasses and jutting hummocks of ice. Much larger chunks of rock fell from the side walls of the crater to the crater floor, landing with heavy thuds all around them. Grave concern etched the men's faces as they crouched instinctively close to the surface of the snow with their arms outstretched in an effort to keep their balance. Their efforts were in vain as a particularly nasty lurch knocked all three of them to the ground. Austin let out a cry of pain as he landed wrong on his outstretched right arm, but his exclamation was drowned out by the massive cacophony of shattering ice.

CHAPTER 2

RICK JONES WOKE with a start. It took a full second for him to slowly comprehend that he was safely seated in the economy section of an airplane in a window seat. During that second, with his heart pounding out of his chest, he had slowed awakened from a dream in which he and his high-school girlfriend, Sally McBride, had been in an earthquake during which Sally had fallen off the edge of a cliff to her certain death. At first he had been gripped by the tragedy of losing Sally, then he had been unsure if it had really happened and finally he had been grateful to realize that it had all been a bad dream. The plane bounced a few more times. Turbulence must have been what had awakened him. He shook his head to try to clear the final vestiges of sleep-induced stupor. A quick glance to his right revealed that the male passenger seated next to him was calmly reading a book like the turbulence had never happened. Rick sighed. *Why don't other people have troubling dreams like I just had?*

Rick jumped as the overhead speaker just above his head suddenly blared, "Ladies and gentlemen, this is your captain speaking. We have a real treat for you today. The cloud cover over Mount

Rainier has just blown off, giving those on the left of the plane a wonderful view of the glacier on top."

Rick had flown on this flight from Chicago to Seattle too many times to be impressed. Mount Rainier was beautiful enough, but he had been looking at it for years from his house in southwest Seattle, at least every time the skies had been clear.

Rick glanced out the window at his side. He was surprised to see that the plane was much closer to Mount Rainier than any flight he had been on in the past. The pilot hadn't been exaggerating when he said that they would have a wonderful view.

CHAPTER 3

THE MOUNTAIN FELL completely silent. Austin opened his eyes and shot his head up from where he lay spread-eagle and face down on the ice. Fear gripped his chest as he immediately noticed the mouth of a deep crevasse in the ice just to his right. The crevasse extended in front of him and across the path that he and the others had been following across the summit. Nick was lying spread-eagle in front of him. Where Seth had been walking moments just before there was now a yawning crevasse.

"Nick, where's Seth?" Austin cried out.

Nick rolled over and looked back at Austin. "I don't know. He's probably in the crevasse."

"So he's dead?" Austin said.

"We won't know until we look. Hopefully, the mountain will hold still long enough for us to take a look and then get out of here." Nick slowly got up and then started edging toward the lip of the crevasse.

"Don't fall over the edge."

"It looks pretty stable." Nick carefully approached the edge of the crevasse and then looked down. "I can't see anything. There's a lot of mist down there."

Austin heard the sound of a jet behind him and briefly looked over his shoulder. It was just some airliner that was approaching the top of the mountain for a flyby look. He turned back to Nick, who was still peering over the edge, trying to find Seth. "Come back, Nick. It's too dangerous."

A roaring sound louder than a hundred jet engines at full throttle burst out of the crevasse, followed by a blast of super-hot steam, sending Nick's body tumbling backward. Nick landed in a heap right in front of Austin. Nick's face had been almost completely scoured of flesh down to the bare bone. His eyes had been scalded until the lids were gone and the corneas were opaque. His tongue was bright red and lolled between the molars on one side of his open and lipless mouth. Austin covered his ears in pain as the roaring sound increased even more. Legs weak with terror, he sank to his knees at Nick's side. The ice under him began to shake and he felt so heavy that he couldn't help but sprawl flat on top of Nick's still steaming body. Barely able to lift a finger, he knew in an instant that he was pinned to the ice because the chunk of mountain that he was on was being accelerating at many times the force of gravity straight into the air. Mercifully, he lost consciousness before he took his next breath, since the breath his body finally did take was a breath of superheated steam that instantly cooked Austin's lungs.

CHAPTER 4

THE SUDDEN AND completely uncharacteristic change in the pitch of the engines as the plane banked sharply to the right and began climbing scared the wits out of Rick. Screams from the other passengers filled the cabin. Most of the starboard overhead luggage compartments popped open, and some pieces of heavy luggage began pelting the hapless passengers on the left side of the plane. The guy next to Rick took a direct hit to the head from a full-sized, fiberglass carry-on. His head slumped lifelessly at an unnatural angle on his chest.

With great effort, Rick turned to look out his window. Where he expected to see Mount Rainier, there was instead just a huge, billowing mass of gray clouds, lit internally here and there by an almost constant barrage of lightening. It only took a moment for Rick to realize that the cloud of ash was rapidly closing the gap between it and plane. They weren't going to make it. To Rick's eye, it looked like the eruption would overtake the plane in less than a minute at their present speed.

With his imminent death staring him directly in the face and with his chest painfully tightening in apprehension, Rick closed his eyes. If he had just taken another flight. But if he had taken an earlier flight, then he would have already arrived in Seattle and would be right in the path of the eruption.

The realization that his mother was stuck alone in the house they shared in Seattle, right in the path of the eruption, hit Rick hard. Rick had lived with his mother in her house for the past ten years to help care for her because of her advanced multiple sclerosis (MS). He had arranged for a neighbor to check on her frequently while he was away on this business trip. With the ash cloud approaching ever closer to the plane, he knew that his mother would never see him alive again. What would his mother do without him there to help her?

The pilot's voice began blaring from the speaker just above Rick, but Rick barely paid him any attention as he couldn't take his eyes off the rapidly approaching eruption. "Fellow passengers, Mount Rainier has erupted. We can't outrun the blast. I'm sorry that—" The pilot's voice cut out and at the same time the cabin was filled with the deafening sound of debris striking the fuselage of the plane. Everything outside Rick's window went gray. The lights in the plane went out and a second later the emergency lights came on. Rick was sure that the engines had stopped cold as soon as the debris from the eruption had hit them. He was amazed that none of the windows had been broken in the cabin by the flying debris. It felt to Rick that the plane was still accelerating upward, although it was hard to tell with the plane being tossed around like a toy by the clouds of roiling ash.

He tried to look around him in the dim light provided by the emergency lighting, but it was too dark to make out much. Most of the nearby passengers were either bent over at the waist with their hands over their ears or were slumped forward and not moving at all, like the poor guy next to him.

Moments later, Rick felt himself become weightless, signaling that the plane had stopped accelerating upward and now was now dropping. Rick had no doubt that death would come quickly in the next few minutes. He just wished that he knew that his mother was going to be all right.

A massive jolt bounced the plane straight up in the air, smacking Rick's head forcibly against the side of the plane and almost knocking him out. Barely conscious, Rick felt the plane came down hard again and then he saw the front of the plane break off from the tail section he was in starting five rows ahead of where he was seated. Catching on something, the tail section slowed to a stop. The forward part of the plane kept going, and it rotated into the maelstrom until it was lost to view. Rick allowed his head to fall against the headrest of his seat and he lost consciousness.

Rick opened his eyes, not sure how long he had been out and not sure for a second if he were even still alive. The tail section of the plane was completely devoid of any human movement or sound and was tilted slightly to the left side. Moments later, a severe shooting pain on the left side of his head immediately announced to him that he was still very much among the living. He rubbed the left side of his head as he looked around the cabin. A haze of dust hung in the air, along with a sulfur smell that burned his throat when he breathed. The scant light from the emergency floor lighting wasn't helping much. The roar of the eruption passing by the open fuselage five rows in front of him was deafening. *Why aren't the superheated and poisonous gasses rushing into the cabin? This doesn't make any sense. Maybe it is because the open part of the cabin is downwind.* Whatever the explanation, Rick was grateful that the rushing rocks and dust were staying put.

He saw a hint of movement in the aisle seat of the row just ahead of him on the other side of the plane. "Hey!" he called out. "Are you okay up there?"

"I think so," a woman said faintly.

"Have you talked to anyone else?"

"I can't hear you," the woman yelled back.

Rick unfastened his seatbelt, stood up and looked at his row mates. Both weren't moving, and their heads were bent forward unnaturally. Rick was pretty sure they were dead, but he still gently shook each one as he passed to be certain. They didn't respond at all. Once in the aisle, he could see clearly where the floor of the cabin ended just fifteen feet in front of him. All he could see beyond that was a wall of swirling ash and rock.

Crouching next to the still-seated female he had tried to converse with, he again asked, "Have you talked to anyone else?"

"No. No one is responding in my row. They're either dead or unconscious."

"What's happening?" a male voice demanded from a few rows back.

Turning to the voice, Rick answered, "The plane crash-landed and tore apart. The front of the plane is gone. Are you okay?"

"I think my leg is broken. I can't get up. Otherwise, I'm okay."

Higher-pitched moaning came from one of the front rows at the same time that someone began coughing in the very back of the plane.

The person finished his coughing jag just as Rick was moving toward the front rows to try to assist a women that started calling for help. A hoarse voice came from the rear of the plane. "Hold on a minute." Rick turned to the back of the plane. A dimly-lit, tall, masculine figure materialized in front of him and said, "Don't you think it's strange that superheated toxic gasses, dust, and rocks are flying past the opening in the fuselage at hundreds of miles an hour, but nothing is hitting the plane like it did when the eruption first overtook the plane? Even stranger, almost nothing is getting into the cabin."

"Yeah, I did notice that, but I can't explain it," Rick said. Now that he thought about it, the speeding rocks from the eruption were no longer striking the side of the plane. That was even more strange. The woman in front moaned again, and Rick turned back to the front seats as he said, "Excuse me. I'm going to check on the woman up there. Tell me your name."

"I'm Kurt. Don't get too close to the gasses. I'm sure they're hot enough to cook you instantly."

Rick was far enough toward the front that he didn't reply. Instead, he followed the moaning to a woman that was hunched forward in her seat, her shoulders shuddering like she was sobbing. She was in the very front remaining row. Bent forward like she was, her head was just inches from the wall of swirling rock and ash.

"Ma'am, can I help you?"

The woman sat up slowly. "I am so sick." She leaned back over quickly, and her shoulders started heaving again. Besides being sick, she seemed to be okay.

Rick turned his attention to the wall of flying ash and rock just in front of him. The products of the eruption were rushing past the front of the plane at a tremendous speed, but none of the ash and rocks were entering the cabin. The wall of ash was at least a foot farther in front of the wrecked fuselage than would possibly be expected if the left side of the wrecked plane were protecting them from the eruption. In addition, the wall of ash was completely flat and stable in its position. It wasn't receding or encroaching on the cabin even a tiny bit.

A large rock hurtled into view, heading straight toward Rick. Lurching to one side, he tried to get out of the path of the rock, but he was too late. However, instead of the speeding rock entering the cabin and killing him and most of the other survivors instantly, the speeding rock disappeared in an instant into the surface of the wall of ash. There was no sound or jolt from the impact. The rock just disappeared. His heart still pounding, Rick faced the wall of ash again and forced himself to relax. *Something unnatural is going on here. Whatever phenomenon is keeping the ash from entering the open end of the plane also explains why the rocks from the eruption are no longer striking the fuselage. As crazy as it seems, it is like there is an impenetrable shield around the whole plane.*

Unable to help himself, he reached out and tenuously put his hand up toward the invisible barrier in front of him. As his hand approached it, he perceived no warmth or even the slightest draft of wind from the eruption.

"I wouldn't do that if I were you," Kurt said from right behind him.

"It's okay. Something is protecting us, and I want to know what it is." Rick extended his hand further and went to touch the invisible barrier, but instantly the whole wall of rushing ash and rock jumped a foot farther away from him. Shocked, he quickly pulled his hand back.

"God is protecting us," the woman said that had been vomiting.

"Like he even exists," Kurt said.

"Oh, he exists, whether you acknowledge him or not," a new male voice said from behind the tall man.

Ignoring them all and concentrating on the wall, Rick said, "Something doesn't want me to touch the barrier."

"Whoever put it there is helping us survive this eruption." It was the younger woman with long hair that had been sitting just in front of Rick. "And, whoever that person is, they know we can't stay in this airplane forever. Try touching it again," she said. "I bet it moves out of your reach again. I think they are expecting us to get out of the plane and save ourselves under the protection of their force field."

Rick turned to Kurt behind him and said, "Hold my hand." Then, leaning out past the torn edge of the floor, he again tried to touch the invisible barrier. Again, it moved another foot out of his reach. Looking down, he could see where the bottom of the fuselage was resting on the ground, about five feet below the floor he was standing on. The luggage compartment below was a jumbled mess of open luggage and its contents. Looking beyond the fuselage at each side of the open end of the plane, he could now see that the invisible barrier extended around the plane. With alarm, he noticed that the invisible barriers were holding back three to four feet of ash and rock and that the depth of the ash was visibly rising. "Pull me back."

As Kurt pulled him back and Rick turned to face him, Rick noticed that there were now four more people standing behind Kurt. It was good to see that at least a few others had survived the crash. However, there were probably even more survivors that were too seriously hurt to stand. *While helping them is a priority, discovering a way out of the wrecked plane is even a greater priority at this point. Otherwise, why save anyone if they're all just going to end up entombed in ash?*

"Doesn't it bother you that we crashed less than a minute after the lead edge of the eruption hit us?" Kurt said. "We had been flying at an altitude that was above the top of Mount Rainier at over fourteen thousand feet. When the blast wave hit us, it lifted us even higher, and then moments later, we crashed. The plane never had time to fall fourteen thousand feet to the ground. The only explanation is that we have crash landed onto something that is at least ten thousand feet above sea level."

"Maybe it's Glacier Peak," the woman in the forward most row said. "It's only about fifty miles north of Rainier, and it's pretty high."

"I don't think there was enough time for us to travel that far," Kurt said.

Rick said, "I'm going down to check this force field thing out. The ash is quickly building up around the plane. We've got to find shelter somewhere before the ash covers us over completely and we suffocate." Kurt helped Rick to lower himself carefully over the torn edge of the floor. Rick used an upright piece of luggage to step down to the floor of the luggage compartment.

Needing answers quickly, Rick wasted no time in moving from floor of the luggage compartment onto the ground in front of the open end of the fuselage. Approaching the wall of ash, he noted that the ash and rock on the other side of the wall were now at shoulder level. There was just enough light to see that rock and ash were still striking the invisible barrier higher up. Although it was hard to tell in the dim light, it still seemed like the rocks that were striking the protective wall weren't bouncing off the wall but were just disappearing into the wall.

With concern, Rick noticed that the ash on the left side of the plane was already piled above his head, which meant it was deeper than six feet. *How had the invisible barrier moved so easily against the tons of ash and rock that were piled up against it?* Determined to find out what was going on, he reached out to the wall of ash in front of him. It moved away from him just like it had previously. Emboldened, he walked up to the wall with his hands outstretched. The wall moved ahead of him and remained always just out of his reach. The rock and ash beyond the wall didn't bunch up like it would have if it had been pushed by a bulldozer. It just disappeared. He stopped walking after about fifteen paces, suddenly concerned that the force field, or whatever it was, would collapse behind him, cutting him off from the others. He hurried back to the open end of the wrecked plane.

"What did you find?" the woman from the row in front of him said. In the dim light, he could see that she was about average height and had long hair that hung to her shoulders.

"Excuse me. What is your name?" Rick asked.

"Amanda."

"Thanks, Amanda. I found that the barrier, or wall, kept moving in front of me. I went about thirty feet and then came back because I didn't want to lose sight of the plane."

"Should we join you down there?" Amanda asked.

"We have to find shelter," Rick said. "Whatever is maintaining this force field has got to be nearby. I could use help in searching for it."

Rick's request galvanized the group of survivors. Assisting each other, they began carefully climbing down the raw edges of the torn fuselage to where Rick was standing.

"Wait for me." It was the man with the broken leg. He was using the seat backs and his good leg to move himself down the aisle toward the open end of the plane. When he got to the forward edge of the floor where there were no more chair backs to support him, he lowered himself to the floor and sat there, grunting in pain. Seeing that there was no way he was going to be able join them on his own, two men helped him over the edge. Rick and Kurt guided him to the ground. Once they had him safely on the ground, and the rest of the survivors were on the ground, Rick asked one of the first two men to act as the injured man's support.

Turning away from the plane to address the group, Rick said, "Why don't a few of you start searching?" Instead of paying attention to him, he saw that all of their eyes were locked in terror at something just behind him and over his head. Sure that a massive rock was moving toward his head like before, he ducked and wheeled just in time to see the open fuselage of the plane behind him lifting in the air. Faint screams from injured passengers that hadn't been able to exit the cabin could be heard as the plane slid out of sight off of what had to be the edge of a cliff.

Silence struck the group. Risk was hit hard by the knowledge that his life would have ended with his fellow passengers if he had stayed on the plane.

The first to speak was the older-looking gentleman that had defended his belief that God was protecting them. "God giveth, and God taketh away. May they enter into his rest."

"Amen," added a few others.

"Why does everything have to do with God?" It was Kurt. "God didn't have anything to do with whether those people lived or died. They're just dead. End of life and story. No one's souls are resting happily anywhere."

"Come on, guys," the woman from the front row said. "Let's

give it a rest. We need to concentrate on finding someplace safe to weather out this eruption."

"We seem to be safe enough now," another middle-aged male said. Rick was frustrated that the light was so dim that he could barely make out the survivor's faces.

Kurt said, "See any food, water, beds, or restrooms? And how do we know how long this protective field is going to last? It could collapse on us at any time. We'd be dead in an instant. I can assure you that the ash that you see erupting around us is hot and deadly."

The group was silent again. Rick spoke up, "Has anyone noticed that we can still see each other, even now that the emergency lights from the plane are gone? The light is coming from somewhere. It's not from the sun, not with all this ash."

"The only explanation for the light and the protective shield around us is that they are being produced by a force outside of nature," one of the men that Rick didn't recognize said.

"Yea, like the military," Kurt said.

"Or God," the older gentleman said.

Rick needed them to stay focused on finding shelter, not arguing. "Okay, let's divide up and walk slowly away from where we are right now in all directions, except for in the direction where the plane just fell off. We need to find out how far this protective field goes and if there is any kind of shelter around here."

Except for the man with the broken leg and his helpers, they all walked up to a section of the wall and stopped, hesitant to adventure into the unknown.

"Nothing ventured, nothing gained," said a middle-aged woman that Rick didn't recognize. The woman turned and walked slowly toward the protective field in front of her. The others hesitated, preferring to wait to see how the woman fared before adventuring off on their own.

"Come on, guys. There's nothing to be afraid of—" Suddenly, only three steps from where she had started, she began flailing her arms like she was trying to keep her balance. Rick quickly moved to her aid, but before he could even move a foot in her direction, she cried in terror as she slowly fell backward and disappeared. The noise of the rushing ash quickly muffled her high-pitched scream.

CHAPTER 5

EVERY LAST MEMBER of the group immediately rushed back to the exact center of the force field where they had all been standing before they had fanned out at Rick's suggestion. Rick arrived last, aghast at what had happened to the woman because of his suggestion.

"That was the last thing that I thought would happen," was all Rick could think to say.

"We all know that," Amanda said. "It wasn't your fault."

"Since you seem to be our self-designated leader at this point, why don't you tell us your name?" the woman from the front most row of seats asked. "I'm Margie."

"I'm Rick. But, guys, we really don't have time for introductions right now. We've got to find shelter, even if it's just a large boulder or a ridge."

"Rick," Kurt said. "You've seen how flat this surface is. It's clearly not a natural surface. This has to be a runway at a military base near the top of some mountain. That would explain the presence of the amazing technology that is holding the ash from the eruption at bay. If we just get looking, we're going to find a hanger or bunker somewhere around here."

"Okay." Rick felt better now that he had someone's support. "For safety reasons, let's get down on our hands and knees and start searching again."

No one moved.

Why and how did I end up as the leader of this group? "Okay, I'll go first." Rick walked up to the wall that he had previously experimented with, got down on all fours, and started slowly forward. As he moved forward, the protective barrier slowly extended in front of him.

Amanda walked over and stopped on his left side. "I want to help, but I'm just too afraid to do it by myself. Can I join you?"

"Sure," Rick said as he continued inching forward.

Amanda got down on the ground at his side and began crawling with him.

Rick couldn't help but glance at Amanda out of the corner of his eye. Even in the dim light, he could tell that she was slim. He noticed that her right ring finger was occupied by a ring. Moments passed until she finally moved her left hand toward him as she searched for the edge of a cliff, and he saw that her left ring finger was not occupied. He chuckled at why, at this extreme moment, that discerning that little fact about the woman had been so important.

They continued moving forward in silence for a moment. Rick asked, "What do you do when you're not trying to escape death from a volcanic eruption?"

"I'm an internist at the University of Washington Medical Center."

"You're a doctor?"

"Yep."

"I know this probably isn't a good time, but I've got this problem…"

"Go ahead," Amanda said with a small sigh that told Rick just how often she'd heard that introductory line as a preface to a request for a free medical consult.

"I got you on that one." Rick smiled. "I've always wanted to ask a doctor that question at some totally inappropriate moment just to see what they would do."

"Okay, you had me going," Amanda said with a smile that was discernable even in the low light. "Now it's your turn. What do you do?"

"Nothing as dashing as being a doctor. I'm just a humble auto mechanic. I have my own shop in Kent. It's not far from—"

"I know where Kent is. I'm from Seattle. So, mister humble mechanic, do you like what you do?"

"Well, that's a long story. If we get out of this mess alive and if you ever have a couple of hours to waste, I'll tell you."

"I do have plenty of time on my hands right now…"

"Hold on," Rick said as he looked past her at a black rectangular shape that he had just noticed out of the corner of his eye behind Amanda. It had definitely not been there a moment before. The rectangle was about four-feet wide and ten-feet long and was slowly extending upward from the ground.

Turning to see what had caught Rick's eye, Amanda cried out in surprise and hurriedly scooted away from the rectangle and closer to Rick. "What is that thing?"

"I have no idea. But the more I see, the more I am starting to agree with Kurt that this has to have something to do with the military."

"Whatever it is, I hope it means we're going to be rescued."

"Just to be safe, let's move back a little until we are sure what's going on."

Rick and Amanda stood and moved away from the rising rectangle. They were soon joined by the rest of the group that had been watching Rick and Amanda's progress and had seen the rectangle rising out of the ground even before Rick.

Kurt said, "See? I told you. This whole place stinks of the military."

"That's just fine with me," one of the older man said. "I just want off this mountain and away from all this ash."

The group fell silent as the rectangle stopped rising at about eight feet in height. The rectangle was featureless. Abruptly, a line of brilliant light emanated from one vertical edge of the narrower side of the rectangle, causing everyone in the group to step back even further. The line of light then traced along the upper and lower edges of the narrow end of the rectangle, like welding torches were cutting through the top and bottom of the end of the rectangle at the same time. A door opened in the narrow end of the rectangle. A man in jeans, tennis shoes, and a dress shirt stepped through the door.

"Hi. How's everybody doing?" the man asked with a big smile on his face.

"Who are you?" Kurt demanded. He had recovered the fastest from the shock of seeing the man exit from the door in the black rectangle.

The man in the jeans smiled even more broadly and replied, "I'm Sam. I'm the manager of this facility."

"Why did you take so long to get up here and help us?" Kurt said. "Because of your delay, a woman died."

"Don't be so critical," Marge said. "We're glad that he's here to save us."

"Please," Sam requested pleasantly but firmly. "Hold your questions until we can get inside. Now, if you'll all follow me." As he started down the stairs, he added, "And, Rick, would you wait and catch the door?"

"Okay," Rick called after him. *How did he know my name?*

CHAPTER 6

"**W**ELCOME TO OUR humble home in the sky," Sam said with a smile after he had quieted the group down. Rick couldn't help but think that his smile was just a little out of place considering what the people in the room had just gone through.

Rick looked around the dark walnut conference table at the group of fellow survivors. Each one was caked with gray ash from head to toe. It was impossible to tell for certain anyone's hair or skin color. There were ten of them seated around the table. That meant that almost 200 others had not survived. Rick blinked at the almost impossible odds that he had survived.

They had followed Sam down the stairwell to a wide hallway with thick rich burgundy carpet, luxurious wall coverings, and cherry-wood crown molding that would have made all but the most exclusive five-star hotels seem plain. It had definitely not been what Rick would have expected from a military base. Two of the men in the group had stayed behind to help the man with the injured leg. They had struggled to get him down the stairs and had been lagging behind the group. Sam had stopped the rest of the group, returned to the stairwell, and asked permission to help. He had knelt down and checked the man's injured leg. Standing soon after,

Sam had then announced that the man's leg would be okay. Almost immediately, the injured man had been able to put some weight on his wounded leg. He had only needed minor support for a few more minutes, and then his leg hadn't seemed to bother him any further. That had been totally at odds with the unnatural angle that the man's leg had been in when he had been helped down to the ground from the tail section of the plane. Rick had been sure that the man's leg was broken.

Sam had then ushered them into this exquisitely adorned conference room and asked them to be seated around the table. He had asked them more than once to not worry about getting ash on the high-backed leather chairs around the table.

"As I told you, I'm Sam, and I'm the director of this facility. I'm so sorry for the tragic accident that each of you has suffered today. I know that some of you lost a spouse, friends, or colleagues in the plane crash, and you must be grieving deeply—"

"Cut to the chase," Kurt said. "Which branch of the military runs this place?" As he was speaking, Kurt reached into his pocket and whipped out his cell phone. After he finished speaking, he immediately turned his attention to the phone.

"This is not a military installation," Sam said.

Looking up from his phone, Kurt asked. "Then who runs it? The CIA, or some secret government research company? And why isn't there cell service here?"

"One question at a time, please, Kurt—"

"How do you know my name?" Kurt asked. "There is no way—"

"I know all of your names," Sam interrupted calmly. "I know more about each one of you than even your mother knows." Some of the survivors around the table gasped. The group's reactions ranged from surprise to suspicion. However, before any of the survivors could protest, Sam hurriedly continued, "This is not a government or a private facility. I know this is going to be hard for each of you to believe right now. But, to put it into the easiest terms that you

can immediately understand, your plane crash landed on a UFO."
The shock and disbelief on the group's dirty faces was immediate
and intense. Sam continued, "You are in an airship that was not
constructed on your world."

Everyone started talking at once. Some stood up and began
demanding an explanation.

"Please take your seats and let's continue in an orderly fashion,"
Sam said quietly yet firmly. Everyone continued talking. "Please."
His mild voice carried unnaturally around the room, like it was
amplified, although there weren't any speakers in the ceiling or walls.
The sudden amplification of his voice startled the survivors into
silence.

"Now please sit down." Warily, each member of the group sank
into their chairs. Sam continued, "I want to get through this part
quickly so that I can get you to your rooms to clean up."

Kurt opened his mouth to speak, but Sam held up one finger
to tell him to wait for questions. However, Kurt ignored him
and blurted out, "Whoever you are, you have no right to hold us
here. I have to be at a meeting this evening, and I demand to be
released immediately."

"I also need to leave ASAP," a dust-encrusted young man from
across the table said. "I need to lock up the record store in Puyallup
since the closer is sick."

"Zach," Sam said gently yet firmly. "Please hear me out. All of
you." He glanced around the room, lingering on Kurt and his furrowed brow. Sam continued, "I assure you that there will be plenty
of time in the hours and days to come to answer all of your questions. First, I think a graphic of what is happening right now in
Seattle will help."

Immediately at the end of Sam's sentence, a perfectly rendered
three-dimensional representation of the Seattle area appeared in the
center of the table in front of them. At one end was the still erupting
stump of what was left of Mount Rainier, and on the other end was

the city of Port Townsend. All ten pairs of eyes were immediately riveted on the exquisitely detailed, full-color and seemingly solid diorama that had suddenly materialized in front of them out of thin air. Only a faint roiling haze above what was left of Mount Rainier was displayed in the diorama. Otherwise, any atmospheric disturbance cause by the eruption had been stripped away, leaving the diorama appearing like what a person would see if they were viewing the area from an airplane on the clearest of days. The diorama began rotating slowly clockwise to give everyone a chance to see what was happening from all angles.

"Look," Amanda said. "You can see the debris from the eruption moving."

"This thing would make Google Earth so jealous," a young man said.

Sam said to the young man, "It is amazing, isn't it, Alex."

The miracle of the detailed map took an immediate back seat for Rick as he searched for the city of Kent where his mother lived. However, instead of finding the city of Kent nestled in its green valley, all he could see was a muddy torrent that filled the valley from rim to rim. It a lahar from the eruption. "Is this being displayed in real time?" Rick asked.

"Yes," Sam said. "I'm not sure I should be letting you see the destruction as it unfolds since many of you have family and friends in the Seattle area that I know you are worried about."

"That's an understatement," a middle aged male said. He was sitting next to Margie.

Margie asked him, "What's your name?"

"I'm David," he replied.

"Can you zoom in on Kent?" Rick asked. It seemed impossible that Kent was completely flooded. It was so far from Mount Rainier.

The map zoomed in to an aerial view of where the city of Kent should have been. The detail was flawless, and Rick could see larger pieces of debris bobbing up and down in the lahar's flow.

"I'm so sorry, Rick. The lahar destroyed your mother's home."

Rick was about to open his mouth to ask if his mother had gotten out of the house and to safety in time when Margie said, "Your diorama has to be wrong. I didn't see Enumclaw."

"The map is correct," Sam said as the diorama zoomed out and then zoomed back in on the western side of Mount Rainier. Instead of tree-filled valleys dotted with small towns, there was just gray. As the image zoomed in closer to where the city of Enumclaw should have been, the gray coalesced into a view of a vast field of nothing but steaming rocks. "Unfortunately, Enumclaw, as well as every other city within twenty-five miles of the west side of Mount Rainier, has been completely destroyed and buried under thousands of tons of ash and rock."

"My dad is dead?" Margie said in a high voice. Tears began flowing freely as she bowed her head in grief.

"I'm sorry, Margie, but your father was in his car, trying to escape the eruption, when he was overtaken by the pyroclastic flows. He died instantly."

"You can't know that for certain," a middle-aged male said from the other side of the table. "With the magnitude of this eruption, communications are down everywhere, and all government services are certainly paralyzed. Even if you are monitoring all the police bands that are still functioning, there is no way that you would have any knowledge at this point of whether her dad is dead or whether Rick's mother's house is destroyed."

"Bart," Sam said, his calm demeanor imperturbable. "I assure you that the image before you is completely accurate and is being displayed in real time by technology that is not available on Earth. All of you were supposed to have died when your plane crashed. The ten of you were fortunate enough to have, as you say, dodged the bullet."

The group of survivors around the table remained silent as they studied the map in front of them, each overwhelmed by the massive loss of life and property that was occurring at that very moment in the Seattle area.

Rick said, "Look. The lahars are smashing into Seattle's and Tacoma's bays and have created huge tsunamis. The tsunamis are traveling up and down the Puget Sound." *It is so hard to watch the tsunamis inundating town after town along the Sound. Thousands of people are dying even as I watch.*

"The immensity of this tragedy is too hard to watch," Sam said. "It's late, and you are all covered in ash. I'm sure that you would like a chance to clean up and then get a good night's rest. We can meet back here in the morning and continue our discussion."

The diorama winked out of existence, leaving just the perfectly finished tabletop.

"But I want to know what's happening," Margie said.

"Me, too," Zach said.

"I insist," Sam said. "Before I escort you to your rooms, I'd like to cover a few housekeeping items. All of your luggage and personal items were lost in the crash. Each of you will find a change of clothes in your rooms, along with toiletries. You may use room service to order dinner and snacks. There are no TVs in your rooms. Your cell phones won't work here. For your safety, you're not to wander around this facility, no matter how curious you might be." After pausing to let his words sink in, Sam continued, "So, if you'll all follow me into the hallway," Sam crossed to the door and opened it, "I'll show you to your rooms."

"So we're your prisoners," Kurt said angrily.

"Heavens no," Sam said. "You're our guests."

"Yea, right. We're guests that can never leave," Kurt said with his brow furrowed again and his eyes narrowed.

CHAPTER 7

RICK LAY IN his bed, alone in his room, alternating between feeling stricken with worry over whether his mother had survived the lahar, feeling amazed that he had survived the plane crash, and feeling perplexed by the strange and lavish facility that he was now in. The advanced technology that was available to this Sam guy was amazing.

They had followed Sam out of the conference room and down the same hall from which they had entered the facility, but in the opposite direction. They hadn't passed anyone as they had made a couple of turns and arrived at a hall with ten doors, numbered one to ten. Sam had assigned Rick number six. After a brief look into a few of the remaining survivor's faces and seeing only fatigue and worry showing through the layers of ash, he had bid them goodbye, entered his room and closed the door. At least Amanda had given him a little smile as he had walked past her to his room. Amanda had been assigned room number two.

Once inside, the strange events of the day became stranger. As soon as the door had closed, a pleasant male voice said, "Hello, Rick. Your clothes are quite dirty. A shower is in order before you get the place filthy."

Thinking that the voice was coming from a member of Sam's staff in the room with him, Rick turned and said, "I am so sorry about the ash. I'll be careful to not get the place too dirty." However, as he looked around the room, he was puzzled to find no one. Curious about where the other occupant of the room was, he headed down a short hallway toward the separate bedroom. He was brought up short again by the voice that seemed to come out of thin air, "If you're heading for the bedroom to look for me, then you're wasting your time."

"Okay, then, where are you?"

"I am the computer that runs this place. I'll be your butler and concierge during your stay here." As the voice was speaking, Rick turned his head to one side and then the other, trying to determine its source. All he was able to determine was that the voice seemed to be coming from all directions at once.

As the voice fell silent, Rick took a quick look around the bedroom, under the bed, in the closet, and finally in the adjoining bathroom. No one was there. He returned to the living room. Looking around the living room and the adjoining kitchenette, he tried to find speakers in the walls or ceiling but found none.

"Okay, no one's here," he said. "But it really freaks me out that I can hear your voice no matter where I am in these rooms, but I can't tell where the sound of your voice is coming from."

"The sound comes from the walls and ceiling, but only in the room where you are currently located. Maybe it would be less 'freaky' for you if I introduced myself. I am Mark."

"Well, Mark, assure me of one thing: You can't see me, right?"

"Why would I need to do that? My sensors tell me exactly where you are at all times and exactly what you are doing." Mark paused, and then in a tone of voice clearly designed to put him at ease, he continued, "Remember, I am a machine. I don't see in images like the human brain does. I just see data points and draw my information from those." Mark's paused again for a moment and then continued, "I understand now. You must be worried that I am going see you undressed." The voice chuckled softly. "That's usually not a concern around here. But now I understand why the others are also hesitating to take showers. Rick, I assure you that you'll have the utmost privacy while you are at this facility. I will not address you while you are completing personal care."

"I'm not surprised the others are hesitating," Rick said. "This whole experience is so unreal. What is this place?"

"I'm sorry, but I am only able to attend to your immediate needs at this time. I am unable to answer any questions about this facility."

"Well, unless I want to stay filthy dirty, I don't really have much choice. Time to hit the showers. No peeking, okay?"

"I already told you that I am a computer. I am not at all interested in watching you while—"

"Are you sure you're a computer? You laughed at your own joke just a moment ago. I didn't think computers were that smart."

"You have no idea just how advanced of a computer that I am."

"If you're that advanced and can think on your own, then decide on your own to tell me what this place is."

"No more questions, Rick. Now, about that shower…"

CHAPTER 8

"**W**HAT DID YOU think about Mark?" Margie asked. "Wasn't that about the creepiest thing you've ever seen? I wanted to get cleaned up so badly from the ash, but I didn't dare for hours. I was worried he would be watching me."

"That was really strange for me, too," Rick said.

After being awakened by Mark the next morning, Mark had informed him that the survivors would being meeting with Sam in one hour. Rick had quickly showered, dressed and returned at the same conference room to find that the only other person in the room was Margie. As soon as Rick had taken a seat opposite her at the table, she had gotten up and sat in the chair next to him.

"I never got to introduce myself to you. My name is Margaret Turner. Everyone calls me Margie."

"I'm Rick Jones. Where are you from?"

"I live in Ohio, but I'm originally from the Seattle area. I'm a writer. I was traveling to Seattle for a conference on historical fiction."

"That sounds interesting."

"It's just a bunch of people talking on forever about the boring books they've written." Vivacious and attractive, she sported a head of flaming red hair that framed brilliant blue eyes and a quick smile.

Rick glanced over to the door of the conference room just as Amanda, who was a brunette now that her hair was no longer covered with ash, and Kurt walked through the door together. Amanda's eyes met Rick's, and she smiled at him. Rick's heart instantly felt like it had skipped a beat, and his chest felt tight. Amanda was way prettier than he had even suspected the day before. Talking to attractive women like Amanda made his mouth go dry, made him stammer, and scrambled his thoughts. When circumstances happened to bring him in proximity with an intensely beautiful woman, it was often easier for him to avoid them altogether.

Rick quickly followed his modus operandi and looked away from Amanda, pretending that he hadn't seen her come in. However, right as he glanced away, he noticed that Kurt had his hand on Amanda's back as he showed her to a chair on the other side of the table. She didn't seem to mind, which surprised Rick a little. He wondered if they already knew each other from before the plane crash. Out of the corner of his eye, he noted that Amanda was wearing a peach blouse with tan dress pants that seemed to be perfectly tailored for her. Kurt sported a solid, light-yellow, button-down, and long-sleeve shirt with dark dress pants. Kurt's clothes appeared to have been perfectly tailored for him.

As Amanda and Kurt settled in their seats across the table from Rick, Amanda smiled again at Rick and said, "Hello, Rick." The way her smile radiated across the table made him feel just like he had when he had fallen off the tricky bars in the third grade and had the wind knocked out of him. With great effort, Rick mustered up a smile and stammered a quick hello in return. Then, because he was sure that if he kept conversing with her that she would see that he found her to be hopelessly attractive, he looked away. He just wasn't used to women as beautiful as Amanda paying attention to him and didn't want to risk rejection.

Turning back to someone that he felt was a lot safer to talk to, Rick commented to Margie beside him, "Their clothes look like they fit perfectly. I was surprised that mine fit so well. How did Sam know all of our clothing sizes?"

"I don't know, but he got my size right, too. He also got my brands of makeup right on, as well as providing an exact copy of the toothbrush that I have at home in my drawer. And, even though this is kind of personal, he had my exact size and brand of bra and panties already in a drawer next to the clothes I am wearing."

"It was the same for me... with the underwear thing," Rick stammered, a little embarrassed by how direct Margie had been and that he had then been too revealing himself.

"You're blushing," Margie said with a smile. She leaned forward, close enough for Rick to get a whiff of her pleasant perfume, and whispered conspiratorially, "Sorry I embarrassed you, but you look so cute when you blush."

Rick blushed even more, and Margie laughed.

"What's the joke over there?" Amanda asked.

"I was just teasing Rick about how this place was so efficient that they even got the brands and sizes of our underwear right. The topic was a little too personal for him, and he blushed so cutely."

As Rick intently studied the grain of the table, waiting for the embarrassing moment to pass, the other survivors filed in from the hallway. Amongst them was the guy who had broken his leg the night before. He was walking without a limp, like nothing had ever happened. *The strange things that keep happening around this place are continuing to pile up.*

The latecomers were all in the same style of dress shirts and slacks of various colors. All of their clothes fit perfectly.

Kurt said from across the table, "They shouldn't know this much about us. It's an invasion of our privacy."

"I'm glad they at least knew our sizes," Margie said. "Otherwise, we might have just been issued extra-large and ugly scrub suits with underwear that didn't fit."

Rick needed Margie to change the subject right now before

Santa called him to light his sleigh with his red face. "So, Margie, do you believe that this is an alien ship, like Sam said?"

"Well, so far, they haven't had sex with us, have they? Isn't that what aliens do to the people they abduct? My aunt was abducted—"

"Hello, everyone," Sam exclaimed as he breezed through the door to the conference room. He was wearing a white shirt, white tie, and white slacks.

I'm so grateful that his entry shut Margie down before she embarrassed me even further.

Sam asked, "How did everyone sleep last night?"

No one answered for a second or two, and then pandemonium broke out as the survivors tried to be the first to ask what had happened to their families, friends, and relatives in Seattle overnight.

"Okay, okay," Sam said as he quieted the group with his hands. "It's really not efficient for us at this point to answer each of your questions one at a time. I will try to answer all of your questions as a group the best that I can over the next hour. After our meeting here, if you still have individual concerns, then I'll talk with you separately."

No one objected.

"Then let's get started," Sam said, "What I have to say to you is going to be hard for many of you to hear, but it has to be said. And, please, hold your questions until I ask for them.

"As I mentioned, this ship that you are on is currently stationary at 20,000 feet above the US-Canadian border, just south of Vancouver, Canada. This ship is almost one-mile long, a half-a-mile wide, and a fourth of a mile tall. It is completely invisible to the naked eye, to telescopes, and even to radar. It emits no exhaust or heat. Any object larger than a molecule that collides with this ship passes through the ship like the ship was never there. As I say this, I am aware that a number of you want to ask me how such a large object can still be invisible. However, time won't permit me to answer that question, or any other technical questions that you might have, until later. Please don't forget your questions. Just ask me later.

"This ship's three main purposes are to assist God in answering the prayers of the individuals on the earth, to be a staging area for the angels that visit the earth periodically to physically assist God in carrying out his designs on the earth, and to assist the spirits of mortals that have died to transition to their next habitation in the world of spirits. We call this ship a station, and I will refer to it by that name from now on."

The older man couldn't restrain himself, "What you're speaking is blasphemy. God needs no one on this Earth to do those things for him. He alone is all powerful—"

"Reverend Porter, please. Let me speak. I am very aware that much of what I'm going to say will be hard for you to accept. In fact, it will be harder for you than for most of the rest of the group. I'm sorry for that. I can't alter the truth to fit your beliefs, especially when you will be able to see the truth here on the station with your own eyes. I will be there along the way to help you with all of this as much as I can. Is that okay?"

The reverend blinked his eyes in disbelief, made to reply, but then stopped and closed his mouth. The muscles of his jaw tightened in a clear sign of silent defiance.

Turning back to the group, Sam continued, "Yesterday, this station was positioned near the Seattle area in preparation for the large numbers of mortals that were going to lose their lives in the eruption of Mount Rainier. The close proximity aids us processing spirits of the dead from catastrophic events where the casualties exceed ten thousand mortals per hour. In addition, the immediacy also allows the angels faster access to those that have been ordained to live, but whose lives are in peril."

This time, it was Rick who couldn't help himself. "You knew in advance that this disaster was going to happen? Why didn't you warn people? So many lives, including possibly my mother's, could have been saved."

Sam held up his hands, shushing Rick and others that were getting ready to speak out. "I appreciate your comments, Rick, but I need to remind you and the rest of the group that we really don't have time for questions right now. I can speak for both myself and for my staff as I express my sorrow for your individual and collective losses from the eruption. At the same time, both my staff and I are specifically forbidden from altering the course of human destiny, unless we have specific instructions from God that we are to do so. Unfortunately, in the case of the eruption of Mount Rainier, we were given instructions not to intervene in the eruption itself and in the destruction that would follow, as much as we wanted to do otherwise.

"Now, let's continue. All of you were supposed to have died when your plane plunged to the ground and crashed after being caught in the eruption. Instead, you crash-landed onto the top of this station. We were so occupied with carrying out our duties to the mass casualties that we failed to notice your plane approaching until it was too late."

"Too late for what?" Kurt said from across table. "To get out of the way and let us die?"

Sam ignored Kurt and continued, "Once we realized that the tail section of your plane was teetering on the edge of the top the station, I had the difficult choice to either let your plane fall off the edge or to allow the remains of the plane to remain on the station just long enough to allow you to escape. It's pretty obvious what I decided."

"But you said that you could only intercede in human destiny when you were told by God to do so," Amanda said.

"You're right. I didn't get permission to intercede to prevent your deaths." Sam paused pensively for a moment and then added, "I guess a little bit of my humanity got in the way of my decision."

"You're admitting that you're human?" Alex asked. "I thought that you said that you were an alien."

"Alex, I never said whether I was an alien or not. In fact, all of God's children look exactly like you and I do. Sure, we all have different colors of skin and hair, just like you do on Earth, and there are a seemingly never-ending number of languages and cultures throughout the thousands of planets. On the other hand, none of God's children on any of his planets have pointed ears like the inhabitants of the fictitious planet of Vulcan, and there definitely aren't any planets of little green men."

"Where are you from then?" Bart asked.

"I would expect you to ask that, Bart, being that you're an astronomer. I am from a planet on the other side of the galaxy in what many of your astronomers call the Centaurus Arm. Your astronomers don't have the ability to see through the galactic bar, which is between my planet and yours. Even if they could see through the galactic bar, your telescopes aren't powerful enough to pick out my solar system's small sun at such a distance.

"I had so much to cover. However, our time is up and we're going to have finish later. I want to take you on a tour of our facility, starting with the—"

"I'm not going on your tour until you tell me when I get to go home." Alex said.

Sam paused, and then said, "I'm sorry to have to tell you this, but none of you can ever go home."

CHAPTER 9

AFTER THE UPROAR caused by his statement had died down, Sam said, "I insist that each of you accompany me on the tour. That is the best way for me to introduce you to the work we do here for the benefit of all humans on Earth. Once the tour is completed, I will do my best to answer your questions."

Miraculously, no one objected, and the survivors stood to follow Sam for the tour. Once in the hallway, the survivors followed Sam down a few short hallways to a closed door.

As Sam held the door open for them to enter, he added, "Everyone please step inside and stand against the wall to the left of the door."

The group filed in and stood quietly against the wall as instructed. In front of them was a non-descript rectangular room, about forty feet by twenty feet, with a central table that was ten-feet wide and twenty-five-feet long. Seated at the table along each of the long sides were eight men and women, all appearing to be about twenty-five years old, and all dressed in white. In front of each of them was an image of a scene that appeared to be happening on Earth. Closer to their end of the table, a woman with black hair was watching a car as it drove along a snow-covered road. The car's headlights were mostly obscured by snow, and its windshield wipers were just barely keeping ahead of the blizzard. A male with a brown mustache next to the woman at the table was watching a group of three young boys playing with a ball by the side of a railroad track. There were no visible monitors, glass panels, or projectors. The images they were watching were perfectly rendered, three-dimensional, full-color images. The people at the table controlled the images without speaking and without any input devices. Sometimes they manipulated the images with their hands, but at other times, the images changed with no apparent input from the user.

At the far end of the table, a blonde woman was watching over an image of a house fire that was quickly spreading from the first floor to the second floor of the home. A small child could be seen in a second-story window, pounding on the glass. The child looked to be a six- or seven-year-old girl and had long, brown hair. As the survivors watched, flames were seen burning more and more brightly behind the girl. The girl glanced over her shoulder at the advancing flames and screamed in terror. With increased vigor, she yanked at the latch to the window but could not open it. In desperation, she again began pounding on the glass with both fists.

"Sam, we can't watch the girl burn to death," one of the female survivors said. Rick hadn't met her yet and didn't know her name.

"Connie, each of the individuals on Earth that my staff members are currently monitoring have been designated by God to have the course of their lives altered by divine intervention. Watch and you will see the power of God at work."

The woman observing the car driving on the icy road suddenly spoke out loud in perfect Spanish, "Carlos, drive slower."

"She just told the driver to slow down in Spanish," Margie whispered to Rick. "They must be in the mountains of South America, since it's winter there now."

In response to the request, the brake lights came on, and the car began slowing down. The effort by the driver came not a moment too soon as the car crested a rise in the road and started down a steep snow-covered hill at a snail's pace. However, the road was so slick that the car began picking up speed. The driver began tapping the brakes, but the car didn't slow. The car started to fishtail and then turned sideways as it kept sliding down the hill. The image expanded ahead of the car, revealing a sharp turn at the bottom of the hill with an abrupt 100-foot drop-off just ten feet beyond the edge of the road. The occupants of the car screamed out loud in terror as the car inexorably kept sliding toward the drop-off.

In the image in front of the male with the moustache, a train appeared on the tracks, barreling down on the place where the boys were playing by the side of the tracks. One of the kids threw the ball over the head of one his playmates. The ball bounced onto the tracks and then into the grass on the other side. The ten-year-old blonde boy that the ball was meant for didn't hesitate. Without checking for a train, he ran toward the track. As he jumped over the nearest rail, the toe of his trailing foot hit the rail, and he tripped and fell across the tracks. His head struck the far rail, and he crumpled into a heap. His momentum carried his body forward until his neck lay on the far rail with his body on one side and his head on the other. His friends leaped to his aid, but then stopped short as they heard the loud horn from the rapidly approaching train. Unable to aid their friend safely, the boys stopped with hands out toward him, screaming in desperation, clearly hoping he would come to and get off the tracks before the train killed him.

"Oh, I can hardly bear to watch any of this," Amanda cried.

Rick felt his heart in his throat. *How could so many horrible things be happening at the same time?*

The woman that was watching the burning house at the far end of the table sprang into action. Instantly, a door-shaped panel appeared in the wall behind her. Flames from a fire could be seen through the opening. Almost as soon as the portal appeared, the woman stood, turned and walked through it. Instantly, the woman appeared in the image on the table, standing behind the girl that was pounding on the window. Flames reached toward the woman and the child but didn't affect either of them. The woman went to the window, lifted the latch, and opened it wide. The child turned to look behind her to see if someone was there that had opened the window for her, but the now open window immediately became a conduit for the super-heated flames from the lower floors. Rushing smoke and flames propelled the girl out the window headfirst, and she fell toward the brick driveway below. Her tiny, outstretched arms would do little to protect her head from the impact.

As the young girl plummeted toward the ground, the woman reappeared on the brick drive below the child. The woman deftly caught the girl and lowered her gently to the ground. Surprised that she hadn't been hurt as she had landed and sure that she had felt arms catch her, the girl sat up on the driveway and looked around. She spoke out loud in Italian, "God, you saved me!" No one was there to confirm her declaration that God had saved her. The woman that had saved her was already seated back at the table.

A snow-filled door opened just behind the black-haired woman. She sprang through the door and instantly appeared between the sliding car and the cliff. Effortlessly, the woman's tiny image on the desktop stopped the sliding car just feet from the edge of the cliff. A moment later, she stepped back into the room through the portal, snow still salting her hair and shoulders. In the car, the occupants could be seen hugging each other in joy at their survival, tears streaming down their cheeks.

Just a moment later, the man with the moustache raced through an open door that appeared just behind him. He was suddenly at the unconscious child's side in the image. The speeding train was just a moment away as the man pulled the boy's limp body completely in-between the rails and then lay down on top of the boy. An instant later, they were both hidden from sight as the roaring train passed over them.

The train continued speeding by as the two friends stood sobbing and hugging each other, clearly sure that their friend had been killed by the train. As the train finally passed, the boy could be seen lying still between the tracks. His friends were overjoyed to see that his head was still on his shoulders. Leaping to his aid, they helped him up. As he slowly came to, he could be heard saying, "What happened?"

One of his friends responded, "A miracle. That's what happened." The friends just cried and hugged him.

The boy that had been knocked unconscious struggled out of their hugs and exclaimed, "Quit hugging me. You are acting like a bunch of sissies."

More than one of the survivors from the plane crash chuckled at the antics of the preteens. At the same time, many wiped tears from their eyes.

"It goes on and on from here," Sam said. "With seven-billion-plus inhabitants on the earth, there's never a dull moment in these angel's staging rooms."

"These workers here don't look like angels to me," Fred said.

"Who cares what they look like? I want to know how those portals work," Alex said. "They're totally cool."

Sam answered, "Since you have now seen the angels at work, Fred, I think that you can answer that question for yourself. And angels never have had wings, in case that is what is concerning you. That misinterpretation has been made on Earth for years as a commonly used Biblical metaphor used to describe an angel's form has been interpreted literally instead of figuratively. As for your question, Alex, I'll have to get to an explanation of the workings of the portals later. We are on a tight schedule and need to proceed with our tour."

CHAPTER 10

THE NEXT ROOM on the tour was the same size as the angel's staging room, but instead of a central table, this room was laid out with eleven eight-foot-wide workstations that were evenly spaced against the outside walls. The workstations contained full-width wooden tables and were separated from each other by floor-to-ceiling, eight-foot-wide and four-inch-thick dividers. Each workstation in the room was manned by a youthful man or woman. All were wearing white, and all were seated in high-backed, comfortable chairs. The plethora of young people on the station was beginning to make Rick feel old.

The survivors filed into the center of the room.

Sam said, "This is just one of thousands of the rooms where members of my staff assist God in answering prayers from individuals on Earth."

"Now you really are committing blasphemy," Fred said. "You profess to serve God, and yet you assume all of his powers. Only God can answer prayers. You are not God."

Sam said patiently, "I am not God, and my staff members are not God. We would never presume to have the knowledge, wisdom, and power of God. At the same time, as a minister, you know well that God has called men on Earth since the beginning of time to act in his name as they assist him with his work. That is the same thing that is happening here."

"This is not the same. The people on Earth are praying to God, not to some man or woman on a spaceship," the reverend said loudly. Some of the workers in the booths turned and looked at Sam with concern.

"Please, we need to keep our voices quiet so as not to disturb the workers." Sam gestured with his hands as he spoke for the group to keep their voices down.

"Fred's not the only one that's bothered by this," Rick said. "I have always prayed to God and felt like he was personally listening. Seeing all of this makes me wonder if any of my prayers have ever made it to God."

Sam said, "I know that this is a delicate topic, and I did hesitate before I decided to bring you here. But now that we are here, let me explain the process. These workers have been called specifically by God to be his eyes and ears for his children on Earth, to love them and care for them as much as he does. They take their work very seriously. They are all from planets all across the galaxy and left behind family and friends when they volunteered for this assignment. In almost all circumstances, they have known the individuals that they have been assigned to care for since birth and will continue to work with them until they die.

"When an individual on Earth prays to any higher power that they might believe in, Mark, whom I'm sure all of you became acquainted with in your rooms last night, receives that prayer and channels it to the worker that is on duty that has been assigned to that individual. Many prayers are simple and don't require answers, such as a prayer to travel safely when we already know that they will arrive safely. Some prayers require immediate attention and are passed to an angel in one of the angel's staging rooms, such as a prayer to be saved from a life-threatening situation. Other prayers require more effort on our worker's part, such as a prayer from an individual to know if they should marry the person they love, a prayer to know which university to attend, or where to live. These are important life-altering questions that need input from God. We pass these requests through the proper channels to God, and he returns his answers back through those channels to the workers. The workers then chose an appropriate method of getting the answer to the individual. As any of you that have prayed know, the answer can come as a still small voice, as a feeling, in a passage of scripture, in a sermon, or as advice from a loved one. Sometimes, God requests that the workers give no answer, and then the worker's hands are tied. They never go against God's wishes. Above all, the workers have the best interest of their charges at heart."

"Can you let us listen to someone's prayer?" Zach asked.

"No. I'm sorry, but prayers to God must always remain private. That is a law that cannot be broken. However, with permission from one of your group, I can let you meet one of the staff that has worked with one of you since you were born. Amanda, do I have your permission to let the group meet one of the workers that has been helping God to answer your prayers since you were a little girl?"

"Well, I guess so. She won't embarrass me, will she?"

"No, she wouldn't think of it. She cares for you like you were her daughter."

Sam signaled a woman from across the room, and she got up from her chair. Like all the workers, the woman appeared to be about twenty-five years old. She wore a knee-length, simple white dress gathered at her waist with a white belt. As the woman approached the group, she smiled broadly. Her gaze came to rest on Amanda, and her eyes lit up.

"Amanda, this is Harriet," Sam said.

"I already know Amanda," Harriet said. "I don't need an introduction."

Amanda hesitated and then held out her hand to shake hands.

"Amanda, I know you too well for just a handshake. Give me a big hug, sweetie." Harriet enveloped Amanda in a heartfelt hug, her eyes closed in obvious pleasure, and with a big smile on her face.

Amanda hugged her back, but not with same degree of fervor.

Laughing softly, Harriet released Amanda. "You don't know me. I understand your hesitance. But, with your permission, can I give you just a peek into how well I know you?"

"Go ahead," Amanda said.

"Do you remember the stormy night from your childhood when you thought that you saw a lost puppy on the lawn outside your bedroom window?"

Amanda nodded. "I do. I was six years old."

"You went outside to rescue the puppy. However, what you thought was a puppy was just a paper bag caught on a stick on the ground that was moving with the wind. But when you went to go back inside, the door was locked."

Amanda continued the story, "It was so cold outside, and I was only in my Cinderella pajamas. The wind was blowing right through the fabric like it wasn't there. My teeth were chattering so loudly. I couldn't stop them." Amanda looked hard at Harriet. "The only way you could possibly know about this is if you somehow listened in when I told my parents about what had happened the next day because I've never told a soul about this since."

Harriet just smiled and said, "You checked the front door, but it was locked. You knocked on the front door, but your babysitter had fallen asleep on the couch, and your knocking wasn't loud enough to wake her over the sound of the wind. With the nearest house a mile away, you were getting pretty desperate."

Amanda said, "Not knowing what else to do, I prayed for help. My Sunday school teacher had told us to pray if we ever really needed help. I knew that I was going to die if I didn't get warm."

"You didn't kneel down or anything, which is just fine," Harriet said. "I heard your prayer. It was God's will that you survived, and so I whispered to your spirit that the basement window was open."

"I heard your voice so clearly. That was you." Amanda gave Harriet a huge hug, tears filling her eyes and streaming down her cheeks.

"Careful, you're going to break me." Harriet smiled sweetly. "You opened the basement window, and you were safe."

With gratitude and happiness making it hard to speak, Amanda said, "I told my parents about what had happened the next day when they returned home. They told me that my guardian angel had saved me. I never dreamed in all the world that I would get to meet that angel."

CHAPTER 11

THE FINAL STOP on their tour was a trapezoidal room with three rows of deeply cushioned seats facing the longer side of the room. The wall of longer side of the room appeared to be made of floor-to-ceiling clear glass. Beyond the glass was a much larger rectangular room that was devoid of furniture, floor coverings, and even light fixtures. It was the same height as the trapezoidal room where they were currently standing. At the moment, it was dimly lit only by the light that was coming from the room where they were now standing.

"Let's all of us step up to the glass wall," Sam said. "Be careful to move toward the wall slowly since it is so clear that it is nearly invisible. I don't want you to run into it and hurt yourselves. Spread out so that each of you has a good view of the room beyond."

"And see what?" Margie said as she arrived at the glass wall. "All I can see is the fog from my breath."

"Look again," Sam said patiently. "Even if you breathe on the wall, it doesn't show your breath. Even your fingerprints won't show on the wall. Pretty cool, huh?"

With Sam's encouragement, most in the group tried to leave fog from their breath on the glass wall or attempted to leave their fingerprints on the glass wall, but to no avail. Connie asked, "This is pretty cool stuff that you have bonded to the surface of this glass. What is it?"

Sam smiled as he said, "Connie, even though you're an expert in geology, this one is going to stretch your imagination a little. This wall isn't made of glass. In fact, none of the walls in the station are made the way you make walls on Earth. These walls are alive. They can assume whatever thickness, shape, surface characteristic, color, hardness, or decoration that we desire. The walls can both radiate and absorb heat, keeping our station at a perfect seventy-two degrees on your Fahrenheit scale. They can even emit light and sound. In the case of this wall, the cells transmit light from one side of the wall to the other, making the wall appear to be clear as glass. When you breathe on the wall or leave fingerprints, the cells assimilate the moisture and oils from your bodies, keeping the wall perfectly clean. Just like your skin, vein-like tubes carry the waste away from the wall."

The few that had still been trying to leave a fingerprint on the wall quickly withdrew their hands.

Connie said, "Amazing. It really is completely organic?"

Sam laughed. "I forget how amazing all this technology is for someone that has never experienced it. To answer your question, the cells that make up the wall are pretty versatile. They produce a carbon nanotube-based frame that allows the wall to be stronger than steel. Even if you had a sledgehammer, you couldn't break through this wall."

"How do you tell the cells what configuration to take?" Amanda asked, stepping back from the wall and turning to address Sam.

"The master computer, whom you all know as Mark, gets a request from one of us and then transmits the specifications for the configuration to the cells in the wall. The cells then handle all the rest."

Sam continued, "As I told you in the conference room, one of the purposes of this station is to assist the spirits of the recently deceased to proceed to the world of spirits. The portals that lead to the world of spirits are at the right end of each of these rectangular rooms. There are seventy-five thousand rooms on the station, each one just like the one that we looking at now. The spirits of the deceased are transported from where they died to the left side of the chamber. They then cross the chamber and enter a portal on the right side of the room that transports them to the world of spirits."

"Are these chambers where near-death experiences happen?" Zach asked. "I have heard of people that have died and come back. They talk about meeting with angels or family members that have given them a choice to proceed to the world of spirits or to return to Earth."

"Yes, these chambers are where near-death experiences take place," Sam answered. "For many of the deceased, the experience of entering the portal to the world of spirits is not intuitive. Overcoming fear of the unknown can be difficult. These chambers are here for us to help the deceased to decide to walk toward and enter the brightly lit portal to the world of spirits."

"A coworker of mine had a near-death experience," Margie said. "She chose to come back and not go into the light. The experience really changed her for the better."

Sam said, "You are correct, Margie. On occasion, a spirit is given a choice to return to their body on Earth instead of proceeding to the spirit world."

Sam gestured to the darkened chamber in front of them. "The spirit of the woman that is about to enter this chamber in front of us has a firm belief that her deceased family members await her in the world of spirits. She shouldn't need any help in proceeding through the chamber and into the portal to the world of spirits."

As Sam was finishing speaking, the large rectangular room beyond the glass began to fill with light. Sam urged them to return to their positions at the wall. As the group watched, the room on the other side of the wall filled with a flawless image of the shoreline of an alpine lake. Tall pine trees could be seen all along the shore of the lake, and light from an unseen sun overhead sparkled on the water. The image was so perfect that Rick couldn't help but feel like he was really on the shore of the lake. Others in the group gasped in surprise at the beauty and clarity of the image. Soon after the image of the mountain lake was complete, a large round circle appeared on the shore of the lake at the right side of the chamber. The light emanating from the circle was a brilliant white, but not so bright that is was unpleasant to look at.

"The observation wall in front of us is displaying the rest of the image of the mountain lake landscape on its other side. The recently deceased won't be able to see us or see this room. The point is to create an image from the person's life that recalls a peaceful time for them, putting the recently deceased at ease."

"Who picks the scene for the deceased?" Amanda inquired.

Before Sam could answer, Rick said softly mostly to himself, "I know where this place is. Does this mean…"

Sam answered Amanda's question, "Watch and you'll see."

At that moment, three men and two women entered the scene in front of them from the portal to the world of spirits. As they moved farther along the shore of the lake and away from the light of the portal, they could be seen to be young, in their mid-twenties, and each was dressed in white. The women wore knee-length skirts with blouses, and the men wore dress shirts and slacks.

One of the women turned to one of the men and asked, "Grant, was the lake by our cabin the right choice?"

"Of course it was, Adele," the man said.

"They're my grandparents," Rick said, his voice tight with grief. "This has to mean that they are here to meet my mother."

Margie and Amanda both moved to Rick's side. Each placed a hand on one of his shoulders. Rick breathed in gasps through parted lips with tears streaming down his cheeks. In spite of his tears, he leaned forward against the wall, trying to get a better look at his family. "The man with curly brown hair is my father. He looks so young. They all look so young. The others are my mom's parents and my mom's grandparents on her mother's side. They've all been dead for years."

On the other side of the observation wall, Rick's father said, "Janice always spoke of the wonderful times that she had at the cabin with her family when she was a child. Meeting us here at the lake will mean a lot to her."

"Sam, can't I talk to them?" Rick asked. "I haven't seen them for so many years."

Amanda moved aside as Sam approached Rick and put his arm gently around Rick's shoulders. "I am so sorry, but you can't talk to them. You asked why they look so young. That is because once spirits are separated from their bodies, all spirits look about twenty-five years old."

"Rick, it's your mother," Amanda said quietly as she pointed to the opposite end of chamber.

All eyes in the room shifted to the left side of the chamber where a young and beautiful blonde woman had suddenly appeared. She was also dressed in white.

"Mom," Rick whispered.

At the same moment, Rick's mother said, "Mom!" to her mother on the shore of the lake. She almost ran to her mother. "I knew you'd come for me."

"Janice, it's so good to see you," her mother said as they embraced briefly.

As soon as Janice and her mother broke their embrace, Janice's husband enveloped her in his arms. "Janice, I missed you so much."

"I missed you too, sweetie," Janice said, a look of pure joy on her face. They ended their brief embrace, and then Janice greeted each of her grandparents with a hug. "Gram and Gramps, it's so good to see you again."

Rick stood speechless, tears continuing to stream down his face.

"Janice," Janice's mother said as she took her daughter's hand. "We have so much to talk about and so much to show you. On top of that, your other grandparents and your aunts, uncles, and cousins are dying to see you." She stopped, giggled, and then continued, "That didn't sound right. You know what I mean. They're all just on the other side of the light."

"You don't have to talk me into entering the light, Mom. I've been looking forward to this moment for my whole life." Hand in hand with her husband and with her mother, and with the rest of her family trailing behind them, she started toward the light, but then she stopped suddenly. "Rick isn't here to greet me. That must mean he survived the eruption."

Janice's mother said, "Rick hasn't passed over yet, Janice. He was supposed to come before you, but all we know is that his passing has been delayed. He must still be alive on Earth somewhere."

"I know that the good Lord will watch over him and keep him safe wherever he is," Janice said. She again started walking toward the light.

"Mom!" Rick called out in anguish just before his mother passed through the portal to the world of spirits and was gone. Moments later, the lakeside scene winked out of existence, leaving just the darkened and featureless rectangular room on the other side of the observation wall.

CHAPTER 12

"**T**HAT WAS A cheap shot, using Rick's mother for your show and tell." Kurt said angrily as he turned to Sam. It had only been moments since the lakeside image had popped out of existence. Rick still stood facing the wall with his head bowed. Margie and Amanda still stood at his side.

"Why don't you ask Rick," Sam said to Kurt, his voice calm as always. "I'm sure that he would have insisted on being here for his mother's passing."

"A little bit of a warning would have been nice," Kurt said.

"There wasn't time to properly prepare him for what he was going to see. I decided that it was best to answer his questions as the event unfolded."

"You've made a lot of decisions for us lately without consulting with us first," Kurt said.

Still completely unruffled, Sam said, "Like saving all of your lives from the plane crash?"

Amanda turned away from Sam and Kurt and back to Rick where he was standing with his forehead against the observation wall. Touching him softly on the arm, she asked, "Are you okay?"

"I'm fine," Rick lied. Straightening up, he turned to face Amanda and Margie. Steeling himself for the sake of the two women, he continued, "It was pretty hard there for a minute, realizing that my mom did die in the eruption. In addition, seeing my father, who I have missed so much, about did me in. But I'm okay now. Mom's gone to a much better place. And, she and Dad are together again."

Amanda said, "She looked like she was so happy to be reunited with her parents and with her husband."

"She has suffered from multiple sclerosis for so many years. It was good to see her walking normally again," Rick said.

As they were conversing, Kurt came over and put his hand on Amanda's elbow. "Amanda, are you ready to leave?"

Rick once again noticed how Kurt was standing close to Amanda and that she didn't seem to mind. *They had to have at least been friends before the plane crash, and possibly more.*

"How were we able to see Rick's family?" Margie asked Sam. "On Earth, humans don't get to see dead people's spirits."

Sam addressed the whole group, "Why don't you all take a seat, and I'll finish what we started downstairs in the conference room."

As the group was taking their seats, David asked, "Sam, why did you say 'downstairs'? We didn't go up any stairs to get here."

The group had taken their seats. Out of the corner of his eye, Rick noticed that Kurt immediately sat next to Amanda, his shoulder touching hers. Margie took the seat between Kurt and Rick.

Sam answered, "David, I am going to leave that question until later, okay?"

David nodded that it was okay.

Sam continued, "Margie asked a good question just a moment ago. She wondered how you were all able to see Rick's mother's spirit. It is a fact that the human eye is unable to see the spirits of the deceased. However, Mark instructed the observation wall in front of us to convert the image of Janice's spirit into an image that you could see with your eyes."

"Were the other members of Rick's family spirits or angels?"

Alex asked. "And where is this world of spirits that you've been talking about?"

"Let's tackle your questions one at a time," Sam said. "The members of Rick's family that you saw are the same spirits that used to inhabit their bodies while they were alive on the earth. Since the spirits of all humans live on after they die, there has to be a place where they can go to wait to be reunited with their surviving family members that are still on Earth. In addition, spirits wait in the world of spirits for the day of resurrection, a time when their spirits will be reunited with a more perfect version of the body that they left behind on Earth.

"The world of spirits is a beautiful and peaceful place, much like the most beautiful parks on the earth, only there are no weeds, insects, pollutants, or litter. In addition, spirits don't suffer from any diseases and can't be injured like the physical bodies on Earth. Whatever suffering and disease that the spirit might have been afflicted with while in its body on the earth, including mental illness, is instantly and completely left behind at death. That is why Rick's mother was no longer suffering from the ravages of multiple sclerosis that had so severely affected her while she was in her physical body on Earth.

"There is a downside to not having a physical body," Sam continued. "Without the pain and pleasure centers in the brain of the physical body, spirits can't feel many things. A spirit can recognize that the sun is shining, but they can't feel the pleasing warmth it provides. While spirits can feel the things that they touch, they don't feel the physical pleasure of human touch. People in the world of spirits are very much aware of this loss of pleasure associated with no longer being united with a physical body. All spirits long for the day of resurrection when they will be able to feel things again like they did when they had a body."

"I guess that's why my mom didn't hug my dad for very long," Rick said. "I thought for sure that they would hug and kiss for a long time since that haven't seen each other for over ten years."

Fred spoke for the first time, "Sam, what are you? Are you a spirit?"

"Ah. Another difficult topic. I'm acutely aware that I'm laying a lot of heavy stuff on you. I know that each one of you has different preset beliefs about life after death, heaven, God, and so forth. At the same time, I want you to know that I will not discuss whether or not any religion on Earth is the 'true' religion or not." As Sam said the work "true," he used air quotes. "While you are here on this station, both my staff and I will not preach to you about any religion unless you specifically and individually ask for it, and you will not be required to attend our church services on Sundays. While you are here, you are welcome to worship God in any way you like, or not at all. God takes the principles of faith and free agency very seriously. You will all need to continue to live by faith while you are here, as much as that is possible. You will not see God while you are here, and you will not be able to access any information in our computer system about God's existence, other than what has been revealed to prophets. Any questions about what I have been saying?"

No one spoke.

"Now to answer Fred's question," Sam continued. "Besides human spirit bodies that you have just seen on the other side of the observation wall, there are three versions of the human physical body that can be inhabited by spirits. First are the human bodies that your spirits all currently inhabit. While they are a masterful creation by our God, they are the least perfected of the versions of the human body that he has created. As you all know, they can get physically and mentally sick, feel pain, get old, be injured, and even die. While in these bodies, God's spirit children feel intense passions, often leading them to make injurious choices for themselves and for others.

"The next version of the human body is a translated human. This is a more perfected version of the human body that is immune to illness, doesn't feel pain from injury, heals immediately from any injury, and lives for thousands of years. Death only comes to a translated human when they are ready for resurrection, which I will explain in greater depth in just a moment. The transition from a translated human body to a resurrected body is painless and takes no longer that the blink of an eye. Humans from Earth can see translated beings with the naked eye.

"I am a translated being. And, since I am sure that most of you are dying to ask me how old I am, I'll tell you so that you don't die of curiosity, to use a human phrase. I am five hundred-thirty-six Earth-years old. My planet has always been a peaceful and God-fearing planet. Because of that, God has been more open with my people about his creations throughout the universe and has given many of us the opportunity to choose to delay death to instead serve him by helping his children throughout the galaxy. I began working for God when I was about three hundred and ten Earth-years old. Since being translated, I have worked all around the galaxy. I assumed command of this station twenty years ago. And, no, I'm not married. As translated humans, we can serve God both as singles and as married couples.

"The last version of the human body that God has created is the resurrected body. This is the body that all past, present, and future inhabitants of the earth will receive after they die and after the judgment at the end of the world. A resurrected body can never die, doesn't age, never gets sick and doesn't feel pain. While all three bodies look about the same on the outside, the difference is that the resurrected body is flawless. It is unlikely that you will see a resurrected being while you are on this station. Resurrected beings only rarely visit us here."

"Are the rest of the staff here translated humans?" Connie asked.

"Yes, they are. They are from planets all over the galaxy."

"Don't our relatives that have died become angels and watch over us?" Zach asked. "My mom always told me that my grandma was with the angels and that she was watching over me."

"My staff is completely made up of translated beings. There are no spirits from the earth that work with us in this station. However, occasionally God does ask us to have a spirit from the world of spirits visit individuals that they might have a particular influence with, like a wayward boy whose life is changed for the better when he is visited by deceased relative in a vision or dream."

As Sam was finishing, a female and a male dressed in white entered the room behind the survivors and stood in the back of the room.

Sam looked over the heads of the survivors at the newcomers and continued, "I'd like to introduce you to two of my staff members that are going to assist me in helping you to get settled here and to help make your time here as comfortable as possible." Sam motioned for the female and male to come forward.

As the two staff members were walking toward Sam, Kurt spoke out, "How do we know that everything we are seeing is not some elaborate scheme by an alien race to enslave the human race? You smile sincerely, you talk convincingly, you wow us with all this advanced technology, and you've even invoked the name of God as your leader, but what proof do we have that there isn't some vast evil going on here? What are you really doing with the human spirits on the other side of the light?"

"Kurt, I am not able to take you through a portal to the world of spirits to show you what a wonderful place it is. That is where faith has to enter in. You have to believe that there is a better place for all of us after our life in our current bodies ends. As for the alien issue, I am an alien by human definition of aliens. I wasn't born on Earth, and I have never lived on Earth. However, you'll just have to believe me and all of my staff that we only have the best intentions with respect to our brothers and sisters on Earth."

Kurt said, "Then why didn't you warn the people of Seattle about the eruption, instead of sitting idly by while over a hundred thousand men, women, and children were slaughtered? Your words sound sincere, but your inaction suggests a darker hidden agenda. I can't believe that any God would condone your inaction, and I'm sure I'm not the only one here that feels this way." A few people nodded in silent agreement.

Sam said, "The tragedy unfolding below us in the Seattle area is unspeakably horrendous. It absolutely breaks my heart to see so many suffer, especially the children. At the same time, as I have already explained to you, we are only allowed to intervene in human crises when given permission to do so by God. That is something that you will have to accept because I can't change it.

"Now, let me introduce these two members of my staff." He gestured to the woman first. "This is Michaela." The dark brunette women to Sam's right smiled as she scanned the group. Her skin was flawless. She appeared to be about twenty-five years old, but like Sam, there was a maturity that shown through her eyes that belied her youthful appearance. Sam then gestured to the male staff member. "And, this is Ethan." Ethan smiled at the group and nodded his head slightly. He was also young and had strawberry-blond hair.

Sam continued, "In order to expedite getting you settled in and oriented here on our station, I have decided to break you into three smaller groups. Michaela, Ethan, and I will each lead a group. Kurt, Amanda, and Alex will be with Ethan. Fred, David, and Bart will be with Michaela. The rest will be with me.

"Before we head to the cafeteria for breakfast, I want to get back to the question that David asked about how we got to this room from the conference room without climbing stairs or going up an elevator. The answer is simple and yet complicated. After we left the conference room, we passed through a transporter that instantaneously deposited us in an identical hall just outside this room, many feet away from where we started. Those of us on this station have lived with this technology for much of our lives, and we don't think a lot about it. We let Mark know where we want to go in the station, and he opens a portal right in front of us that leads to that location. Of course, Mark makes sure that the other end of the portal is opened in a safe place so that we don't exit the portal on top of someone or into the middle of a pot of boiling water that someone is carrying in the kitchen. Once the portal is open, we just walk through. Unlike the transporter systems that your film industry has dreamed up for years, you don't notice or feel anything. The process is instantaneous."

Bart said, "Are you telling us that you vaporized us and then reconstituted us instantaneously thousands of feet away without us noticing anything? That is not physically possible. Even if it were, the energy requirements would be immense."

"Hold on, Bart," Sam said. "You are attempting to understand what happens here at this station only by the physics of the physical universe that you live in. To avoid a lengthy discussion that you and Michaela can have later, let's just leave it at this. The laws of physics of the universe that is known to you don't allow for instantaneous transportation of matter through space. Instantaneous transportation through space is instead accomplished through the laws of physics that govern the spiritual part of the universe. Those laws are quite different than the laws that govern the physical universe."

"And this spiritual universe is in the same space-time continuum that the physical universe occupies?" Bart asked.

"Yes. Just recently your scientists have been allowed to begin to discern the presence of what they have named dark matter and dark energy, although they don't really have a good idea of what either one is. In reality, they are seeing for the first time, although indirectly, the presence of the spiritual universe."

CHAPTER 13

THE YOUNG BRUNETTE in cut-off jeans and a short T-shirt bent over at the waist to put a dishwashing tablet into the soap dispenser of the dishwasher in her kitchen. Rick couldn't help but notice the perfect proportions of her trim figure.

"Hey, that's my sister you're looking at," Margie said. "Guys, keep your thoughts out of the gutter, please." After everyone had split into their three separate groups, Sam had suggested that they try out the computer system in one of the vacant angel's staging rooms to check on someone that they knew on Earth. Margie had suggested that they look in on her sister, Samantha, who lived in Houston.

Margie's sister shut the dishwasher door as she stood up and then started the cleaning cycle with the push of a button. Taking off her apron, she then headed down a hall that led away from the kitchen. Rick could see that she had the same eyes as Margie and a similar mouth to Margie's. The computer system followed Margie's sister down the hallway. Stopping to grab a bath towel from a hall closet, she headed for a bedroom. Once in the bedroom, she kicked off her slippers and reached behind her head to pull off her T-shirt.

"Sam, this is getting a little personal. Don't you think you should keep us from watching things like..." The image on the screen was replaced by a view of a red, covered bridge over a small river in what looked like a New England countryside. "Image Blocked" appeared in red letters in the center of the screen. "Oh," Margie continued after a pause. "I guess you already took care of that possibility."

Sam said, "Mark is acutely aware of the intensely pleasurable feelings that earthly beings can experience when presented with an unclothed human figure. Viewing of any sexually oriented images or video, recorded or live, on the station's systems by any of the survivors will be blocked."

Connie asked, "What about the angels, or even you, for example? What keeps you from secretly checking out someone that you are attracted to?"

"We just don't look. I know that sounds hard to believe from your perspective, but translated humans aren't exactly like earthly humans. One of the changes is a subtle dampening in arousal related to members of the opposite sex that we only know casually. However, once translated beings fall in love, they imprint on their long-term partner and their degree of sexual attraction is then no different than any earthly human, but it's only with their long-term partner. That isn't saying that translated beings don't find companionship with members of the opposite sex to be appealing. It's just that the attraction is much more to the person than to their physical body. It makes it so much easier to fall in love for the right reasons when sexual attraction isn't getting in the way."

"You expect me to believe that? Males are males," Margie said.

Rick smiled. Margie had quite the sense of humor.

"You'll just have to take my word on this one," Sam said.

"I wish more men were like that," Connie said. "Being interesting to a guy only because of your anatomy gets really old."

Sam and his group finished with their introduction to the computer system in their angel's staging room and then headed to the cafeteria. Ethan's group was already there. Michaela's group was forced to walk to the cafeteria since Bart refused to enter a portal. As a result, Michaela's group arrived at the cafeteria twenty minutes later than the rest.

Lunch was excellent, compliments of Mark. They were informed that Mark could create any dish in the universe. Mark started with subatomic particles and then constructed the needed atoms, molecules, proteins, carbohydrates, fats, and flavorings, according to recipes stored in his memory banks. Sam informed them that the food that Mark produced was always flawless in taste and presentation.

Immediately after lunch, the survivors left in their groups to be introduced to their assigned angel's staging rooms. Each group had been assigned to a different room that was not currently in use. The room that Sam's group was assigned was identical to the angel's staging room that they had visited at the beginning of their tour. The table in the center of the room was sectioned off into six work areas, three on each side. Once Mark turned the system on, the image to be viewed was presented in the air just above the table as a three-dimensional hologram. There was no visible screen or projector.

Sam turned to the others in his group, "You are welcome to use this angel's staging room when it is not in use, which will be pretty much all the time. We have thousands of similar rooms at our disposal and only rarely need to put them all to use. We were using all of them for the first few hours after the eruption yesterday, but that was the first time since the 1970 Bhola cyclone in what was then East Pakistan."

"Besides spying on our family, what else can we do with this system?" Rick asked.

"For writers like Margie, this system contains real-time recordings of all world events from an infinite number of viewing angles and with an almost infinite degree of magnification."

"You've got to be kidding," Margie said, her eyes suddenly bright in anticipation. "You mean I can really find out who shot JFK?"

"That and about every other historical mystery that you can possibly imagine."

"Okay, I'm in," Margie said. "Where do I sign up?" She paused. "Wait a minute. If I do find out who killed JFK, who built Stonehenge, and where the lost city of Atlantis is, who will I tell? I can never go back to Earth."

Sam didn't respond.

Margie remained silent for a few moments, her excitement flagging a little. "Well, it doesn't mean that I still don't want to know the answers to the millions of questions that I have always wondered about. I just wish I had someone to tell about what I find."

"You can tell your fellow survivors; you could tell one of my staff; or you can record it either in text or audio," Sam said. "Mark can help you with that."

"It's just not the same as telling the whole world." Margie sighed. "Maybe I'll write a book about what I find and hope that someone on Earth gets a hold of a copy someday."

"You do that. I'd like to read it myself," Sam said. He then turned to address the others, "Connie, you'll be fascinated by delving into the history of the creation of Earth. Rick, you'll find that there are detailed diagrams for any machine that has ever been invented on Earth. And Zach, you'll find thousands of hours of recordings of songs and histories from the careers of musicians throughout history."

"Cool," Zach said.

Connie said, "I guess I am interested in your take on the creation of the world. I hope it is well balanced and isn't just a whole bunch of mumbo-jumbo Bible talk, like 'God created the world in seven days.'"

"Oh, I'm sure that the geologist in you will be more than satisfied with what you will find," Sam said with a smile.

Rick asked, "Are we going to be allowed to use the portals that we saw the angels use?"

"It was only a matter of time until someone asked that. To be honest, we're not sure how much access we should give you to the transporter system as it pertains to traveling to Earth." Sam paused for a moment, looking off into the distance. "Okay, for starters, we will allow you to visit places on Earth as long as there is no chance that you will run into another human being and as long as you don't move farther than one hundred yards from the transporter's exit. If you attempt to contact someone or attempt to escape, Mark will instantly transport you back here."

"That's cruel," Margie said. "Let us look, but not stay. That's like giving a baby one lick of a sucker and then taking it away."

"You can't return to live on Earth, especially with what you now know about this station." Sam paused. "Okay, as a demonstration, let's take a few minutes to check out a remote section of the Amazon."

Sam turned toward the outside wall near where he was standing. A moment later, a portal appeared against the wall. Through the opening, the group could see a small clearing in a jungle that was surrounded by a thick green wall of vegetation. Sunlight filtered in through a canopy of trees. Sam asked them to follow him and then he walked through the portal without any hesitation. He took a couple of steps across the clearing and then turned around.

"Come on, guys." He motioned them forward with his hand. "There is nothing to be afraid of."

"In for a dime, in for a dollar," Maggie said as she walked through the portal and joined Sam. Zach and Connie followed.

Upon seeing that the others hadn't been instantly melted into a mass of smoking protoplasm by passing through the portal, Rick brought up the rear. Rick's nose was immediately assailed by the smell of decaying vegetation. His body felt like it was being suffocated by stifling heat and humidity and his ears were being assaulted by the noise of a thousand humming insects. A canopy of green treetops extended as far as he could see in all directions. A large snake began uncoiling from a branch of a tree just thirty feet from where they stood, its eyes never looking away from their group. The ear-splitting scream of a jaguar resounded throughout the jungle.

The group looked around warily as Margie said, "Uh, Sam? Are you sure we're safe here?"

"Mark is keeping an eye on the jaguar. It's moving away from us."

"How do you know that for sure? Do you have a telepathic link with Mark?"

"Another perk of being a translated being." Sam smiled and then slapped the side of his neck with his hand.

The buzzing sound of insects intensified. "Ouch," Alex said. "These bugs bite."

Soon, they were all swatting at bugs, trying to keep from being bitten.

"Sam, get us out of here," Connie said.

"Head back through the portal," Sam cried out.

Rick didn't have to be coaxed any further. He had never thought that he would be grateful to leave Earth and get back on the station, but at the moment, there was no question that he was. The others quickly followed him; Sam brought up the rear.

Back in the angel's staging room, Margie said to Sam, "Thanks for the object lesson. Was that designed to convince us not to try to visit Earth?"

"No. I'm so sorry. I didn't think that the bugs would be so bad. I picked the Amazon because I knew that Connie had always wanted to visit the Amazon."

"Yeah, but someone forgot the bug spray," Rick said.

"Sam, how did you know I've always wanted to visit the Amazon?" Connie asked.

"When I learned that ten of you had survived the crash, I hurriedly acquainted myself with your lives so that I could better help you adjust to your new life here." Rick noticed that Sam had hesitated for just a moment when he had replied and had then looked away from Connie while he spoke. *Was he telling the truth?*

It was almost dinnertime when Michaela burst into the staging room where the members of Sam's group had each been lost for the past two hours in searching what Margie had already dubbed the "GWW," or the galaxy wide web.

"Sam! Fred's on the outside, and he's threatening to jump."

Sam was out the door in an instant, with the others close behind. Rick figured that they must have entered and exited a portal in the hallway outside their staging room because they arrived at the stairwell they had come through the night before within seconds. Bounding up the steps to the door to the roof, they exited into bright daylight. As Rick followed Sam onto the roof of the station, he quickly spotted Fred twenty feet off to his right, standing still and looking down. Beyond Fred, the horizon was obscured by massive clouds of billowing black and gray ash from the still erupting Mount Rainier. Even from this distance, Rick could see that the clouds of ash were being lanced on and off with stabs of lightening, and he could hear the faint rumbling of thunder.

Led by Sam, the group slowly approached Fred.

As soon as they came within six feet of where he was perched on the edge of the station, Fred exclaimed, "Don't come any closer, or I'll jump."

Sam said. "Fred. I know that this is all very strange for you—"

"Don't try to talk me out of this, child of Satan. I won't follow you into hell."

"This station has nothing to do with Satan, and we are not Satan's followers."

"You're trying to deceive me, just as Matthew predicted in the Bible when he said that false Christs and false prophets will appear and perform great signs and miracles to deceive even the elect. You haven't deceived me. You are trying to divert the children of God away from him and entice them to hell. But you won't get me. You might have orchestrated the eruption and the plane crash in an attempt to bring me and my fellow travelers into your scheme to encircle us about with the chains of hell, dragging us down into the eternal pit of fire and damnation. But you can't keep me from dying for real, bypassing your trap, and entering into the safety of God's kingdom."

As Fred was speaking, Amanda had come up behind Margie and Rick and had stopped at Rick's left side. She leaned over to Rick and said softly, "It doesn't sound like we can talk him out of jumping, does it?"

"Fred. Don't do this," Margie called out.

"By your very words, you have shown yourself to be on his side now. You have all become his servants. You are all damned to hell, and I am not going with you." Without another word and without looking back at them, Fred stepped off the edge and disappeared.

CHAPTER 14

"HURRY UP. THEY could come back anytime." Kurt hunched close to Alex. They were alone in their group's angel's staging room.

Minutes before, Kurt and Alex's group leader, Ethan, had learned from Michaela that Fred was missing, and he and Amanda had left the room. As soon as they were gone, Alex had said, "Even though I might not be able to check out hot women on this system, I wonder if it will let me check out even more tempting things." His hands had flown through a series of images on the table in front of him, with no single image being displayed for more than a few seconds.

"What do you mean?" When Alex didn't answer, Kurt continued, "I'm amazed that you already know the system so well. That skill could really be an asset."

"This is just a computer," Alex said. "Sure, it's way more advanced than anything I've ever worked on before. But it's still just a computer. No computer system has ever denied me what I wanted before, and this one is no exception."

"You don't say. Can you have it look into a bank vault?"

Alex chuckled. "I hadn't thought of that possibility yet. What bank vault do you have in mind?"

"Let's go for broke. How about the Federal Reserve Bank of New York's vault? It sits on the bedrock eighty-feet below street level and supposedly holds more gold in one place that any other vault in the world. It's worth about three-hundred-billion dollars. Even taking a peek at the gold in the vault would be pretty much impossible for anyone on Earth and stealing some of the gold would be even more impossible."

Even as Kurt was speaking, Alex brought up a three-dimensional image of an eleven-story, gray-stone building with its flanks pierced with evenly spaced rows of small windows. It even looked like a bank.

"Taking a gander at the gold will be child's play. Just watch," Alex said. He zoomed in on the base of the stone building until their point of view came to rest on a burnished steel wall. A walkway through the wall extended about twelve feet to a floor to ceiling metal grate that was currently closed. Wheels with spokes, similar to ship's wheels, were mounted on each side of the entrance to the walkway. "The wheels are part of a locking system that is used to open and close the metal grate."

"Can you get look inside?"

"Sure." The view moved down the hall just like they were seeing through the eyes of someone that was physically walking down the hall. The only difference was that their vantage point didn't have to stop at the tightly-spaced bars but moved right through them and into the room beyond. Without being asked, Alex panned around the room, revealing side-chamber after side-chamber, each filled with thousands of gold bars.

"Whew, would you look at that." The excitement in Kurt's voice was palpable. "Can you open a portal into the vault just like Ethan did to that mountain meadow where he took us in the French Alps?"

"I'm way ahead of you," Alex said. "Give me just a moment here."

"I can't believe that Fred is threatening to jump. He is way too intense. Religious types all act so high and mighty, but their religion sucks all the fun out of their lives. Wherever he is, I hope that it takes Michaela and Ethan a long time to find him."

"Got it." Alex turned around in his chair, got up, and moved toward a portal that had opened just behind him, revealing a doorway-sized image of the vault. "We need to hurry. We should only take one bar since we'll have a hard enough time hiding it from the others once we return to this room."

"Will we be able to get back once we go through the portal?"

"Don't worry. Mark won't let us escape that easily."

Kurt let Alex go through first. Alex turned around once he was through and saw that Kurt was still on the other side of the portal. "Come on. We don't have all day."

Kurt took a deep breath and walked through the portal. "These portals give me the willies. I kind of agree with Bart."

"Well, you're not going to get any gold by staying in the angel's staging room." As he spoke, Alex had hurried over to one of the side chambers and grabbed a bar of gold. "This stuff is heavy," he said as he turned and almost ran into Kurt. "Come on, let's get out of here."

Kurt said, "Now that I'm here, I want to enjoy the view for just a moment. On top of that, I think I'm going to take a bar for myself. How did you think that we were going to divide up one bar between us?" He grabbed a bar of gold and hefted it easily with one hand.

"Suit yourself. I'm out of here." Alex hustled back through the portal. It didn't take long, and Alex appeared behind him in the staging room.

As soon as Kurt was through, Alex closed the portal from his seat at the table. Kurt sat next to him. "What do we do with the bars? I don't think that holding them behind our backs is going to get us very far."

Without a reply, Alex opened a portal into his room on the station. As he rose from his chair to pass through the portal, he heard Ethan's voice outside the door to their angel's staging room. He motioned fiercely to Kurt to bring his gold bar over to the portal.

Alex yanked the bar out of Kurt's hands, heaved both bars through the portal onto the floor in his room, dove into his chair, and shut the portal.

A moment later, Ethan entered the room. Seeing Kurt and Alex at the table, he said, "Fred just jumped to his death. Sam wants us to be there in the portal observation room to see him pass."

CHAPTER 15

"TAKE A SEAT, please." Sam stood in the front of the portal observation room. His back was turned to glass-like wall. "For those of you that weren't there, Fred leaped to his death from the top of the station just a few minutes ago." As Sam was speaking, the portal room behind him began filling with light. Sam turned to face the portal as the walls and floor of the portal room turned brilliant white. From Rick's vantage point, it seemed like the walls of the room had dissolved and that the featureless bright white landscape went on forever in all directions.

The brilliance of the landscape was outdone moments later as an even more brilliant white light began shining from a portal to the world of spirits that had just opened. Less than a second later, a man dressed in a flowing, white, full-length robe strode into the portal room from the world of spirits. Unlike the spirits of Rick's family, the man's body glowed with a light that was just as bright as the still-open portal to the world of spirits. The group in the observation room was completely silent in awe and anticipation.

Fred appeared at the right side of the portal room. He looked first at the man in front of him in the room and then briefly around the portal. His gaze lingered in the direction of the observation room. Apparently unable to see them, Fred returned his gaze to the man in white. "Who are you?"

"I am John, one of Christ's original apostles. God sent me to help guide you to the light." John's voice was gentle and loving, and it made Rick feel a warmth in his chest.

"How do I know that you're not with Sam and his demons?"

"Fred, you are in a good place where demons have no influence. The peace you feel should reassure you that this is true."

Fred paused for a moment. "It is true that I am feeling only peace. Just moments ago, before I died, I had feared greatly for my soul. I was so concerned that if I stayed on the station with Sam, I would end up trapped forever by Satan in hell. To escape, I jumped from the station to my death. But, as I fell, I recognized that by committing suicide, I had murdered one of God's children. I have always preached against the evil of committing suicide. As the ground rushed up to meet me, my heart ached in my chest with concern that I was going to be thrust down to hell anyway for committing such a grievous sin. But now, I recognize that the peace that I am feeling is the peace that only God could bring to my soul. Has God forgiven me for what I have done?"

John walked toward Fred and enveloped him in his arms. "Fred, you will not be held accountable for jumping from the station. You truly believed that you were sacrificing your life to avoid becoming a slave to Satan. Come with me and enter into God's rest."

"I'll go with you," Fred said, nodding his head. He suddenly stared in the direction of the group behind the transparent wall. "But just tell me for sure that Sam isn't behind a wall over there, rubbing his hands with glee that he has trapped me in a counterfeit kingdom of Satan."

"Trust your heart, Fred. You know that you are making the right choice."

Turning slowly away from the group of survivors and back to John, Fred said, "You're right. I'm ready to go with you."

Arm in arm, Fred and the John stepped into the light and were gone.

"Was that really John from the Bible?" Connie asked. "He's over two thousand years old."

Sam answered, "Yes, it was John. John is a resurrected being. Because of our concern that Fred would refuse to enter the light because he believed the portals to be a work of Satan, we had to bring in what you call on Earth 'one of the big guns.' John agreed to travel here to help out since Fred has always related well to John's writings in the Bible. In addition, we chose an eternal white background because we felt that anything else would be construed to be part of one of the portals Fred saw on our station. We elected not to have his family meet him in the portal because it was also too much like what he had just witnessed at Rick's mother's passing. He might have then rejected his family members as being Satan's followers disguised as his family. As you can see, it all turned out okay."

"How can resurrected beings can enter the world of spirits when we can't?" Rick asked.

"Humans from Earth and translated humans can't enter the world of spirits, at least until after death. Resurrected beings have previously died, passed through the world of spirits and then been resurrected. They are able to reenter the world of spirits at any time."

Kurt said, "John looked just like any one of us. What makes him so different from you or even from me? How do we know for sure that he's one of these magical resurrected beings and not just a man that the observation wall displayed to us as shining brilliantly?"

"I assure you that John is a resurrected being," Sam said. "It wasn't just an optical illusion."

Kurt asked, "If he is resurrected, then he can't be killed, correct?

"Nothing can kill a resurrected being."

Kurt fell silent.

Sam said, "Okay, time for dinner. I'm sure we all need a break from the stress of losing Fred."

As the group moved toward the door, Rick overheard Kurt talking to Alex off to one side of the room, "Sam is trying to trick us into believing all the crap he keeps spouting. He's an alien and so are all of his staff. We can't trust them. They're up to something, but I can't tell what it is yet."

Alex said, "I agree. This whole place doesn't make sense. There has to be something dark going on behind all this."

Kurt nodded as he said, "As for these resurrected beings, I say that if it walks and talks, then it can also die. Stick with me, and you'll see that these aliens can be snuffed out just like anyone else."

CHAPTER 16

"IT'S SO AMAZING to see it all right there in front of me," Amanda said. "So many diseases could be cured and so many lives could be saved with just a fraction of the information that I have discovered. The only problem is I can't get the information back to Earth where it can be of help."

Amanda and Rick sat across from each other in the cafeteria. The survivors had eaten together as a group for the first few meals. However, as they had become engrossed in their individual discoveries on the station, they had started eating only when they were hungry. Now, they only occasionally ran into each other in the cafeteria.

At the moment, Amanda and Rick were the only occupants of the dining room. Amanda had arrived a few minutes after Rick, picked up her meal, and then had joined Rick at his table. They had been conversing about the discoveries they had each made while using the station computer's amazing search engine.

"What are some of the diseases that you've learned how to cure?" Rick asked. He still found it hard to look at her since her beauty still made it hard for him to breathe.

"The computer system here has the cures for diabetes, heart

disease, and all kinds of cancer. As far as I can tell, it has the cures for every disease known to man."

"That's incredible. But then wouldn't you be out of a job?"

"That's okay with me. I'd give up my job in a heartbeat if I just could stop all the suffering that my patients go through."

"What kind of cures are these?"

"The cures listed in the system for the majority of human diseases are achieved by repairing errors in the non-coding parts of our DNA."

"I thought that most diseases came from errors in the genes that coded for proteins and not from errors in the non-coding parts of our DNA. Isn't that the whole point of the Human Genome Project?"

"You surprise me, Rick. How does a car mechanic know about the Human Genome Project?"

"Hey, just because I'm a car mechanic, it doesn't mean I don't have a brain. It might come as a surprise to you, but I did start college as a pre-med student."

"So what happened? Why didn't you finish?"

"My mom developed MS soon after I was born. In spite of the best efforts from her medical providers, she progressively got worse throughout my childhood. After my father died of a ruptured brain aneurysm in my senior year of high school, her MS got a lot worse. By the end of my freshman year in college, she was so bad that I had to quit school to take care of her. I moved back in with her and opened an auto repair shop just a block away from her house so that I could always be nearby. Even though she needed me at home with her, I had to work long hours to pay the bills that Medicare and her Social Security payments wouldn't cover."

Amanda reached out and put her hand on top of Rick's. Her touch thrilled him and made it hard for him to think. *Does she like me, or is she just being kind?*

"Rick, you're a truly a hero in my eyes. You unselfishly gave up everything for your mother. I'm sure that she was grateful for your help. And I want to say again that I'm so sorry for your loss at her passing."

Rick noticed small tears forming in the corners of Amanda's beautiful eyes. She took her hand away from his to wipe away the tears. His hand ached at the loss of her touch, but at least his brain recovered to a degree from its stupor so that he could think again. "Thank you. I miss her a lot."

Amanda smiled. Her eyes were still filled with tears, making them sparkle even more. What was it about Amanda? It had been hard for him in the presence of other beautiful women in the past, but it was worse than ever with Amanda. He had to change the subject quickly or he was going blurt out something embarrassing. "I'm interested to know more about the cures for diseases that you found that are in the non-coding part of human DNA."

"Okay. The computer here has the exact sequences for defects in our DNA that cause all known human diseases. Most aren't single base-pair mutations like we have been looking for. Instead, the defective sequences are thousands and even tens of thousands of base-pairs long. According to the computer, every one of these defective controlling genes was placed in the human DNA on purpose to make us prone to disease, suffering, and death. The computer then lists the correct form of each defective gene and lists ways that the defective genes can be corrected. Most of the information is way over my head and would take me forever to figure out, but there are scientists on Earth that could use this information to save so many lives. I know that we're not supposed to ever be able to communicate with anyone on Earth, but I've been thinking about writing some of it down, going through a portal to a lone mailbox somewhere, and sending it to someone that would know what to do with it."

"Sam will never let you do that. If scientists on Earth were meant to have that information, then Sam would have already allowed it to happen."

"It's just plain wrong that Sam is playing God and keeping information of this degree of importance from the earth."

"I don't think that it's Sam's decision. I think it's God's decision."

"What kind of God would let his children suffer and die unnecessarily when he has the cures to all diseases right at his fingertips? That's a God that I'm not sure that I can believe in."

"Me neither," Kurt's voice chimed in from the food-service area.

Rick realized that Kurt must have slipped in unnoticed while he had been engrossed in his conversation with Amanda.

Kurt continued, "Sam and his staff are meddling in the lives of the people on Earth in ways that really scare me. They are supposedly doing it in the name of some all-knowing God. Yet, we can't see or hear this God. They refuse to prove to us that he exists. To me, that means that they are just using the name of God to justify their wrongdoings."

Rick said, "I haven't noted any evil intent in any of Sam's actions. Sam seems like a genuinely nice—"

"He killed your mother," Kurt said as he sat down next to Amanda, his shoulder touching hers.

It wasn't lost on Rick that she didn't move away.

Kurt continued, "Sam could have warned the Seattle area about the impending disaster and saved so many lives. For all we know, he might have even caused the eruption because his unseen God told him to do it. And he is holding us against our wills and won't ever let us leave. I could go on and on, but if that doesn't sound like evil intent, Rick, then what is?" As Kurt finished, he grinned triumphantly at Rick as he put his arm around Amanda's shoulders.

Even though he was grinning, Rick was puzzled that Kurt's eyes remained cold as ice. Amanda still wasn't making any effort to move away from him. Rick couldn't think of anything to say in response to Kurt's argument. It was true that Sam was holding them prisoner, but Rick was sure that Sam hadn't caused the eruption. However, Rick didn't have the heart at the moment to argue with Kurt since Kurt had clearly already won Amanda's heart. The disappointment and sense of failure hurt like he had been suckerpunched in the stomach.

Turning to Amanda, Kurt said, "So what were you two talking about?"

"I was just explaining to Rick that I had found cures for diabetes, heart disease, and more in the computer."

"I heard you say that the cause for most human disease was purposely inserted by Sam's alien race into the non-coding portion of human DNA. From my time at MIT as a grad student, I learned quite a bit about epigenetics." He stopped and stared right at Rick with a smug look on his face. Turning back to Amanda, he continued, "So what were the gene alterations that you discovered, chromatin remodeling, altered RNA signaling, or DNA methylation?"

"Wow," Amanda said. "Those terms are new to me. You'll have to explain them to me."

Kurt said, "Even better, after we eat, why don't you show me the gene-based cures that you have discovered? I'm sure I can help you understand them better, and maybe together we can figure out a way to get around Sam and get some of the information to Earth."

As Amanda excitedly explained to Kurt about her discoveries and how much they might help different patients that she had seen in her practice with incurable diseases, she glanced less and less at Rick. Feeling totally outclassed by Kurt, unwanted by Amanda, and acutely embarrassed that he had imagined even for a moment that she might be interested in him, Rick suddenly stood, muttered a goodbye, and turned to leave.

"Rick, do you really need to leave so soon?" Amanda asked. "It would be nice if you hung out with us for a little longer."

Rick looked back at her, sitting there looking absolutely radiant with Kurt's arm around her. That, along with the look on Kurt's face that clearly said, "Get lost, loser," only reinforced the urgent need he felt to flee. "I need to get back to looking at some specs on some 1920s engines. I'll catch you both later."

Without looking back, he left the dining room. *Why are some guys born with all the good looks and charm? It seems that no matter how*

I try to be attractive to women, some smarter, funnier, more talented, or more charismatic guy with a more handsome face and a brawnier physique shows up and steals the women away.

Arriving back at his group's angel's staging room, Rick noticed that Zach was still on the other side of the table, watching the same young woman that he had been watching when Rick had left for the dining room. The young woman was still curled up in a comforter on the same sofa in her posh hotel room and was still watching TV.

"If you watch Tye long enough, I'm sure she'll finally get off the couch."

"Dude, you don't have any clue why I do what I do."

"Now I've been reduced to being a surf bum."

"Sorry, man. It's just something that kids my age say. No offence meant."

Rick grinned as he walked over to where Zach was sitting. "What is it about this woman that is keeping you from investigating all of the other amazing stuff that's stored in this system? Surely you're interested in what music kids your age are listening to in other parts of the world?"

"I already checked that out. They listen to some weird crap when they're not listening to American music. I gave up on that idea. I like our music better."

"If I'm not mistaken, I think you mostly just like the music from one young woman, right? Have you even eaten since you last woke up?"

"I'm really not hungry." Zach was silent for a moment. "You're right; I'm probably a little obsessed with Tye. I can't help it. She's so beautiful and so cool. When she sings, it's like an angel is singing."

"Have you ever met her? I mean, in person?"

Ignoring him, Zach shrunk the image of Tye on the couch and put it on the left side of his work area, next to an image of a stage in a stadium somewhere. A tiny stage crew in the image was preparing for a concert. Without asking, Rick knew that the stage crew was preparing for one of Tye's concerts.

Zach spoke louder, "Show Tye's public release video of her singing 'Your Love Lights Me Up.'" Instantly, a three-dimensional view of the same young woman appeared in front of them, although she was now heavily made up and was wearing a short, tight miniskirt with a low-cut top. Along with four other similarly-clad young women, she moved toward the front of the image from the depths of a mist-enshrouded mountain top, dancing to a strong beat that Rick hadn't heard before. She began singing. Rick was surprised that her voice was truly quite good. Rick watched for a few moments in silence.

"This song made it to number three on the charts. It should have been number one. It's my favorite."

"She is pretty good."

"She's more than good; she's the best. One thing that really gets me about being stuck here is that I can't update my website that is dedicated to Tye. There are so many pictures and 3D videos stored here in this computer system about Tye that the world has never seen. I am dying to be the one to introduce them to the world on my website. Tye would be so impressed. You know, I did get an email from her once."

"Oh, yeah?" Rick was genuinely surprised.

"Oh, yeah. It said, 'Please cease posting non-public domain pictures of Tye on your website, or legal action will be taken.' That tells me that she has been checking out my website and that she knows who I am."

Rick didn't know whether to laugh or not.

Tye finished her song, and as the music began to fade, she stood and stared into the distance.

"Freeze," Zach said. The image obediently froze in front of them. He stood up from his chair and said, "Magnify to only show Tye, full size, standing in front of me." Tye's image grew quickly until only Tye was visible while her image moved toward them until she was standing on the ground in front of the table. The detail was incredible. If Rick hadn't known, he would have thought that the real Tye was now in the room with them. She was close enough to Rick that he stepped back to where he felt like he wasn't invading her personal space, which seemed really weird since she wasn't really there. Zach didn't move back at all, but he just stood right in front of her image with a look of rapture lighting up his face.

"See? She's a goddess."

"All I can see is a girl who is young enough to be my daughter and that you're salivating over her a little too much." Rick continued a little louder, "Mark, turn off the life-sized image. Zach's already obsessed with Tye enough, and this is just making it worse."

Mark's voice spoke from everywhere, something that was still hard for Rick to get used to. "Zach, is it okay that I turn off Tye's full-sized image?"

Zach looked at Rick sharply for a moment, his brows knitted in frustration over Rick's meddling, and then he turned back to Tye's image. After a moment, he spoke softly, "I guess so." As soon as Tye's image blinked out of existence, Zach turned to Rick. "Why did you have to do that?"

"Zach, you're way too obsessed with Tye. It's not healthy. You don't even know her."

"Dude, who are you to tell me what to do? You're not my father."

"Hey, Zach, calm down. You're an adult, albeit a very young adult, and you can choose to do what you want with your time. I was just trying to save you some heartache since you're here and she's there on Earth and there is no way that you and she will ever meet."

Zach said with a wail of despair, "I know. I know."

CHAPTER 17

"**Y**OU REALLY DO believe that your God created the earth and then moved it here to its present orbit?" Connie asked.

"Yes, in very simplified terms, that is exactly what I am trying to tell you," Sam replied.

To Connie, the guy was either a really good liar, or he was so deceived that he actually believed the lies that his God-based society was feeding him. "To start with, most of us on Earth with any degree of intelligence have gone way past belief in the creation theory. There is just too much evidence to the contrary."

Sam smiled. "So you're lumping me in with all the other folk on Earth that possess a lesser intelligence?"

"No, that's not what I'm saying. You are plenty smart, probably way smarter than me."

"Have you ever given thought to the fact that humans have always had a knack for adopting widespread beliefs that are later proven completely false? They have held to these beliefs so fiercely that they have historically imprisoned and even killed those that disagreed."

"It is true that over the centuries we scientists have believed in some pretty bizarre ideas. But, in recent years, science has pretty much proven that life on Earth evolved from single cells and not from creation by a supreme being. Scientists have worked hard to eradicate theories that are not based on fact. Now you're trying to convince me that God has the power not only to create the Earth, but also to perform the impossible task of moving it thousands of light years across the galaxy.

"I really love how your mind thinks. You are so fun to talk to."

"Hey, quit trying to soften me up with compliments. It makes me mad because it really does work, even though I'm not sure I want it to work."

"If you'll just give me a chance, I will open your mind to the real truths of the earth, along with enough evidence for each truth so that you won't be able to deny their truth."

"And you won't try to convince me that I have to believe in God at the same time?"

"You already know the rules I have to follow—Wait a minute." Sam was suddenly all business. "Sorry, but I've got to leave right now."

"What's wrong?"

"Nothing that you need to worry yourself about. I'll be back as soon as I can."

CHAPTER 18

ALONE IN HIS angel's staging room, Alex looked longingly at the image on the top of the table in front of him. It was his grandparent's cabin in Vail, Colorado. He had spent many summers mountain biking, four-wheeling, and fishing with his family. It was summer now, and the image looked so real and inviting. Sam had said that they could go anywhere on Earth as long as they didn't come in contact with another human, as long as they didn't try to contact anyone on Earth by any means, and as long as they didn't go too far away from the portal. Well, there wasn't anyone at the cabin so maybe he could drop in and hang out for a while. Maybe Sam and Mark would even forget that he was gone, and he could escape. It was time to test Mark out to see just how secure their prison was.

Using his hands to manipulate the menus in front of him, Alex requested that a portal be opened to the driveway of the cabin. He was relieved to see the portal appear right behind him. That confirmed that no one was at the cabin at the present. Sliding his chair out, he headed for the portal. His heart beat hard in his chest. If he could just walk through the portal, then why couldn't he just walk away and disappear once he was on the other side?

Once through the portal and on the driveway, he breathed deeply of the mountain air. It felt so good to be out of the station and back in his old stomping ground. Pulling out the key that was hidden under the rock to the left of the front door, he let himself into the cabin. It smelled a little musty inside, like no one had been there for a few weeks, but it was home, and he didn't care. Reflexively, he checked the fridge for a snack. It was empty. *Darn it.* He opened the pantry but found only canned foods. He wasn't that hungry. After a few more minutes of walking through the cabin, he began to realize that being there alone wasn't as fun as being there with family. The place was just too empty. He turned off the lights, locked the front door, and replaced the key under the rock. The portal to the angel's staging room was still open in the driveway, but he wasn't ready to return just yet.

Looking around, he figured that he would head toward the nearby stream where he had gone swimming so many times when he was a kid. Maybe Mark would lose track of him, and he would be able to escape.

Arriving at the stream a few minutes later, he found it just as he had remembered it. In midsummer, as it was now, the flow in the creek had quieted down to a gentle babbling with quiet pools here and there. The old tree bridge still stretched over the stream. He hopped onto the tree trunk and walked confidently across the log, just like he had so many times in his youth. Halfway across the stream, he was suddenly back in the angel's staging room. The portal to the cabin must have closed an instant later because when he turned back to the wall to see what had happened, there was only the blank wall of the staging room staring back at him.

"So we really are prisoners, aren't we?" he said out loud.

"I'm sorry if the sudden transportation back to this room surprised you," Mark said. "I was just following Sam's instructions for an occurrence in which one of you exceeded the distance limit for travel away from a portal."

"That's still called being a prisoner from where I'm from. Who gave you the right to lock us up like this?"

"I'm sorry, but you'll have to take that up with Sam."

CHAPTER 19

KURT PUT HIS fork down next to his unfinished piece of hot apple pie a la mode. "Man is the food good here. I thought I had room for my favorite desert, but I can't eat another bite."

Amanda had also been too full for desert. "I consider myself a pretty good cook, but why cook when you can have food like this all the time? I'm going to have to be careful, or I'm going to get as big as a house."

"Yeah, right. I bet that cute little waist of yours doesn't have an extra ounce of fat on it." He stretched and then let his arm again fall around her shoulders.

Amanda smiled as she said, "That was smooth. I bet you're quite the lady's man back on Earth." His eyes were so blue and looked so intelligent. With his arm around her shoulders, she could feel the hard muscles of his arm through his shirt. His closeness made it just a little harder for her to breath.

"Oh, I've dated some, but I've never met anyone quite as enchanting as you."

"You're also quite a flatterer." She looked up at his eyes, expecting him to be looking at her. But his eyes were looking down at her cleavage. She quickly checked to be sure that her shirt hadn't been pulled down or wasn't gaping open for some reason, but she was well covered. With irritation, she asked, "Hey, Kurt, what color are my eyes?"

He glanced up at her eyes, but his eyes were unfocused, and his pupils were dilated. Instead of answering her question, he murmured, "Kiss me." He began to pull her closer.

Kissing him wasn't completely out of the question for Amanda. It was just a little too fast. Why had he suddenly grown so amorous?

Her question went unanswered as the door to the dining room suddenly opened, and Sam bustled in. Kurt instantly loosened his arm from around her shoulders, and Amanda scooted away from him on the bench seat they had been sitting on. Amanda blushed. She didn't dare look at Kurt to see if he were just as embarrassed as she was.

"Hi, guys," Sam called out as he approached them. "How's dinner?"

CHAPTER 20

RICK WAS STILL smarting from how easily Kurt had made him feel like a loser in front of Amanda. *Kurt did it on purpose to make himself look good to Amanda.* And, it had worked. Amanda had pretty much ignored Rick after Kurt had arrived.

After leaving Zach with his obsession, Rick had returned to his end of the table. The view that he had been looking at when he had headed to the dining room to eat an hour ago was still being displayed. It was the destroyed chapel where his mother had gone to escape the lahar that had destroyed Kent. She had survived the lahar, but had died from the effect of a massive side wave that had resulted when two massive tsunamis had collided with each other in the Puget Sound just west of Kent. It was more than he could take right now so he closed the view.

He had lied to Amanda and Kurt. He hadn't spent any time since he had arrived at the station looking into information about cars. He hadn't become a mechanic because he loved cars. It had just paid the bills. He had really wanted to be a doctor, but fate just hadn't let him. Caring for his sick mother had come first. Furiously at first and then more slowly as he reach more meaty content, Rick searched the system for what Kurt had mentioned in the cafeteria, epigenetics.

He discovered was it was the study of how the body controls the expression of genes. He also researched the role of the non-coding sections of DNA that Amanda had mentioned. He wasn't stupid. If the subject of human disease and genetics came up again with Amanda and Kurt, he was going to be ready.

CHAPTER 21

THE SACK OF money was heavy but stealing it had been child's play. *If the criminal masterminds of the world could only see me now.* Alex heaved the sack of over his shoulder and headed toward the still open portal. In the bag was over $500,000 dollars in bundles of $100-dollar bills. He was rich!

After walking though the portal from the Citibank vault back to the angel's staging room, he quickly opened another portal to his room on the station and heaved the bag of bills onto the floor of his room, just like he had done with the gold bars. He closed the portals to the bank vault and to his room on the station, and then he calmly seated himself at the table. He had the system bring up one of his favorite Eminem music videos.

Minutes later, the door to the room banged open, and Kurt stormed in. "I am sick to death of Sam controlling every little aspect of our lives here. If I don't get out of this place, I'm going to have to hurt somebody."

Alex spun around in his chair. "What did the bad old Sam do today?"

"I was about ready to make a serious move on Amanda in the dining room when he suddenly showed up."

"What was on your mind at the time?"

"As hot as she is, do I have to tell you?"

"No, but the very fact that you were thinking it must have shown on your face enough that Mark figured out what was on your mind and alerted Sam." Alex motioned for Kurt to get closer so that he could whisper in his ear.

Kurt hesitated for a moment, but then he complied with Alex's request.

Alex said, "We went through the portal, stole the gold, and Sam didn't show up to stop us. I think as long as we don't talk loud enough for Mark to hear us and don't let our intentions show on our faces, then Mark won't be able to discern what we're up to and notify Sam. Otherwise, he would be here right now because we are whispering, wondering what evils we're conspiring to commit."

"Are you sure?" Kurt whispered back.

"Yeah, I'm pretty sure."

"Then this is a good time for us to start making plans to get off the station. And, as we leave, we have to destroy it. Sam and his kind are bent on the enslavement of the chosen race, as well as all other humans. I've killed many times before to save the chosen race, and I'll kill again in a heartbeat to save them now."

"I'm totally with you on Sam being evil and that we need to destroy the station, but what's this about a chosen race?"

"You don't understand now, but you will. Like me, you were also born one of the chosen. This alien race has no right to imprison us."

"Chosen or not, we aren't going to be able to escape by just walking through a portal and disappearing. While you were gone, I tried to wander away from a portal at my grandparent's cabin in Vail. I made it about one hundred yards, and then I was suddenly transported back into the angel's staging room."

"Crap. I was going to have you help me try that later today. I guess that idea's out."

"Unfortunately, it is. That's why I said that I don't exactly know how good Mark is at keeping an eye on us. It seems like he is watching sometimes and other times not. With Mark watching us so closely, what do you think we can do?"

"You know how we grabbed those two bars of gold?" Kurt said. "I know where we can find some C4 plastic explosive down on Earth. We go through a portal, grab the C4, and plant it in the engine room of the station. I checked on the engine room earlier today. The door was open, and no one was in there. Since no one was there, I think they trust Mark to run it all."

Alex said, "If you blow the engines, then won't we die in the crash?"

"No, stupid. We put a timer on the C4 and then escape through a portal to somewhere on Earth right before the C4 blows and the station goes down. Since Mark will die with the station, he won't be able to transport us back."

"What about the people on the ground? A ship this big is going to kill a lot of people when it hits the ground."

"You thought of that, too. The chosen often think alike. It would be so cool to crash the ship into a big city to scare the world into believing that an alien invasion is coming. But it would be more impressive if it were a city that has not already been half destroyed, like Seattle has been. I did find out that the ship has started moving east since about two hours ago. It's moving at a leisurely twenty-five miles per hour. I just don't know where it's heading to."

Alex said, "I'll try to find out where the ship is heading, and then we can plan the timing for the explosion. But, can we skip the 'Destroy the Big City in the Name of the Aliens' thing? Killing Sam and his crew is good enough for me."

"Quit being such a sissy. We will take out this ship when and where I say we're going to take it out. Try and stop me, and I'll make sure that you go down with the ship."

CHAPTER 22

RICK WAS SEATED in his staging room, viewing the terrible destruction that was still ongoing from the ash that was falling thicker and thicker over the Seattle area when Mark suddenly announced, "Rick, Bart has passed away and will be passing through a portal room in just a few moments. Please enter the portal behind you that will take you directly to the portal observation room."

Shocked, Rick stood, walked through a portal that was already open behind him, and entered a portal observation room. Sam was already there.

"Sam, what happened?" Rick asked.

Before Sam could answer, Margie entered the room from another portal nearby, and a second later Amanda and Connie arrived as well. All three rushed to Sam as Amanda asked, "Sam what happened to Bart?"

Sam said, "I'll explain later. Take your seats." As he spoke, David and Zach entered the room. Moments later Alex, Kurt, Ethan and Michaela arrived.

Soon after Sam had directed them to their seats, a forest scene with tall pine trees and a log cabin off to one side appeared in the portal room beyond. A young women entered the scene from the world of spirits and walked to the center of the scene and stopped next to a wooden swing. The ropes for the swing extended above the portal room and out of sight.

Bart appeared to their left in the portal room. "Mom," he said as soon as he saw the woman. "It is really you?"

"Yes, it is."

"How do I know that you're not just an alien projection meant to deceive me? With their technology, I wouldn't put it past them."

The woman walked toward him as she said, "Bart, don't be afraid. I know what you're thinking: there isn't a God, and all this is the work of aliens bent on enslaving the human population. You were always so headstrong, even when you were a toddler. But you always trusted me. So I'm asking you to trust me again. There is a place of beauty and peace beyond the light." She gestured to the portal to the world of spirits behind her. "Your grandparents are all there. We're all so happy. You have nothing to fear."

"Prove it to me first. Show me what the world of spirits looks like."

"Bart, I can't do that. You need to choose to enter the world of spirits to experience it for yourself. Don't you feel the peace in your heart? It's real, and it never fades. That feeling is not being fabricated by aliens. Come with me. I've missed you so much. We have so much catching up to do." With a loving smile on her face, she reached out her hand for him to take.

Bart looked to his right where he was sure the other survivors were watching. He sighed, waved at them, and gave them just a little bit of a smile. His mother was still holding her hand out for him. He looked back at his mother and with a much bigger smile on his face, he took his mother's hand.

"Is that what is going to happen to all of us?" Margie asked. "If so, then why don't we just get it over with now and go through a portal to the world of spirits?" Margie had been the first to break the silence that had settled on the group of survivors as soon as Bart had passed through the portal to the world of spirits and the portal room had returned to its plain, dimly-lit state.

"Bart died accidentally while viewing his favorite planet through a portal in his staging room," Sam said. "As long as you're cautious as you use the station's systems, the same thing won't happen to you."

Rick asked, "How did he die?"

"More importantly," Kurt said, "How do we know that you didn't just have him killed?"

"I'll show you how he died," Sam said. The portal observation window in front of them immediately filled with a view of Bart in his staging room, seated as his table. He was observing a glowing yellow ball the size of a basketball in front of him just above the surface of his work area. Sam continued, "Michaela, please tell us what we're seeing."

Michaela said, "Bart was a little obsessed with the extrasolar planet that he called Sophie 199. Bart discovered Sophie 199 two years ago and named it after his daughter."

The image of Sophie 199 was illuminated on one side and dark on the other. Horizontal bands of color of various widths, similar to Jupiter's, encircled the planet in orange, brown, and red. Five large, target-like, red circles interrupted the bands of color in different parts of the sphere.

As they were watching, David approached Bart on the screen and said, "So what is it?"

"This, my friend, is my planet, Sophie 199," Bart said. "I discovered her two years ago after scouring the heavens for months for a new planet. At the time, hundreds of planets within three hundred light years of Earth had already been discovered. It was getting harder and harder to find a star within the reach of Earth-based telescopes that had not been carefully examined for the presence of planets. This planet and its star are two hundred and ninety-nine light years from Earth."

In the video, David yawned and stretched. "Cool," he said with as much interest in his voice as if he had discovered a mosquito smashed on his windshield. "I think I'm going to get some sleep while the markets in the US are closed for the evening. I'll see you in about eight hours." David trudged off one side of the screen and disappeared.

Michaela approached Bart in the video from where she had been sitting at another workstation on the other side of the table. "I'm glad to see that you're happy with the ability you have to view the planet that you discovered. I'll leave you to your exploring while I get some lunch. Unless you want to join me."

"You go ahead," Bart replied, his eyes never leaving Sophie 199's glowing surface. "I have plenty of exploring to do." As Michaela walked off the same side of the screen as David and disappeared, Bart began zooming in on various levels of the atmosphere of Sophie 199 in a separate viewer to his right of the image of Sophie 199.

Michaela said to the survivors, "I left Bart alone, and I wish I hadn't. He found a point in Sophie 199's atmosphere that was about the same atmospheric pressure on Earth, although with a gravity of three times that on Earth. He then opened a portal to that point in Sophie 199's atmosphere."

They all watched as Bart turned to look through a portal see what the atmosphere of his planet looked like. There was just a dark gray color beyond the open portal.

Bart said, "Mark, can you turn on a light on the other side of the portal?"

Instantly, the view beyond the portal was lit up by a light source emanating from just above the portal. Bart said, "This station is an explorer's dream come true." The swirling gases beyond the portal took on a slight yellowish hue in the light. A sudden flash of light lit up the clouds of gas even more brightly for just a moment, followed a few seconds later by a clap of thunder. Bart laughed out loud as he stood up from his chair and went to walk toward the portal. Unbeknownst to him, a shoelace from his left shoe had gotten tangled in the roller of the chair he had been sitting in. As Bart went to move his left foot forward toward the portal, the trapped shoelace pulled taut and stopped his left foot's progress, causing him to fall forward. Trying desperately to stop his forward progress toward the open portal, he tried to bring his right foot in front of him, but the effort was too late. He kept falling toward the portal. Desperately, he flung his arms out to try to grasp one of the walls on either side of the portal, but his right hand missed and passed through the portal. Immediately his hand and forearm were pulled toward the floor of the portal in the higher gravity of Sophie 199. This unbalanced him even further, causing him to fall forward even faster. As soon as his head passed through the portal, it accelerated rapidly toward the portal's platform. His head struck the floor with a sickening thud. His body went completely limp.

The video in front of the survivors ended.

"That is horrible," Margie said. "Did you have to show us the whole gruesome thing?"

"As you could see, my staff and I had nothing to do with Bart or with Fred's deaths," Sam said. "You all saw Fred jump, even though we all tried to stop him. Bart's shoelace got tangled in his chair, causing him to trip and fall."

Kurt said, with his voice bristling with barely suppressed anger, "Yes, but how do we know that you didn't plant the suggestion in Fred's mind to jump and in Bart's mind to open the portal that would end up getting him killed?"

"Because, just like anyone of you, I know that doing so would be taking the life of an innocent person," Sam said. "And if I were that evil, God would know instantly; I would be arrested, and I would be tried for murder."

The room was silent.

Connie spoke up, "A lot of us here were having a hard time believing that there was even a God before we came to this station, much less spirits and a world of spirits. But now we are forced to accept that at least humans do have a spirit that goes on after life.

So what are spirits made of? And what and where is this place you are calling the world of spirits?"

"If you don't mind, I'll need more than a few minutes to answer your question."

Kurt said. "Alex and I are fed up with your explanations. They are really just thinly veiled lies to keep us from the truth: that you're an alien that is bent on enslaving humans. I just haven't figured out yet what you're doing on the other side of the portals with all the life forces from all of the humans you have captured."

Alex quickly said, "Kurt, give the man a chance to speak. I'm sure that everyone else here is interested in what he has to say."

"Okay. Fine," Kurt said, "I'll sit here and waste my time."

Sam completely ignored Kurt's outburst. "To answer Connie's question, I have to start at the beginning. I understand that what I am about to say doesn't fit well with many of your different views of God and the universe.

"In the beginning, many billions of years ago, God took the unorganized matter that made up this galaxy and used part of it to create the protons, neutrons, and electrons that became the atoms of what you know as the periodic table. The unorganized matter that he used was composed of subatomic particles that your scientists have recently discovered and that you classify as quarks, leptons, and bosons. Your scientists have identified eighteen subatomic particles so far and have predicted the existence of twenty-five more. However, almost two hundred subatomic particles made up the unorganized matter. God used only some of those subatomic particles to make the physical matter that makes up your physical bodies, your planet, and the universe that is visible to your scientists.

"He used other subatomic particles and made a completely different type of matter. This matter occupies the same space-time continuum that the matter in the visible universe does, but it is so different in its quantum laws that it is almost completely undetectable to human scientists. I will refrain from calling this alternate form of matter 'dark matter' as your scientists have recently called it, and I will instead refer to it as spiritual matter.

"One of God's crowning achievements was creating spirit children from spiritual matter. As spirit children, we lived with God for eons of time until it became our turn to be born on our respective planets. Since spirits will be born and die on your Earth for about 7,000 years, there has to be somewhere for the spirits of the dead to wait until all the spirits that have been assigned to come to Earth have had a chance to do so. Hence, God created a beautiful planet made of spiritual matter that orbits a spiritual sun not far from here where the dead from Earth can live until the resurrection at the end of the seven thousand years. The world of spirits is a beautiful and peaceful place. There is no evil there. All humans ever born and since passed on are there, reunited as families and friends. There is no sickness, death, or pain." He paused. "I think that is enough. There is so much more for you to learn, but it doesn't all have to be in one day."

"Whew. That was enough to make my brain ache," Dave said.

"Now I understand how you could move our Earth across the universe," Connie said. "It's all pretty farfetched, to be sure. But, at least now there is a plausible explanation for the crazy technology that you've got around here, and especially the portals."

Kurt shot out of his chair. "Guys, it's all lies. There is no world of spirits, no God, and no happy ending. The whole thing is a freaking alien plot. I'm not sitting here listening to this crap for another moment. Anyone else who thinks like I do, let's blow this place." With that, he turned and stormed out of the room.

All eyes were suddenly on Alex. He said, "Hey, do you see me following him out the door?"

"If you'll all excuse me," Sam said. "I'm needed elsewhere."

"Darn it, Sam," Margie said. "I still have a million questions to ask you, like who made God? Is there more than one God? Did I have a spiritual mother? Do I ever get my memories back from my life before this? And how do the dinosaurs fit into all this?"

"I guess I'll have to get back with you later with the answers to those questions," Sam replied.

"I'd like to be there when you do," Rick said.

Most of the others echoed the same interest. Sam left, and Alex followed soon afterward.

Amanda got up, walked over, and sat down next to Rick. "Hey, stranger."

Rick was shocked she had come over to talk to him. "Why do you say that?" he stammered.

"You rushed out of the lunchroom the other day and I haven't seen you since. I was hoping to talk to you further about the information that I have found in the computer system. Is that something that would interest you?"

"Sure it would," Rick said, his heart beating so fast that he was sure that everyone in the room could hear it. Rick could barely believe that Amanda was sitting next to him. After what had happened in the dining room, he had figured that any relationship with her was out of the question. But since Amanda hadn't left with Kurt, maybe she really wasn't Kurt's girlfriend. He asked, "What did you think about what Sam said?"

"Wow. That was a lot to take in. However, there was a ring of truth to a lot of it. Nothing he said really contradicts anything in the Bible, as far as I can tell. But I'm no expert since I have been too busy to attend mass on a regular basis for years."

"I'm far from being an expert, either. But my mother always taught me to believe in God, and I still do after all these years. I figure that all of God's miracles can be explained by the same laws of science that he used when he created everything. We just don't know all of those laws, so the lay person calls God's work magic, or miracles, while the scientists try to explain it all away by laws of nature."

"After what I've seen on this station, the scientist in me is really in awe." She paused. "You know, Rick, I was really enjoying talking to you earlier today in the lunchroom. I wish you hadn't left me alone with Kurt."

"Why do you say that?"

"He's really starting to give me the creeps. After you left, he started talking about a master race. I only know one group that talks like that."

"The Aryan Nation."

"Exactly. You know what I'm talking about. There's a coldness to him that makes me not what to be alone with him."

"Now you've got me concerned, too. He does get angry and defiant at the drop of a hat. Do you think that he might resort to violence against Sam and his staff?"

"No," Amanda replied. "Not as long as he is stuck here with the rest of us. He loves himself too much to die for his cause."

"But if he can find a way off the station, who knows what he might do before he leaves."

"I'm pretty sure that Sam is keeping an eye on him with all of this advanced technology of his. Sam won't let Kurt do anything to this station."

"Just in case, I'll try to keep an eye on him as well," Rick said.

"Okay but be careful. I don't want you to get hurt."

"It kind of sounds like you care about me." Rick said with a smile.

"Of course I care about you."

"Thanks. I care about you, too. I'm also getting hungry. Why don't we try again and have dinner together? It would be fun to learn a little bit more about you. You already know my life story, so I don't know that I'll have any more dark secrets to share."

"Don't worry. The doctor in me will dig deep and find something."

"Doctor, shouldn't I get a second opinion first before I let you do that?"

"Don't worry. I'm a physician. You won't feel a thing."

CHAPTER 23

"**A**LEX. HOLD UP," Kurt whispered. He was lugging the heavy box containing the detonators for the plastic explosive Semtex that they had just stolen from the warehouse of the company Explosia. The company had been manufacturing explosives in a suburb of Pardubice, a city in the Czech Republic, since 1920. Fortunately, the factory had not been well guarded on the weekend, and they had been able to open a portal right next to the Semtex.

While Kurt had a lot more experience with the explosive C4, Alex had been unable to find a warehouse or military depot in the United States that wasn't guarded twenty-four hours a day. With the guard nearby, the station's portal system wouldn't allow them to open a portal close enough to get to where the C4 was stored.

Once in the warehouse at Explosia, it had taken Alex only seconds to find a hand truck to easily transport a fifty-kilogram box of the Semtex back to the portal. Kurt had been left to grab the detonators with their remote controls.

"What? A fifty-pound box is too heavy for you?" Alex was standing next to the portal waiting for Kurt.

"The box is slippery, you jerk." Kurt lifted the box of detonators above the top of the box of the Semtex and then dropped it unceremoniously.

Alex dove for the falling box of detonators but was too late as it slammed into the box of Semtex. Alex held his breath in terror, but nothing happened. "Why did you do that?" he said.

"You're such a baby," Kurt said. "Anyone knows that plastic explosive will only explode when it is set off by both the high heat and extreme pressure caused by the explosion of a detonator. Pressure alone, such as stomping on it or shooting it with a bullet, will not detonate it. Heat alone, such as a flame, will not cause it to explode. You can even light plastic explosive on fire, and it will just burn slowly."

"How was I supposed to know that?"

"I've used plastic explosive to blow up a lot of stuff," Kurt said. "I haven't told you yet that I have been a member of a secret subgroup of the Aryan Nation for ten years. We target anyone who threatens the supremacy of the white race. My lifetime kills are at forty-seven, the highest in our group. The next closest person in my group is way behind me at eighteen kills. No one is as good as I am. And that's why I'm not afraid of these freakin' aliens. Instead, they should be afraid of me." As he finished speaking, Kurt pulled a switch blade out of his pocket and popped open the wicked-looking blade. Rotating the blade, he gazed admiringly at it like it was made of solid gold. "Especially now that I have this," he added.

"Awesome, dude," Alex said, although inside he felt sick. *This guy is a psychopath.* No wonder Kurt wasn't bothered by the idea of taking out a whole city when they blew up the station. Kurt thought of people as mere cattle to be slaughtered. Alex, on the other hand, had no grudges against anyone, no matter what race or persuasion they were, as long as they minded their own business. And he definitely hadn't ever killed anyone. Nor did he plan to do so at any time in the future. Carefully hiding his fears, he added, "Put the knife away, and let's get going before someone comes along."

"Right." Kurt smoothly closed and pocketed the blade. "I'll tell you more about my secret group later. We're always looking for new recruits."

CHAPTER 24

CONNIE COULDN'T BELIEVE what she was seeing on the station's advanced display in front of her. She'd been curious about how the eruption was affecting the Seattle area, but she hadn't been prepared for the extent of the destruction.

After leaving the portal observation room where she had observed Bart's passing, she had returned to her group's room. Taking her usual seat at the table, she had used the station's computer to get updated on the continuing destruction caused by Mount Rainier's eruption.

The eruption had settled down to a steady ejection of ash from the massive crater, interrupted by occasional small eruptions of lava, both as lava bombs and lava flows. The falling ash continued to cause problems in the northwestern US. Crops had been destroyed. With the sun's rays being reflected back into space by the clouds of ash, normal summer temperatures had dropped by more than forty degrees. Early frosts were expected, threatening harvests of many fruits and vegetables that hadn't already been destroyed by the ash.

Desirous to know the extent of the loss of human life, Connie called up the statistics from the station's computer, not sure at first if the numbers would be available so soon after the eruption. But the system immediately indicated 628,997 lives had been lost from the direct and indirect effects of the eruption and an additional 213,451 lives would be lost in the next six months. *Of course the station's computer would have extremely precise and up-to-date information,* she thought to herself. What didn't it have? At the same time, the staggering loss of human life made her heart ache. If this society on the station was so advanced, then it was deplorable that they hadn't acted to prevent the deaths in the Seattle area. Didn't they have any compassion? If they were really emissaries of a loving God, how could he let so many of his children die so horribly?

She decided to use the station's computer system to see how this disaster compared to past natural disasters throughout the world. After a few moments, she was able to arrive at a list of all of the natural disasters that had ever occurred in the world, sorted by the number of lives that had been lost. The following list appeared in front of her:

Earth's Worst Natural Disasters					
RANK	LOCATION	EVENT	DATE	DEATHS	NOTES
1	Pangaea	Great Flood	2301 BC	27,691,988	
2	USA	Hudson Canyon Tsunami	-2 days	5,000,000	Estimated
3	China	Yellow River Flood	1931 AD	3,578,917	
4	Suukrmini	Abrucuri Earthquake	2817 BC	2,188,156	
5	China	Yellow River Flood	1887 AD	1,966,141	
6	Egypt & Syria	Eastern Med. Earthquake	1201 AD	1,143,294	

7	Netherlands	Dyke failure	1228 AD	997,100	
8	Bangladesh	Bhola Cyclone	1970 AD	888,387	
9	China	Shaanxi Earthquake	1556 AD	831,289	
10	China	Tangshan Earthquake	1976 AD	634,778	
11	USA	Mount Rainier Eruption	2021 AD	628,997	In progress
12	India	Calcutta Typhoon	1737 AD	309,654	
13	China	Kaifeng Yellow River Flood	1642 AD	279,755	
14	Syria & Turkey	Antioch Earthquake	526 AD	249,611	
15	Haiti	Porte-au-Prince Earthquake	2010 AD	237,446	
16	Indian Ocean	Indian Ocean Tsunami	2004 AD	236,891	
17	Syria	Aleppo Earthquake	1148 AD	235,116	
18	China	Haiyuan Earthquake	1920 AD	233,991	
19	Iran	Tabriz Earthquake	1780 AD	231,517	
20	Hitaunii	Babbag Hurricane	2498 BC	225,556	

Her eyes stopped for a moment on the great flood of 2301 BC. *Hadn't the primordial continent of Pangaea broken up into the present-day continents far before Noah?* In addition, she was pretty sure that the whole Noah's ark thing was a myth. She'd have to get on Sam's case on that one. There had to be a mistake in the data.

Looking down the list for Mount Rainier's recent eruption, her eyes passed by the entry for the Hudson Canyon Tsunami and continued down the list for about a half second longer. Suddenly, her mind snapped to attention. What it the world? Five million deaths were estimated to occur two days from now in the Hudson Canyon Tsunami, making it the second worst disaster to ever strike the earth? She blinked in disbelief as her pulse quickened. Where on Earth was Hudson Canyon? What could occur in a canyon on land that would cause a tsunami that would kill five million people?

Using the system, she found an article within seconds on the submarine Hudson Canyon in the continental shelf off the coast of New Jersey. It had been formed by runoff from the Hudson River over millions of years and was an astounding three quarters of a mile deep. The article stated that a huge section of the wall of the canyon was going to collapse in two days, causing the deadly tsunami. She pushed back her chair and headed out into the hall, determined to find Sam immediately. Sam was going to have to stop the tsunami from ever occurring.

CHAPTER 25

"**N**O. NO. NO." Zach shouted. "Get up, Tye!"

"Hey, Zach, keep it to a dull roar, okay?" Margie asked from the other end of the table. Looking up at Zach, she noted the look of anguish on his face. Immediately concerned, she asked, "What's wrong?"

Still staring in disbelief at the image in front of him, Zach said, "I don't know. Tye slipped and fell. Now she won't get up."

Margie stood and walked toward Zach. Margie could see the singer that he was so obsessed with lying still on her back on a small extension of main stage at a concert. Other members of her cast kneeled around her. Moments later, the fans in the audience surged toward the stage, overwhelming the ring of protective bodyguards. The most aggressive fans pulled themselves up on the stage at the same time that the first members of Tye's backstage security team arrived at her side. Seeing the frenzied crowd rushing to the aid of their beloved fallen singer galvanized the security team into action. They snatched Tye's still form from off the stage and rushed her back to the main stage, barely staying ahead of the charging fans. The station's video feed automatically followed them as they quickly exited the rear of the stage down a set of stairs.

Margie watched as the bodyguards deposited Tye's still unconscious body on a table behind the stage. The wail of an ambulance
could be heard in the background.

Zach just stood and sobbed silently.

Margie put her arm around him, but he didn't respond to
her gesture.

"She just can't die," Zach wailed. "If she dies, I don't know what
I'll do."

"Let's go and find Sam and ask for his help," Margie said.

CHAPTER 26

"I THOUGHT I WAS going to be an actor when I was a sopho-more in high school," Rick said.

"I'm not surprised," Amanda said. "You're definitely hand-some enough."

"Yeah, right," Rick said, sure that she was just saying that to be nice. He had never thought he was handsome.

"No, I really do think that you're handsome. Why are you always so worried about yourself? You really need to learn to like yourself for yourself. There is no one else in this world that you need to impress. Except maybe me." Amanda smiled. "But you have already done that."

Rick opened his mouth to reply, but the door to the dining room opened with a bang.

It was David, and he looked worried. "Has anyone seen Sam? I need to talk to him ASAP. My son was hiking in the Grand Tetons. A large rock has fallen on his legs and pinned him to the ground. If he doesn't get help, he's going to die."

"We haven't seen Sam," Rick said.

"How do I find him then?" David asked.

"Find who? Because if you're looking for Sam, so am I," Connie announced from behind David as she entered the dining room. Her brows were furrowed, and she wasn't smiling.

"Join the crowd," David said.

"Guys, all we have to do is ask Mark," Amanda said. She turned to address the middle of the room and called out, "Mark, how can these guys get a hold of Sam?"

"I just alerted him that you need him," Mark answered from everywhere. "He will join you shortly."

"This place still gives me the creeps, and especially Mark," David said. "I don't like the idea that Mark is always listening to us. I like my privacy."

"Hey, that's just the generation that you were born in," Connie said. "If you were a modern teen, you would have thought nothing of giving up your privacy to Instagram, Twitter, and your cell phone."

"Sam," David exclaimed as Sam came through the door. Rushing over to Sam before Sam could reach the table where the others were sitting, David continued, "My son is dying. Please save him."

"David, your son is not going to survive his injuries. God has asked us not to intervene. Even though I want to, I can't help him."

"Yes, you can," David nearly yelled. "I saw what the angels can do in the angel's staging room. You have to send an angel to save my son."

"David, I'm so sorry—"

"You sadistic jerk," David yelled. "Kurt is right. You're just a cold-hearted alien hiding behind our world's religions while you get your kicks out of torturing humans." David stormed out of the room and slammed the door.

Sam sighed as he approached the three others at the table where they were still seated. "Am I still welcome here?"

"Sam, it's your ship," Connie said. "I think that you're welcome anywhere."

"I mean, am I welcome to join your conversation? It appears that more and more of the members of your group are unhappy with me.

I can understand their feelings to a point because they don't have the bigger perspective on the whole thing like my staff and I do."

"This whole thing is getting harder and harder for all of us to swallow," Connie said. "From our perspective, your race saves a few of us here and there, but then steps back and allows many more to die in disasters, small and large. How can we admire you for that? I have just discovered that a massive tsunami is going to strike the eastern coast of the United States in the next two days. You system says that an estimated five million men, women, and children are going to die in a matter of minutes. Why haven't you told us about this? I'm sure that you already know about it."

"What are you talking about?" Amanda asked in alarm. "My brother lives in downtown New York City. Sam, is she right?"

"Yes, she is correct."

Connie asked, "And you are going to let the tsunami happen and let five million people die, right?"

"I don't have a choice. It is not God's will that we stop the tsunami. Believe me; it tears me up inside to know that so many are going to die."

The group was silent for a moment until Rick spoke up, "Then help us to understand, Sam. Why does God let so many humans suffer when he has you right here with untold technology that could save all of us?"

"It goes back to the beginning, before Earth was ready for you to live on. You and all the other spirits that were ever to be born on Earth were presented a plan by which God would provide you with physical bodies to make you more complete. With no memory of your previous life with God, you would be born on Earth into less perfect bodies that would experience strong passions, disease, and ultimately death. You might think of the bodies that you have now as test models for God's spirit children to see if they, in moments of suffering, anguish, or passion, will call on him for help and comfort, or will turn their backs on him. Those that would obey God would be resurrected after death and would be able to return to live with God forever.

"There was a risk to the whole plan," Sam continued. "Those that wouldn't obey God would still ultimately receive a resurrected body, but it would not possess as many capabilities. In addition, they would live out the rest of eternity away from the God that they had turned their backs on.

"Many of the spirits didn't like the plan that was presented. They didn't want to take the risk of ending up in lesser versions of resurrected bodies. They also refused to be born on a faraway planet in bodies that would subject them to suffering and death. For their refusal to follow God's plan, they were not allowed to be born on Earth and were not allowed receive physical bodies. At the same time, many other spirits accepted God's plan and agreed to come to Earth. Sure, they were afraid of the risk of failure, pain, suffering, and death that having a human body would bring. But they loved their God and trusted that he knew what was best for them. Therefore, everyone that has ever born on the earth chose to follow God's plan, knowing full well the consequences. They did it because there was a wonderful future ahead of them after their earthly experience, a future in which they would receive resurrected bodies and would be reunited with their God."

Connie said quietly, "So, telling us that we chose to suffer is supposed to make it easier for us just to say, 'There goes another one,' when a few or millions of humans die?"

"I think it makes it a little easier to accept," Rick said. "Especially now that we have seen with our own eyes that life doesn't end with death."

Amanda said, "It is still hard for me to accept the fact that you have cures for virtually every human disease on this station, and yet you won't share it with the human race. That is so cruel."

Sam said, "But if God removed all suffering from the human experience, then that would defeat God's plan for our existence on

Earth to be a test of our love for him and a test of our obedience to him."

Connie said, "After spending the past days with you and seeing the incredible technology on the station, we can't deny that there is more to the universe than any of us ever imagined." She hesitated and then continued, "Sam, I know that everything that you're saying is probably true. It just isn't that easy to throw out all our past beliefs and accept yours."

"Give it some time, Connie," Sam said gently. "It's not a race."

CHAPTER 27

"**F**ORGET GOING TO Sam," David said bluntly to Margie and Zach in the hallway outside of the cafeteria after Zach had explained why they were looking for Sam. "He won't do anything to save my son so I doubt he will help you when you're not even related to Tye."

"But she's really hurt," Zach said. "He's got to help her before she dies."

"Sam is not the nice alien that he portrays himself to be. Along with all of his staff, he seems to get his jollies out of seeing humans suffer and die."

"Are you sure?" Margie said. "He's been pretty nice to us."

David said, "It's like the Hansel and Gretel story, if they still tell that these days."

Zach and Margie nodded that they knew the story.

David continued, "He's just fattening us up for some evil scheme he's hatching. I heard Alex talking about it. Alex knows how to open portals to the earth like the angels do. I'm not going to sit around and watch my son die. I'm going to help him myself."

"But what can I do to help Tye?," Zach said. "She's headed to surgery right now for a severe head injury with internal bleeding.

I heard her surgeon say that she might not make it. Even if I go through a portal, I can't get close enough to help her."

"I'm sorry, but that's your problem. I need to focus on saving my son. If you want, you can come with me and watch as Alex teaches me how to open the portals."

As David wheeled and headed toward Alex's staging room, with Zach following closely behind, Margie said. "You guys go on without me. I'm going to head back to my staging room."

CHAPTER 28

KURT AND ALEX were wheeling the hand truck of explosives from the warehouse through the portal and into their staging room when they came face to face with David and Zach as they rushed into the room. All four of them stopped and stared at each other and at the boxes on the hand cart.

Zach broke the tense silence, "So what you guys got there?"

"None of your business, kid," Kurt said. "Now you guys beat it, and don't tell a soul what you have seen." A switchblade appeared suddenly in Kurt's right hand. He held the blade up right in front of Zach and David's faces as he continued, "If you do talk, I'll make sure that you are just one more name on my list of lifetime kills."

"We get the message," David said. "Calm down and put away the knife. We have no love for Sam and his cronies. You can count on our silence."

"Good. Now get lost." Kurt closed the switchblade and put it back in his pocket.

"Wait," Zach said. "We need Alex to teach us how to open portals to Earth to help us save dying friends and family members."

"Your needs are not our needs." Kurt said. "Get lost before my blade comes out to play again, only this time for real."

Alex said, "Kurt, let me show them what they want to know, and then they can leave. It'll just take a second."

Kurt hesitated a moment. The tenseness in his eyebrows softened a little. "Fine. But make it quick."

Alex quickly showed David and Zach how to navigate to the proper screen and then what gestures were needed to open a portal. He was done with the demo in less than a minute.

David and Zach left the room hastily.

CHAPTER 29

MARGIE HAD COME to the realization that the amount of historical information stored in the station's database was so infinitely large that it would take her many lifetimes to write a history of all of the amazing events that had happened on the earth. Yesterday, she had finally decided to focus on only one area of the earth's history. After spending a day delving into the love story of Cleopatra and Mark Antony, she was pretty sure that she wanted to write the history of the world's greatest love stories. She would start with the most famous ones that she already knew about and then would search for others that had been lost in history but were likely to be just as amazing.

Zach burst through the door. "Margie, how is she?"

"The surgeons are just getting ready to cut." She had been keeping an eye on Tye while Zach was out of the room.

Zach rushed to the image of the imminent surgery where a scrub nurse had just handed a scalpel to the lead surgeon. A square patch of Tye's shaved scalp was visible through the drapes and was marked with purple lines, indicating the places where the surgeon was to cut. Bracing his hands against her scalp, the surgeon lowered the blade to the surface of Tye's skin.

"I can't stand to watch him cut her!" Zach said.

Zach was just beginning to look away when suddenly Tye sat up on the surgical table. Zach startled in surprise. Tye's eyes were open, and the ventilation tube was no longer in her mouth, but she looked confused. Tye said, "Margie, she's…"

"She's in cardiac arrest," shouted an unseen person from the video.

"Oh, crap!" they heard the surgeon say. "We're too late." He chucked the scalpel onto a nearby surgical stand. He reached right through Tye's still-seated spirit body and he ripped the surgical drape off of Tye's still-prone physical body. The surgeon said, "Start CPR and get me the defibrillator."

With a confused look on her face, Tye looked down at the surgeon's arms that were extending right through her chest. She grimaced and then she jumped off the operating table. She backed away from the operating table where the surgeon and his assistant were now pressing hard and repetitively on a dying person's chest. "Who are they trying to save?" she said out loud to herself. Standing against the wall of the operating room, she stood quietly and observed the drama.

"She's dead. Oh my…" Zach buried his face in his hands. Marge rushed over to console him.

The defibrillator arrived, and the surgeon began shocking Tye's lifeless body with progressively stronger shocks. With her body paralyzed for surgery, her muscles barely twitched with each shock.

A bright light began to appear against the wall just to Tye's left. As Tye turned to look at the light, Zach yelled as he bolted from the room, "She is going through the portal right now and I'm not going to be there…" His voice faded down the hall.

Tye's resuscitation continued in miniature on the desktop, even after Tye's spirit entered the bright light and then the bright light on the wall winked out of existence. Margie knew that Tye wouldn't be coming back to life, no matter how hard the surgeons tried. It was too difficult to watch the surgeons going through the motions for nothing. With a flick of her finger, she closed the image. She then immediately opened a view of Zach. She was shocked to see Zach standing on a broad white sandy beach. A calm blue lagoon lay to his left. To his right, low hills covered with lush tropical foliage quickly gave way to mist-enshrouded cliffs streaked with numerous waterfalls. The sun sparkled off the sand.

Zach was oblivious to the beauty around him and was instead completely focused on Tye's back side on the other side of the portal room as she stepped into the bright white light of the portal to the world of spirits.

"Tye," Zach yelled, but she was already gone before the words left his lips.

Out loud he said, "I just missed her. I have to be with her." Without hesitating, Zach sprinted to the portal to the world of spirits, clearly determined to follow after his love. As he approached the portal he dove headfirst toward the portal.

Instead of passing through the portal, Zach's head and then the rest of his body smacked against it like a ton of bricks. His body slid down the wall of the portal and crumpled in a heap on the sand. A moment later, the portal to the world of spirits winked out of view.

CHAPTER 30

"YOU HAVE SUCH cute dimples when you smile," Amanda said to Rick.

Rick blushed and smiled again.

"They are cute," Connie said with a smile. "They give a man charm."

"All they give me is embarrassment," Rick said.

Amanda yawned. "I am really getting tired. I guess I'm due for a night's rest, although I must say that I have long since lost track of when day and night are supposed to be."

Connie said, "I think that we're all on different time zones at this point. This is the middle of the day for me."

"Well, it's not for me," Amanda said as she stood to leave.

"Hey, Amanda, do you need me to walk you to your room?" Rick asked.

"Like this is a scary place with monsters lurking around every corner," Amanda said.

"Okay," Rick said, disappointed, but trying hard not to let it show. "I'm sure that you're capable of making it on your own."

"Hey, I was just teasing," Amanda said. "Don't take things so seriously. I'd be honored to have you walk with me to my room."

She waited until Rick stood, and then she scooted over to him and took his arm.

"Hmm," Connie said. "Are you two going to need a chaperone?"

Rick turned bright red again. Seeing his reaction, Amanda chuckled. "Oh, don't worry about us. Rick's too shy to try anything."

The walk to Amanda's room took all of five seconds since Mark opened a portal from the hall outside the dining room to the hall next to Amanda's room.

"That was quick," Rick said. "I'm not sure I like all of the conveniences that this place offers, especially since I had wanted to spend longer talking to you as we walked."

"Well, then you'll just have to come in."

Rick instantly blushed again.

Amanda laughed. "I'm not going to attack you, if that is what you're worried about." Still laughing, she opened her door. Taking Rick by the arm, she led him to the couch in her sitting room. She sat and patted the cushion next to her for Rick to sit down. Rick obliged and sat down a few feet from Amanda.

"You surprise me, you know," Amanda said.

"Oh, how's that?"

"I saw how you took charge up on the roof right after we crashed. You seemed like a no-nonsense kind of guy. But now, when it comes to a woman that you're interested in, you clam up and act like a shy schoolboy."

"I just haven't had that many highly-educated and beautiful women like you pay attention to me. I half expect to wake up and find that it's all a dream and that you're not really here."

"Rick, believe it or not, being thought of as beautiful is not all that it's cracked up to be. All my life, I've ended up with oodles of attractive men circling about me like sharks, hoping to get a piece of me. Kurt is the epitome of what I am talking about. Guys like him crowd around me so much that I can barely see the nice guys, like you, that are waiting on the edge of the crowd. The nice guys are unwilling approach me because they think that they don't have a chance when they compare themselves to the jocks that are pursuing me so ardently. That's exactly what you did when Kurt was circling in for the kill."

"But I had no idea at the time—"

"Rick, I'm interested in you, not Kurt. You have nothing to worry about. So, what had you wanted to talk to me about?"

"Well, I was interested in the cures for diseases that you have been researching in the computer system here."

"That is fascinating, for sure. But right now, I'm more interested in getting to know you better."

"I think you already know about everything there is to know about me. Let's talk about you instead."

"All right," Amanda said. "What do you want to know?"

"Why did you decide to become a doctor?"

"Because I love helping people. It was as simple as that. I could have become an attorney, accountant, airline pilot or a CEO of a big company. But none of those professions appealed to me. My favorite thing is just talking to people."

"Wow. You really are too good to be true."

"I bet you say that to all the girls."

"No, I don't. You really are—"

"Rick, stop. You really can't tell when I am teasing you, can you?"

"Well, I wasn't sure…"

Amanda slid closer to him on the couch. As their thighs touched, all intelligent thought left Rick's head.

"You think I'm sexy, don't you?" Amanda purred huskily while at the same time a wry grin lit up her face. She walked her fingers up his shirt to his collar bone, leaving a feeling of pleasant tingling.

"Stop it," Rick said with a smile. "I'm concentrating on just being attracted to you for your mind, and you're making it very difficult." He put his arm around her shoulders.

Amanda snuggled up to his chest, closed her eyes, and smiled. "I've been waiting for you to do this for days. What took you so long?"

CHAPTER 31

"**W**E'RE ALONE NOW that Ethan is finally gone," Kurt said to Alex. They were in their angel's staging room. "Show me where the station is located right now and where it's heading."

Alex manipulated images in front of him until a map of the US was displayed with the location and trajectory of the station overlaid on top of the map. "As you can see, the station is following a gently curving course that will take it directly over Sioux Falls, South Dakota; then Chicago, Illinois; and then on to New York City. Assuming that the station continues its present leisurely rate of travel, it will arrive in the New York City area in about a day and a half."

"Perfect. I couldn't have planned it better myself."

Alex was afraid to ask, but he just had to know. "So what are you planning exactly?"

"I didn't like President Obama one bit. He's living in Washington, D.C. now. But the people that made him a three-term Illinois senator and then helped to propel him onto the national political stage deserve to pay for inflicting him on the rest of the country. We're going to bring the station down right on top of downtown

Chicago, President Obama's home city. Since this ship is a mile long and almost as wide, a direct impact with the city should kill three- or four-million people. Maybe we'll get lucky and take out five million."

"Wow. That's a lot of people." The more that Kurt revealed of his past and of his plans for the future, the more that Alex wished he had never gotten involved with him in the first place.

"All I need you to do is tell me exactly when to set the detonators to go off so that the ship will crash directly into downtown Chicago."

CHAPTER 32

"LET ME BE sure that I understand you," Connie said. "You're saying that God populated this planet with dinosaurs as part of his plan to prepare a layer of coal, oil, and natural gas around the world for us to use as energy?" As a scientist and geologist, Connie couldn't help but continue to pump Sam for information about Earth and its supposed creation by a superbeing that no one had ever seen. Sam and she had stayed in the dining room after Amanda and Rick had left and had been talking ever since.

"You are definitely one of the most insatiably curious earthlings that I have ever met," Sam said.

"And you are one of the most patient aliens that I have ever met."

"Well, if you really aren't bored to tears by all my explanations…"

"I'm not bored at all. You really are enjoyable to talk to, and not just because I'm fascinated with the subjects we're discussing."

"Far be it for an alien male to have any clue about the behavior of female humanoids on your planet. But, if I'm not mistaken, you're flirting with me."

"Fine. Now that you've pointed out my forward behavior, I guess I'll have to tone it down."

"Please don't."

Connie stared hard into Sam's eyes. "You know, I just don't get it. You're hundreds of years older than me, even though you look like you're no older than twenty-five. What in the world, I mean in the galaxy, do you find interesting about little old me?"

"It's you, Connie. It's your eyes when you smile; it's your laugh when you think something is amusing, and it's your mind that is as sharp as a tack, to borrow a metaphor from Earth. I could sit and talk to you forever."

"The women on your planet must be pretty dull because the men on Earth haven't been exactly been falling over themselves to spend time with me."

"That's their loss and my gain."

Connie laughed. "Okay, funny guy. Now how about my answer to the dinosaur thing?"

"Okay but promise that you'll stop me if I'm boring you. As God prepares planets for his spirit children to be born onto, he has to prepare a layer of hydrocarbon-based energy to assist them in moving past the Stone Age, as your scientists call it. Can you image what human existence would be like if there weren't an easily accessible and plentiful layer of coal, natural gas, and oil all around the earth? You would never have been able to move into the Steel Age. Wood would have been your only source of energy. Sure, there are other sources of energy available on the earth. But humans would never have been able to harness energy from coal, oil, natural gas, wind, the sun and the atom without first being able to produce steel."

"I'll grant you that the plentiful deposits of oil, gas and coal around the earth are truly a scientific longshot," Connie said. "We already know that the other planets in our solar system don't have them."

Sam said, "The need to lay down such a thick layer of plant material on land and algae in the oceans while at the same time coming up with a way to use up the oxygen that the plants and algae would produce is what led God to create warm-blooded dinosaurs.

With their very high metabolic rates and their massive worldwide numbers, they used up part of the oxygen produced by the vegetation, converting it back into carbon dioxide for the plants to use again. Dinosaurs were only part of the equation. A large part of the oxygen produced by plants was also converted back to carbon dioxide by bacteria in the soil. The world was cloud covered during this portion of its creation to help maintain a uniform temperature around the world, to provide daily precipitation to support the vegetation, and to suppress fires. Also, during this period, a greater percentage of the earth was covered with shallow seas, promoting ocean-based plant life. Volcanic activity was maintained at a low level so as to avoid burning any of the vegetation.

"After hundreds of millions of years," Sam said, "An adequate layer of decayed vegetation on land and in the shallow seas covered the earth. God caused the climate to change worldwide, causing layer upon layer of sand to cover over the layer of vegetation and algae, starting the process of converting it into oil, coal and natural gas. After the layer of vegetation and algae had been completed, God had no further use for the hydrocarbon-producing biosphere of dinosaurs and pre-historic plants. Like he most often does, he destroyed that biosphere with repeated asteroid impacts that cracked the world's crust, causing a worldwide massive increase in volcanism. The earth was dark for years. What the thick layers of ash from volcanism didn't kill, the lack of sunlight and cold temperatures did. God then introduced the present mammalian-based biosphere and let it mature in preparation for human habitation. The different biospheres that God introduces on planets are some of his most amazing creations. They are vastly complex, containing tens of thousands of species of land and sea plants and animals, as well as a vast number of bacteria, fungi, and algae. Amazingly, each biosphere is designed to be resilient and to adapt to the environments of different planets in slightly different ways. Earth's present biosphere on another planet might still have Dodo birds or might have a greater percentage of sulfur-based life deep in the oceans. No species is ever really extinct to God since he has the genetic code for all species ever created and can reintroduce them at will."

"Wow," Connie said. "You have an answer for everything. What you're saying sounds like a fairy tale, or the ranting of a misguided Bible-thumping preacher, except that I know that it's coming from you. You have more scientific knowledge in your head than every scientist on the earth combined."

"I am just regurgitating what I have learned. As time permits, there are so many additional topics that we can discuss, like the purpose of ice ages, the falsehoods surrounding your scientists' theory of evolution, and the science behind rapidly healing any ailment of the human body."

"You know me too well. I would like answers to those questions also."

"However, right now, I have a few important matters to attend to."

"Anything that I need to know about?"

"Maybe at some point. Sorry to have to leave right in the middle of our conversation. We'll talk more later."

Sam stood and walked through a portal just a feet away from their table and disappeared.

Connie made a mental note to ask Sam how Mark always seemed to know what he wanted without any obvious communication. She was pretty sure what the answer was going to be, but it seemed so improbable, so she wanted to hear it from Sam himself.

CHAPTER 33

RICK DECIDED TO go for broke. He had already hazarded a few kisses on Amanda's forehead as she rested her head on his shoulder, and she hadn't resisted. Instead, she had snuggled even closer into his shoulder. He couldn't help himself. He just had to kiss her.

"Amanda?"

"What, Rick?"

"Can I kiss you?"

"Don't spoil it by asking. If you feel like doing it, then do it. I'll let you know if it's okay or not."

"But I don't want to do the wrong—"

"You're so insecure. Let me explain it to you as simply as I can. I am snuggling up to you and your sexy chest because I want to. I like you, or I wouldn't be doing it. You just have to accept that. Now let's pretend that you didn't ask me if you could kiss me, and let's try it again."

She snuggled against his chest once more, her head resting on his shoulder. Emboldened by her words of encouragement, he leaned his head down as he lifted her face up to his.

"What are you trying to do!" Amanda said. "Make me swap spit with you? That's gross."

Rick jerked his head back up and let go of her chin in confusion, like her face was a hot potato.

A big grin spread across Amanda's face. "I got you with that one. Now kiss me before I have kiss you first." She closed her eyes and waited.

Completely disarmed and at her mercy, Rick swallowed his fear, closed his eyes, and softly kissed her on the lips. She responded by pressing her lips to his, first gently and then more ardently. Swept away in passion, he held her in his arms as he kissed her back with equal fervor.

"Guys." Rick jumped at the sound of Sam's voice, and Amanda let out a cry of surprise. Sam was standing not three feet away from them in front of the couch.

As Rick untangled himself from Amanda, Sam said, "Things are getting a little steamy around here, don't you think?"

"Sam, you've got to quit showing up like this," Amanda said. "It scares me half to death."

Rick said, "You have been spying on us." His cheeks were red with embarrassment.

"Mark does all the day-to-day work of keeping tabs on you for me. As instructed, he did tip me off just a few minutes ago that the two of you..." Sam paused.

Rick jumped right in. "Nothing was happening. What is the problem with our spending time together?"

"I'm just fine with you spending time together. But rules are rules. You can't have sex on this station unless you're married. And you aren't allowed to get married as long as you are on the station."

"We weren't going to have sex," Amanda said. "At least, that wasn't on my mind. Was it on yours, Rick?"

"No. No it wasn't. I-I was just enjoying the moment." Rick blushed an even brighter red.

"So, I take it this means that you're going to pop in on us any-time we get affectionate?" Amanda asked.

"I'm afraid so," Sam replied. "I hope that we can still be friends in spite of it."

"I'm okay with your chaperoning," Rick said. "At this point in my life, I'm fine waiting for marriage before having sex anyway. But what is this about not being able to get married while we're on the station?"

"Rick, I'd never thought you'd ask," Amanda said.

"Not that I am thinking about marriage, or anything like that," Rick stammered.

"Aha!" Amanda said with a wry grin on her face. "Now I've got you squirming. You really were thinking about marrying me, weren't you?"

"I wasn't, I promise." Rick was so confused that he didn't know what to say.

"Amanda, I'm sure his thoughts were pure," Sam said. "I just showed up to make sure that they stayed that way."

Rick said, "Now that you have both thoroughly embarrassed me..."

Amanda and Sam smiled guiltily.

Rick continued, "Sam, please explain this marriage rule to me."

"It's simple. If we were to allow you to get married, then you would be allowed to cohabitate. That would invariably result in chil-dren being born. However, we can't let you have children here on the station because then those children would have children, and after a while, we would have a whole colony of earthlings on the station."

"Then just let us off the station," Amanda said. "We'll promise to not tell anyone about the station. Then, you won't have to worry about some of us getting a little too cuddly."

"As I told you at the beginning, this is the first time in the galaxy that humans from a test planet have ever physically set foot on an angel's station. Under anything but the most extreme circumstance, humans from test planets are not allowed to know that we are here. The last thing that I can do is to let you return to Earth. Over the years, one of you would talk to someone about your experience here. We can't afford that."

CHAPTER 34

"SO WHO DIED this time?" Connie said as she pulled out a chair from a table in the cafeteria. The table was already occupied by Amanda and Rick. "It seems like every time that Sam gets us all together, someone has died."

Amanda said, "I was worried it might be you since Kurt and Alex are already here." As she finished speaking, she glanced over to the other side of the dining room where Kurt and Alex were huddled and talking quietly. Just as quickly, she glanced away.

"You're sweet to be worried about me," Connie said. "I was a little slow getting here because I took a few extra minutes to finish reading a fascinating article about the Earth's spinning magnetic core." She looked around the room for a moment and then said. "Hey, Margie, Zach and David aren't here yet either. Do you think something has happened to one of them?"

Rick said, "Your guess is as good as mine."

The door to the dining room opened, and Sam and Margie entered. Margie walked to Rick's table and sat in the empty chair next to Rick.

Sam stopped at a point equidistant from each table. Sam said, "Thanks everybody for coming. I have bad news. Zach died a less than an hour ago when he attempted to follow a person's spirit through a portal to the world of spirits. He felt no discomfort in the least. In fact, he had to be informed that he had died by an acquaintance in the world of spirits."

"I watched him enter the portal room for the singer he had been obsessed with," Margie said. "The singer passed through the portal to the world of spirits just as he arrived, and he sprinted for the still open portal in an effort to follow after her. He dove for the portal at the last second, but instead he hit the portal head first like it was a brick wall and then crumpled to the floor. From what Sam says, his spirit left his body at that moment and entered the world of spirits. We won't get to see him pass through a portal." Margie paused. "It would have been nice for all of us to have been there to see him off."

Sam said, "Unfortunately, another one of your group is near death. We are due in one of the portals in just a few minutes to see David pass through to the world of spirits."

"You knew about Zach's and David's impending deaths but did nothing to intervene. How typical," Kurt said.

Sam turned to Kurt. "I was not allowed to intervene."

Kurt said, "You just as well should have killed them yourself, you murderous creep. You could have prevented their deaths, but you didn't. That's murder in my book. Are you going watch us all die, one by one, while you get off in some perverse way on our suffering?"

"I grieve for their loss as much as anyone," Sam said. "All life is precious."

Amanda said, "It can't mean the same thing to you as it does to us since you know that a massive tsunami is going to strike the Eastern Seaboard of the United States in two days. It's going to kill five-million innocent men, women, and children, and you're not going to lift a finger to save them. If the people in the tsunami's path are really God's children, then he should do what any earthly father would do: save them. Instead, your plan of inaction has left me wondering if there ever was a God. Is the God of my youth really just the head honcho of an alien race that delights in human suffering and death?"

"It's about time someone else smelled the stink in this whole operation." Kurt smiled at Amanda.

Amanda shook her head in exasperation and looked away from Kurt.

"We need to get to the portal, folks, or we'll miss David's passing," Sam said.

"I'd like to be there to say goodbye to David," Connie said.

"Alex and I don't want any part of your sick voyeurism, Sam," Kurt said. "We're out of here." With Alex in tow, he left the dining room.

CHAPTER 35

ALEX DIDN'T LIKE it one bit that Kurt had included him when he had stormed out of the dining room. Why hadn't he had the guts to say no to Kurt and stay in the dining room with Sam and the others? He knew why. If he hadn't followed Kurt out of the dining room, Kurt would have killed him for abandoning him sooner or later. How he wished that Kurt hadn't picked him to help Kurt carry out his plans. Right after Kurt had stated that he and Alex were not going to accompany Sam to watch David pass, Alex had glanced briefly at the other survivors at the other table. He had been met with only cold stares. It looked like his best bet was to stick with Kurt, at least for the time being.

Outside the dining room, Kurt first requested that Mark open a portal to their sleeping rooms and then turned to Alex. "With Sam taking the rest of the survivors to one of the portals, this is a perfect time to place the plastic explosives in the engine room. I figure we have about fifteen minutes to do it. Working together, we'll finish in plenty of time."

Alex didn't dare refuse. "I'm with you, boss."

They hurried into Kurt's room, opened the boxes of plastic explosives and detonators, and grabbed as much as they could stuff into two pillowcases. Back in the hallway, Mark opened a portal for them to the hallway outside the engine room. Both the hall outside the engine room and the engine room itself were unoccupied.

The spacious engine room was dominated by a central, clear, twenty-foot sphere that contained shining, swirling plasma. Every hue of the rainbow was represented in constantly shifting bands of color. Two large clear tubes containing the same colorful plasma extended parallel to the floor from each side of the sphere and to the walls. Nothing else was holding up the huge sphere. Two floor-to-ceiling flat-screen displays were mounted on each side of the room and were covered with graphs and boxes of text that were unintelligible. They had to be the control panels for the engines.

Alex stood mesmerized by the advanced display of technology with his mouth slightly open. "Wow."

"Come on." Kurt said. "It'll just be a bunch of broken glass when we are done with it."

"Wait a minute," Alex whispered near Kurt's ear. "Don't you think that Mark is monitoring what we are doing and saying? I don't think that he's going to let us just march in here and fill this place with plastic explosive without trying to stop us."

"If their technology really was so awesome, then they would be flooding in here right now to stop us. In reality, the very fact that they aren't here at this minute is a big sign that they have grown lax with their security. They think that they are so powerful that they can't even imagine that someone would waltz in and blow them out sky. Now quit quaking in your boots, and let's get the job done."

Alex's mouth was dry with fear. If there were just some way he could be anywhere else besides in this room with this megalomaniac. "Okay," he said weakly. "What do you want me to do?"

"I'll place the plastic explosive. You insert the detonators. The detonators are already set to go off at the right time, correct?"

"Correct. They are set to go off in about twelve and a half hours, right when the station is exactly over downtown Chicago."

Kurt tore open a plastic bag of Semtex, grabbed a wad of the off-white clay-like substance, and began kneading it in his hands. At the same time, he studied the colorful sphere in front of him.

Alex asked, "Are you sure that you can just play with it like silly putty?"

"I already told you that you that it is very safe. It will only go off when the detonators explode. Now get out the detonators and get them ready, or else I'm going to be forced to do it by myself. At that point, I'll have to consider you to be of no value to me. And I think you already know what I do to things that useless to me."

"I'm on it, boss." Alex busied himself with laying out the detonators.

"Now where to put this stuff so that one of Sam's goons don't find it?"

"The sphere and tubing are clear as glass," Alex said. "The only place that the Semtex won't be obvious is next to the wall where the tubes enter into the wall. We could shape it like a molding meant to hide a less than perfect opening in the wall for the tubes."

"Great idea," Kurt said as he moved to one side of the room. After molding the Semtex into a thick, flexible rod, he wrapped it around the tubing where it entered the room through the wall. "Get me some more Semtex," he barked.

Alex sprang to action and grabbed the pillowcase of plastic explosives. Opening the pillowcase, he snatched another package of Semtex and molded it into a similar rod.

Kurt grabbed the rope of Semtex from Alex and added it to what he had already applied. Working quickly, the men finished encircling the end of the tubing where it entered the wall and then smoothed the surface of the Semtex to look like a purposefully-placed plastic molding. Alex inserted a detonator into the Semtex on the back side of the tubing, out of sight. He then pushed a button on the small display on the detonator. Red LED letters began counting down from twelve hours, twenty-nine minutes, and forty-four seconds. After ten seconds, the display extinguished. Working together, the men quickly formed the Semtex into an identical molding on the other side of the room where the other glass tube entered the wall. Alex inserted an identical detonator into the Semtex and activated it.

"These wireless detonators are really cool," Alex said. "After I set the first one, the rest will wirelessly sync their clocks to it so that they will all go off simultaneously. In addition, if someone tries to pull out any one of the detonators, it will send a wireless signal to all of the rest of the detonators to immediately explode."

Kurt said, "Perfect. We now have about ten pounds of Semtex on each side of the tubing. That's probably enough to destroy the sphere and send the ship plummeting into the heart of Chicago. But, just to be sure, I want to put all the rest of the Semtex that we brought behind the sphere."

The two men ducked under the large tube on the right side of the sphere and inspected the backside of the massive glowing orb. On the lower portion of the back side of the sphere, they discovered four widely-spaced metallic plates attached to the sphere. From the center of each plate, a thick cable angled toward and disappeared into a square opening in the wall directly behind the sphere.

Kurt said, "I don't know what exactly these cables or conduits are for, but they look important. We need to take them out."

Working together, the remaining twenty pounds or so of Semtex was divided into four parts and then molded and smoothed over each metal plate on the back of the sphere so that a casual observer would think that they were just plastic coverings for the metal plates. Once the plastic explosive was in place, Alex quickly inserted and activated four additional detonators. While he was working, Kurt picked up every piece of garbage that he could see.

Back in front of the sphere, Kurt said, "Anyone walking in this room would never be able to tell that there is anything different about the room."

"We do nice work."

"Now let's get out of here before anyone suspects anything."

CHAPTER 36

"DAVID HAS GOTTEN himself into quite a predicament," Sam said to the group in the portal observation room. Amanda sat by Rick on the front row. Margie was seated on Rick's other side and Connie was sitting next to Amanda. Michaela and Ethan were sitting together on the back row.

"I'm sure that you're very interested in seeing what is happening, but you must know that it is hard to look at and will only get worse. If you don't want to see David like this, then step out into the hall and I'll call you back when the gruesome part is over."

Rick looked at the Amanda and asked, "Do you want to step out?"

Amanda replied, "I'm okay."

Connie and Margie said that they were okay as well.

Rick said to Sam, "We're all staying."

"Okay," Sam said. "Let me give you a little background. David's son, Bruce, has been hiking alone in the Grand Tetons in Idaho. Using our system, David has been checking on Bruce's progress every day. While hiking off trail in Paintbrush Canyon last evening, Bruce grabbed onto a large rock to help pull himself up a steep part of the canyon. Without warning the rock came loose. Bruce lost his balance, fell to the ground and the rock rolled on top of his legs and pelvis. The rock is too large for Bruce to move. And, try as he might, Bruce has not been able to pull himself from under the rock.

"David checked on Bruce's progress this morning and was horrified to discover what had happened to Bruce. David went to Alex to ask how to use the portal system. David then opened a portal as near to Bruce as Mark would allow him to do so. However, due to inexperience, David had not realized that the portal he opened was set to open fifteen feet above the ground and then slowly descend. In his haste, David went through the portal and fell fifteen feet to the ground, fracturing his right hip. In great pain, David crawled for the next four hours to get close to where his son is lying trapped under the rock."

Rick asked, "How did he do that without Mark returning him back to the station, like you told us would happen?"

"I asked God if we could intervene to help David and I was told no. David and his son were both going to die from their injuries, and we were not to interfere. Once we knew this, I instructed Mark to allow David to join his son. They are together now."

The whole portal observation wall in front of them filled with a view of David slowly and painfully dragging himself toward where Bruce lay trapped under a huge rock in a mountainous canyon. Any beauty to be found in the pines and rocky terrain was completely lost to the tragedy in the center of the image.

"Bruce," David called out from the screen. He grimaced from the pain from the effort at calling out to his son.

"Dad, is that you?" Bruce called back.

"I'm coming," David yelled, causing another grimace from the pain. "Hold on." He pulled himself in the direction of Bruce's voice as fast as he could.

"Dad, why is it taking you so long?"

"I broke my hip," David said as he continued painfully pulling himself toward his son. "Sorry, Bruce. I came to free you, but now I can't even walk."

Bruce arched his neck to get a look at his dad. "At least you're here. How did you find me? And how did you even know that I was trapped and needed help?"

"It's a long story." David was almost to his son.

"We've got all the time in the world, Dad."

David finally reached his son's side. David put his arms around Bruce and hugged him tight. "I love you, son."

"I love you, too, dad." Bruce's lips were cracked and dry and his face had been burned by the sun. His eyes were bloodshot.

The two men embraced in silence for a few moments.

"Dad, your tears are getting me wet."

David chuckled. "It's just that I'm so happy to see you." With an exhausted heave and then a grimace of pain, David rolled onto his side on the rocky ground next to Bruce. "I haven't hugged you like that since you fell off your bike and broke your arm when you were seven."

"I could have used a few more hugs like that one since then, you know."

"I know, son. I know. I haven't been very supportive of you since… you-know-what."

"It's alright, dad. I did some things that I'm not proud of. I knew how disappointed you'd be if you found out what I was dealing drugs, but that didn't stop me. So when I finally did get caught, I immediately started treating you like you were already disappointed with me before you even said a word. Sorry about that."

"Hey, I'm the one that needs to say sorry. I'm sure it was hard getting kicked out of school and even harder in jail. I could have been so much more supportive."

"Well, I guess it was a good thing that I got crushed by this boulder to bring us together." Bruce tried his best to laugh though his cracked lips. "Which reminds me, how did you have any idea what had happened and where to find me? Have you been following me all along?"

"This is going to sound pretty wild, but you asked, so here goes. Would you believe me if I told you that aliens abducted me, that I used their equipment to locate you, and that I escaped from their ship by using one of their transporters to beam me down to this location?"

"No!"

"Well, that is exactly what happened. Except that somehow the portal, that's what the aliens call their transporters, opened up way above the ground. I was in such a hurry to get to you that I didn't look down before I stepped. I hit my head when I fell to the ground and got knocked out. When I came to, my right hip was killing me, and the portal was gone."

"Dad, there aren't any aliens. Don't start getting all crazy on me. I'm having enough trouble just coping with figuring out what to do about this boulder on my legs. I thought about cutting off my legs to survive, like that guy in Utah that cut off his hand. But I realized pretty quickly that without legs I wouldn't be able to hike out of here, even if I did survive the blood loss."

David looked at the boulder. "It is huge." He scooted over to the side of the boulder. He first tried moving it with his arms, but to no avail. He then tried pushing it with his one good leg, but the only result was a searing pain in his broken hip. "I can't budge it."

"I doubt that you could have budged it even if you hadn't broken your hip."

"If I hadn't broken my hip, at least I could have gone for help."

Both men were silent for a moment.

"Dad, no one is going to find us."

"Maybe someone will come along."

"I've been hoping that all day long. But the trail is over a mile away. Beside the occasional passing jet and your voice, I haven't heard a human sound for days. That's why I chose this place: for its solitude. Like I said, no one is going to find us. I am going to die here."

"No you're not," David said. "You've got to hang on. Someone will come. Maybe one of the other humans on the alien ship will come looking for me when they can't find me. I'm sure that Mark, the alien's artificial intelligence, will show them where I am."

"Stop, Dad. There aren't any aliens. No one is going to materialize right in front of us and save us."

"I was on the alien ship until just a few hours ago. The stuff that I saw there was amazing."

"Really? I think your hip fracture is affecting your mental capacity. Regardless, I need to finish what I was saying. Dad, you need to crawl to the trail and save yourself. It might take you two or three days, but you can make it. Someone will find you on the trail and get you to a hospital."

"And you'll probably be dead by the time I can lead them back to you. I'm not going anywhere without you."

The men fell silent again. After a few moments, the bushes across a clearing rustled for a few seconds.

"What was that?" David asked.

"I'm sure it was just the wind…"

The rustling sound came again.

"Okay, that wasn't just the wind," Bruce said. "It's probably just a rabbit."

"Who's there?" David yelled.

The rustling stopped. Shortly afterward, an irregular clicking sound could be heard that seemed to be getting closer and closer. As the clicking sound drew closer, coarse breathing could also be heard. The men craned their necks in the direction of the sound but saw nothing.

A moment later, a grizzly bear cub rounded a clump of tall grass at a gallop and headed straight for them.

"Oh, crap." Bruce said. "We're in big trouble now."

"Why? It's just a cub."

"Where there's a baby bear, there's always an extremely protective mama bear."

The grizzly bear cub moved in closer to sniff at David's neck. David pushed the cub away. The cub yelped and moved away, but only a few feet.

Just moments later, a deep growl sounded from the direction where the cub had first appeared. Both men craned their necks toward the sound. Sure enough, it was the cub's mother, looking very agitated. She was pawing the ground, huffing and clicking her jaw.

"This isn't good. She preparing to charge," Bruce said softly. "If she does, roll over, cover the back of your neck, and play dead."

"What about you? You can't roll over."

"Save yourself. Don't worry about me."

David was going to reply, but he was interrupted when apparently the baby bear overcame its fear and it padded over to David's midsection. The cub put its front paws onto David's abdomen and then tried to climb up onto David's stomach.

"Get away from me, you stupid bear," David said with a forced whisper.

The baby bear startled at David's forced whisper and let out a yelp.

The mother bear immediately charged toward the men. The cub scooted away from David as soon as the mother charged. David tried to roll over on his stomach, but his hip pain slowed him down, and the enraged mother bear was too fast. She caught him before he could roll completely over and rolled him on his back. David held his arms up in defense, but she swatted his arms out of the way, lacerating each deeply with her claws. Then she immediately lunged at his throat with her mouth, silencing his screams as she crushed his windpipe. David's body went limp. Still enraged, she left David's dying body and quickly pounced on Bruce. He had wrapped his arms around his head and throat and was playing dead. The bear swiped Bruce's arms away from his head and neck and then crushed his windpipe with her powerful jaws, just like she had his father's.

David's spirit stood up and watched as the bear continued to maul his son.

Bruce lay motionless on his back with his eyes closed. He was bleeding profusely from deep lacerations over his arms and chest and from deep bite marks over his neck and face. Positioning himself in front of the bear, David raised his arms and yelled, "Get away from my son." The bear didn't even look up. Moving to the side of the bear, David put out his hands to push the bear off of Bruce, but instead, he fell right through the bear. He landed on the rocks on the other side of the bear, unhurt. As he got up, he noticed Bruce getting up on his feet from where he had been lying, his physical body still trapped by the boulder and still being mauled by the bear. Bruce turned to face his father with a puzzled look on his face.

"Bruce, you're okay now."

"What is going on here? Am I dead?"

"Well, I think that the bear made short work of us."

Bruce turned back to the scene of the mauling. The bear was tearing open his abdomen with her claws, and loops of his bowel were spilling out onto the rocks. "So that is really me. I really am dead." He paused for a moment. "Why don't I feel pain or sadness?"

"I honestly don't know the answer to your question. I do know that I feel the same way." David paused. "Remember that alien ship that I told you about? One of its functions is to be a conduit or portal for spirits to leave this world and decide to move on to the world of spirits. For some reason, there is a moment of decision that is required of all the recently dead. They must choose to move onto the world of spirits or not. I have watched four people pass through the bright light that marks the entrance to the portal to the world of spirits. It's really a wonderful and awesome thing to see. I just never imagined that it would come so soon for me."

As David finished speaking, the view of the mountainside canyon on the screen was replaced by a three-dimensional representation of a beautiful garden beyond the portal observation wall with a shallow brook flowing gently along one side and a fence covered with climbing vines on the other. David and Bruce were standing on one side of the garden.

A swing set stood in front of them on an expanse of grass. A beautiful young woman with long red hair sat in one of the two swings. As soon as she saw the two men, she smiled and waved.

"Mom," David exclaimed.

"Grandma," Bruce called out at almost the same time.

The woman said, "I thought you'd both recognize me in my backyard." She rose from the swing.

The two men didn't need an invitation to approach her. David reached her first and gave her a tender embrace. As they released each other, the woman turned and hugged Bruce.

"Mom, you look great. You look so young," David said.

"What? Did you want to see me as I looked at age sixty-five? Well, for your information, folks here are just fine with leaving behind their old bodies. All those wrinkles and sagging skin. You'll just have to get used to me like this." She smiled radiantly.

"Grandma, I always thought you looked like you were twenty," Bruce said.

The woman laughed melodiously. "You were always such a flatterer, Bruce. My, it's good to see you both again. It has been so many years."

"It's good to see you again, too, Mom," David said.

"Oh, I'm sorry about the horrible way that you boys died. David, you were supposed to die days ago in a plane crash, but somehow you didn't come through the portal. Dying in a plane crash would have been bad enough. But then somehow you ended up with Bruce and both of you died in a bear attack. Are you guys doing okay?"

Bruce answered, "Bear? Was that a bear?" He chuckled at his own joke. "I feel great. I don't have a one-ton rock on my legs anymore."

"I only feel peace," David said. "No fear, regret, or sadness. I can see now why the others that I saw pass through the portals were so happy. In fact, the rest of the survivors from the plane crash are probably right over there behind a glass wall." As he spoke, David moved to the right with his hands outstretched.

As David moved slowly toward the invisible glass wall, a glowing light appeared beyond the swing and quickly increased in intensity.

"David, it's time," his mother called after him. "The portal is open."

David ignored his mother and keep moving slowly toward the observation wall, his hands still up in front of him to avoid running face first into the wall.

"How long will the portal stay open for him?" Margie asked from the other side of the observation wall. David had been searching for the observation wall that divided the observation room from the portal room for over a minute.

David finally found the transparent wall of the observation room. He stood with his hands flat against the wall and with his nose up to the wall's surface, trying to peer through the wall.

"The portal will stay open as long as it is needed," Sam replied.

David said, "Guys, are you there?" Hearing nothing, he continued, "I know that you're there. I just want to say goodbye, and I want to tell you that death is nothing to fear. We have all watched this miracle unfold for others, but now that I am going through it, I can only say that it is wonderful. I'll see you on the other side someday."

David turned away from the wall and rejoined his mother. She took him by the hand. Then, with Bruce holding her other hand, they moved through the portal and were gone. The scene in portal room instantly disappeared, leaving behind the usual featureless and dimly-lit room.

"Now there are only six of us left," Rick said.

The room was silent.

Connie broke the silence. "We were all supposed to have died in the plane crash. The spirits from the world of spirits that we have seen in the portals say that they had been notified that we were all going to die in the plane crash. But we didn't. Miraculously, we survived. For me, it is such a rush to realize that I have a second lease on life. And this place we have end up in is so amazing. However, now that we are dying off one by one in a very short period of time, this whole experience on the station seems to be just delaying the inevitable. Maybe we're all going to die like the others." She stopped and then continued with tears in her eyes. "I don't want to die."

"You're not going to die," Sam said.

Amanda turned to Sam. "How can we be sure that you're not letting us die to fulfill some God-ordained destiny that was frustrated when it missed us once and is now coming back for a second try?"

"I promise you that God, my staff, or I had nothing to do with these deaths. They were just accidents, plain and simple. Of course, I knew that they were going to happen, but I was not allowed to intervene."

"If something is going to happened to one of the rest of us," Margie asked, "Can't you at least warn us in advance? I really don't want to die now that I have started writing my book on Earth's greatest love stories."

"I can't prevent accidental deaths without God's permission, but I can assure you that as long as you're here on this station, you won't suffer from disease. In addition, any non-life-ending trauma will heal quickly. You will grow old, however. But, at the end of your life, you'll pass peacefully and painlessly to the world of spirits."

"I'm good with that," Margie said. "Just keep me alive until I can finish my book. Now, if you'll excuse me, I'm going to get back to my writing." She turned to the other three survivors in the room. "Be careful, please. I really don't want to see one of you in one of the portals."

"You do the same, Margie," Rick said. As Margie left the room, he turned to Amanda and asked, "How about we take the long way back to our rooms? We'll tell Mark to not open a portal for us. I really need to stretch out my legs and get some exercise."

"Sounds good," Amanda said. "I could use some exercise myself." Amanda and Rick left the room, hand in hand.

CHAPTER 37

"IT'S GOOD TO see them together. They make a cute couple," Connie said after Amanda and Rick had left the portal observation room.

"They are very happy together," Sam said.

"Sam, I've been thinking about our survival. Why did God tell you to intervene and save us from the plane crash, but not the others that were sitting right next to us on the plane? What have we all done to deserve to live?"

Sam didn't answer her question.

"Wait a minute," Connie said. "The master of all answers to all questions suddenly clams up. What is it? You can't answer my question?"

"No, I can answer it. I was just deciding how much to tell you."

"Hopefully, you're going to tell me everything. I can't live with the stress of knowing that you're holding back anything from me."

"Okay. Here's the truth. And I pray that you'll forgive me once you know it."

"I'm all ears."

"You were supposed to die in the plane crash. All of you were. I never got a directive from God to intervene in your deaths."

"What? Then why did you?"

"It all goes back to the day in Cancun when you tried to save that little boy from choking to death."

Connie looked at Sam incredulously. "How do you know about that? It was decades ago."

"I was working in an angel's staging room that day. God had directed that I was to intervene to prevent the child from dying. I was informed that a bystander was going to try to help the choking child, but that their efforts would fail without divine intervention. When I got there, you were trying so hard to save the child. No matter what you did, the smooth stone that he had breathed into his windpipe wouldn't dislodge. Tears streamed down your face as you silently called on God to save the child."

Connie said, "I had tried every lifesaving technique that I knew, but the kid still couldn't breathe. He was unconscious and turning blue. Exhausted, I had put him on the sand and had taken a two-second break to catch my breath before I resumed my efforts to try to dislodge the stone by pounding him on the back. Suddenly, without the child moving at all or without me doing anything, the stone popped out of his mouth and onto the sand. That was you!"

"You were amazing that day."

"You saved the tail section of the jet to save me," Connie said. Tears welled up in her eyes and began streaming down her cheeks. "You were supposed to let me die, but you couldn't." Trying to blink back her tears, she continued as best she could in a broken voice, "You love me, don't you? That's why you did all of this."

"I do love you, Connie," Sam said quietly. "I have loved you every minute since I first saw you."

Connie leaned toward him with her arms stretched out to hold him. As he encircled her in his arms, she tucked her head against his neck. Sam kissed her gently on the top of her head.

She lifted her face to his and they kissed tenderly. He started kissing her more ardently, but Connie held him away from her. "Wait a minute. Before this whole things goes in that direction... and don't think that I'm not interested in that whole kissing thing. It's just that I have to talk first before I can kiss you like that. Maybe I'm different from the women on your planet. It's like the movie I saw years ago. I can't remember… Oh, I know. It was *Earth Girls Aren't Easy*."

"Connie. Stop. I have loved you for twenty years, ever since I first saw you. Never once during that time did I not find your keen intellect, your heart, your laugh, and your giving personality completely captivating. I can wait as long as you need until you're ready to kiss me again. I'm not going anywhere."

"I don't mind kissing you at all." She reached up and kissed him tenderly on the lips again. "I just need to ask you some questions first. Please indulge me in that, okay?"

"Okay."

"First, why are you interested in me? I don't get it. I am forty years old, and you are five hundred and thirty-two years old. You've traveled all over the galaxy, and you know ten thousand times as much as I do. You must have interacted with millions and millions of attractive women, many who are younger and smarter than me."

"Connie, when I was a young man on my home planet, I never dreamed that I would be single for so long. I had assumed that I would soon meet my eternal companion, like almost all of my friends, and that I would settle down and have a family. However, like I already told you, I just never met the right woman. I did date hundreds and hundreds of wonderful women, many of whom had all of the qualities that I would ever hope for in a wife. But, with each one of them, there was always something missing. Since being translated, I have dated on and off. Again, I have never met the right woman. Until I met you that day on the beach. Whatever was missing with all the other women was there with you then and is still there with you now."

"Thank you. I think we do have something pretty special."

"To finish answering your first question, I was attracted to you from afar, but I just didn't know how I could ever meet you. It's against the rules for translated beings to get involved with the individuals on the planets they are assigned to. Even knowing that, you would be shocked at how many times I daydreamed of being behind you in line at a grocery store checkout or sitting next to you in the library and then introducing myself. But I never did it because I was always too afraid of getting caught and transferred to the farthest reaches of the other side of the galaxy, far away from you.

"When I learned that you were going to die in the plane crash, my heart sank. I had waited too long to get to know you. Now the opportunity was going to pass from my reach forever. Without telling anyone on the station of my real intent, I maneuvered the station to be at the perfect place during the eruption to allow your plane to safely crash on the roof of the station. When some of the members of my staff questioned what I had done, I told them that I just hadn't been able to let the people on the plane die."

"And your staff went for it?"

"I'm afraid not. A few of them saw through my plan and openly denounced my saving you to my face. I'm sure that they have reported me for what I have done. There is a good chance I might even get transferred because of it. At the worst, I might even be asked to resign from working as a translated being. In that case, I would simply move straight to the world of spirits that is assigned to my home world. Still, regardless of the risk, I would have done the same thing a thousand times over, and even more so now that I have gotten to know you personally. I'm not leaving your side ever again, if there is anything that I can do about it."

"You know, for a man, you do talk a lot," she said with a smile.

"Does it bother you?"

"Sam, I wouldn't have it any other way." She gently touched him on the cheek with her fingers. "I have to confess that there is something special about you also; something that I have never felt before. I'm looking forward to seeing how our alien and Earth girl romance unfolds."

CHAPTER 38

ALEX CAREFULLY RAISED the line of white powder on the back of his hand to his nose. He snorted the whole line expertly, leaving little behind. The powder instantly irritated his nasal lining, making his eyes water and his nose wrinkle. Leaning his head back with his eyes closed, he waited for the feeling to pass. The line of powder was an old friend, but one that he hadn't visited for a while. That was why it was bothering his nose more that it had when he had been snorting heavily years back. Multiple expensive episodes in rehab at that time had saved his job and had kept him out of jail. However, once a cokehead, always a cokehead. For the years since rehab, he had been just one stressful event away from embracing the mind-numbing bliss of the white powder again. Now, with constant concern for his life because of Kurt and with complete access to an unlimited supply of cocaine, he had no longer been able to resist.

After the stress of placing the Semtex in the station's engine room, his anxiety level had been so high that he had been trembling when he had gotten back to their angel's staging room. Kurt, on the other hand, had been as calm as a cucumber and had gone to his room to sleep. As soon as the door had closed behind Kurt, Alex had easily located a small-time dealer that he had brought coke from in the past and had opened a portal directly into the room where the dealer stored his cocaine. Hurrying through the portal, he hadn't wasted a moment as he had grabbed the first bag he had seen and had torn it open. He had lined up the huge snort on the back of his hand within seconds. Sure, it had been a lot of coke, but he had figured that his heart was immune to the stuff since he had snorted so much of it in his lifetime.

The cocaine easily passed through his nasal membranes and into his blood stream. Almost immediately, he felt a rush of elation and confidence, two things that he had been sorely lacking with Kurt around. After savoring the rush for a moment, he realized that he had to get back before someone discovered that he was gone. Grabbing another unopened bag of his old friend, he reentered the angel's staging room via the portal. He was grateful to see that the angel's staging room was still unoccupied. Opening a portal to his bedroom, he hopped through, leaving the angel's staging room empty and no one in the whole station the wiser.

CHAPTER 39

"WELL, HERE WE are." Rick said as they arrived at the door to Amanda's room. Even though it had taken them twenty minutes to get there, to Rick it seemed like the time had gone by in the blink of an eye.

"You want to come in?" Amanda asked.

"After what happened last time, Sam will just come barreling into your sitting room as soon as we are on the couch."

"Come on. Don't give up so easily. Let's test him to see what we can get away with before he shows up."

"Amanda Thomas. I had no idea you were such a risk taker."

"When it comes to someone telling me I can't spend quality time with a man I care about, I start feeling like a grounded teenager. Rebellious." She opened the door to her room and motioned Rick inside. "Have a seat on the couch while I use the ladies room," she said as she hurried ahead of him and down the hall.

As Rick sat on the couch, he heard Amanda opening drawers in her bedroom for a few moments and then he heard the bathroom door shut. After a few minutes more, he heard the toilet flush. To his surprise, he then heard the shower come on. What was she up to? He sat there for a few more minutes, listening carefully for any clues as to what she was doing, but he didn't hear any more sounds besides the running water.

"Rick," Amanda whispered from down the hall. "Come here."

Rick approached the bathroom door.

The door to the bathroom was cracked open a little and steam was pouring out of the opening. The light in the bathroom was off.

"Don't say anything and get in here," she whispered.

Rick couldn't believe what was happening. Did she want him to take a shower with her? He froze. On one hand, he totally wanted to sprint into the bathroom and take her naked body in his arms, but, at the same time, he was sure that Sam would show up the moment that he was in the shower with her. That would be extremely embarrassing. On top of that, he wasn't quite ready to make love to her yet. He liked things to move a little slower than this.

"Come on, silly. I don't bite."

"Amanda…"

"I'm not naked. It's okay."

That changed everything. Rick slipped into the dark and steamy bathroom. As Amanda shut the door, he couldn't help but exclaim softly, "What in the world are you up to?" By the light of a dim night light, he could barely see the outline of her face inches in front of his.

"I'm trying to see if we can trick Mark. He said he never spies on us when we are in the shower. I'm hoping that the dark and the steam will make us impossible for him to see."

"This is crazy."

Amanda laughed. "You didn't know what you were getting yourself into with me, did you?"

"You definitely are one surprise after another."

"If you don't like it…"

"I think you're tons of fun. Now you're the one that's paranoid."

Amanda punched him on the arm playfully in the dim light.

"You hit me," Rick said playfully.

"I'm going to do a lot more than that if you don't get with the plan and kiss me right now. I didn't go to all this trouble for nothing."

Rick reached out for her in the dim light, found her shoulders, and went to kiss her. However, he ended up kissing her nose instead.

"Ew! Sick. You tried to stick your tongue up my nose." Amanda giggled at her own joke. "Let me help you." She found his head and pulled his lips to hers. The kiss was gentle and sweet. As their lips parted, Amanda said, "Where was the fire and passion that you kissed me with on the couch?"

"Knowing that Sam could knock on the door at any second kind of puts a damper on any fire and passion. As creative as you are, I don't think that a little steam and having the lights off will fool Mark."

"Well, then just hold me. That's the best part anyway."

Rick took her in his arms, and she nestled her head against his shoulder.

After a few moments, Rick said, "Amanda?"

"What?" she said softly.

"When I am with you, I feel so happy. You're fun, smart, and beautiful. I know it's fast, but I can't help but tell you that I'm falling in love with you."

"Rick, I really care about you, too."

Rick wasn't surprised that she hadn't said that she loved him. They had barely just met. She probably needed time to think about it. "Amanda?" he asked.

"What?"

"Can we go back to the couch before I melt into a puddle of water on this floor? It's really hot in here."

"Aww. Come on. Admit it. It's just the passion that you feel for me."

"No, it's the steam from the shower. Either I'm going to have to strip naked this very moment, or I'm going to have to run out the door."

Amanda took her arms from around him. "It is hot." She flipped her hair from where it was stuck to the back of her neck. "Maybe my idea wasn't so good after all."

Rick opened the door, and they both spilled out into the hall, along with half of the steam in the bathroom. Amanda's hair was limp and stuck to her forehead. Rick's face was dripping wet.

"Ah. Fresh air," Rick said as they moved down the hall. Rick plopped onto the couch.

Amanda stayed in the center of the room. "Hey, Mark," she called out to the walls around her. "Guess where we've been?" The room was silent. "Aha! You couldn't see us in the bathroom. For all you know, we just had amazing sex, and now I'm pregnant with triplets."

Mark's disembodied voice came from everywhere, as usual. "Rick's testosterone and adrenaline levels remained constant the whole time you were in the bathroom. It is not possible for a male—"

"Okay. Okay. You are all-seeing and all-knowing," Amanda said. "Now, please just go away and give us some privacy."

Rick said from the couch, "Amanda, you know he can't do that. He's a computer. He doesn't have feelings. Sam told him to keep an eye on us, and that's exactly what he is going to do."

Amanda sank onto the couch next to Rick. "You're right. I was just hoping we could spend some unsupervised time alone."

"Well, we do have the next fifty years or so to spend together. That is, as long as you're okay with me hanging around for that long."

"Are you proposing to me already? Just a moment ago you said you were starting to fall in love with me, and now—"

"I'm not proposing." Rick blushed.

"Just checking." Grinning, she continued, "But if we can't get any more physical than this without triggering the chaperone, then it's going to be a long fifty years."

"You just agreed that you're going to be with me for the next fifty years," Rick said. "You accepted my proposal."

"No, I didn't. You're just trying to trap me into marriage. I should have known."

"Come on. Would being married to me really be all that bad?"

"No, but it's all just theoretical. We can never marry and never have kids, thanks to Sam and his diabolical plan. This place is more of a prison than anything else." She covered her mouth as she yawned.

"Okay, time for your beauty sleep," Rick said. "As if you needed it." Rick sat up on the couch.

"Don't go."

"I have to. You're so pretty that I'd better leave before I do something crazy, and Sam has to pop back into the room. Get a good night's rest, and I'll see you first thing in the morning."

CHAPTER 40

ALEX'S EYES POPPED open in an instant as he felt someone shaking his shoulder. He sat up, inhaling sharply, with fear making his heart race. Slowly, his eyes focused in the dim light on Kurt's face. Alex's brows knitted in irritation. "Don't ever wake me up like that again. Why didn't you knock?"

"I did. But you didn't answer. I had to use a portal to get to your living room."

"What was so important that you had to wake me up from a dead sleep?"

"I couldn't sleep. My eyes popped open a few hours ago, and I have been lying in bed thinking about the opportunities that the portals provide for us. We're going to be leaving soon. It seems a shame not to use the portals to help ourselves to some of the wealth that is so carefully guarded around the earth, but that is completely defenseless to us here on the station. Since time is short, I want to be sure that we get a chance to help ourselves to as much as we can."

Alex swung his legs over the side of the bed. "What did you have in mind?"

"Gold weighs too much. Paper bills are too heavy if you get enough of them. On top of that, they can be traced. Uncut diamonds have a much greater value per pound and can't be easily traced. I know that the Diamond Trading Company has a large number of rough diamonds stored in their vaults in preparation for their every fifth week show for their preferred buyers. The shows, or 'sights,' as they call them, will be taking place in the UK, South Africa, Botswana, and Namibia simultaneously about twenty-four hours from now. The diamonds are already in vaults at each site. We should be able to walk in via a portal and just pick them up. No one would ever be able to figure out how they were robbed. I could then use some of my contacts to fence the diamonds, little by little, over the next few years."

Alex didn't know what to say. On one hand, he was mortified with Kurt's plans to wipe out most of the population of downtown Chicago. On the other hand, he had to hand it to Kurt for coming up with a pretty good get-filthy-rich-quick scheme. Could they really pull this one off, along with blowing up the station and getting away before the station plunged to the earth? If they did, he'd never have to worry about coming up with the cash to buy cocaine again. Just as cool, he'd never need to work again either.

"Come on. Cat got your tongue? There's nothing to this plan. The diamonds are ours already."

"I'm in," Alex said. "But, are you sure that we will be able to fence the diamonds without the Diamond Trading Company tracing them to us and then sending hit men to kill us?"

"You have no idea how good my colleagues are. They never fail me, which is why they are still alive."

"When do you want to grab the diamonds?" Alex asked with a yawn.

"Right now. Get out of bed, sleepyhead."

CHAPTER 41

"**N**OW THAT WE have some time, could you please enlighten me on how God accomplished the seemingly impossible task of moving the Earth here from wherever it was created?" Connie asked. "You were going to tell me earlier, but then you had to leave. I still can't see how you were able to provide the huge amount of energy required to accelerate and decelerate the earth for the trip and how you did it without leaving the atmosphere and oceans behind in space."

They were seated on a red- and white-checked blanket in a grassy area on the shore of Moraine Lake in Banff National Park in the Canadian Rockies. The sun was shining brightly overhead in the clear blue sky. The turquoise water of the lake sparkled with the glint of a million diamonds. When Sam had invited Connie for a picnic to any uninhabited area on Earth, Connie had requested a mountain lake. Sam had chosen this mostly uninhabited location, being sure to check first that no hikers or campers were in the area. The remains of their picnic lunch sat to one side of the blanket.

Sam said, "After God had completed Earth's preparation, it was gradually moved out of its stable orbit around its sun. Temperatures dropped hundreds of degrees below zero, freezing the oceans and the atmosphere. Once the earth was completely frozen, it was safely transported through space at many times the speed of light. Earth was then gently placed in its current orbit around your sun. Within a matter of a few years, the ice had melted enough that Earth was reseeded and repopulated with plants and animals."

Connie was quiet for a moment. "What you're saying goes against everything that I have learned and observed as a scientist. For my whole life, I have been pleased at the victories that science has achieved over religion in proving that there is no supreme creator, and that evolution did it all. But now, in the face of overwhelming evidence coming from a vast and highly advanced society of human aliens, the foundations of my beliefs as a scientist are crumbling."

"Out of those ashes will rise a bright knowledge of the truth. Of all the people that I know, you value truth above all else."

"You know that about me, do you? Is there anything about me that you don't know?"

"I don't know what you are going to say next, what you are thinking about right now, and what you are planning to do with the rest of your life. Maybe that is why your mind is fascinating to me."

"As long as you don't cut my brain out my head to study it, like aliens supposedly do to abducted humans, then I'm okay with that."

"Why cut it out to study it when Mark can give me a three-dimensional accounting of every single cell in your brain?"

"That's an invasion of privacy."

"Believe me, ninety-nine percent of all human memories are boring enough that no one is ever going to be interested in seeing them again, including the individual that experienced them. That final one percent can be pretty fascinating, however. Like the time you took that shot on the goal to win the regional-final soccer game your senior year of high—"

"That's enough, wise guy. I really don't want to relive every embarrassing moment of my life. Let's just leave the heartbreak of that missed shot in the dark recesses of my past memory."

CHAPTER 42

"IT'S SO COOL that all of these diamonds are just lying around for us to pick up," Alex whispered.

"I don't think that The Diamond Trading Company has ever had any suspicion that someone would materialize inside their vault and snag their diamonds," Kurt said as he finished filling his canvas sack with diamonds and then pulled the draw strings.

Alex finished doing the same with his canvas sack, stuffing it full of individually packaged and labeled diamonds. "We've got as much as we can carry. Let's get going."

The two men grabbed their sacks and returned to the angel's staging room via the still-open portal. Just as they entered the room, Ethan came through the door to the angel's staging room. Alex and Kurt froze like kids with their hands in the cookie jar.

Ethan walked up to them slowly, his eyes darting to the men, the open portal to the vault, and their canvas sacks. "What do you have in the sacks?"

"We just picked up a few supplies on Earth that we needed," Kurt replied hastily.

"From a bank vault?" Ethan asked. "Open the sacks and let me see what you've taken." Ethan relieved Alex of his sack and set it on the ground.

As Ethan was working on untying the drawstrings on Alex's sack, Kurt slipped behind him slowly. Quick as lightening, Kurt grabbed his knife from his sheath, yanked Ethan's head back by his hair, and sliced his throat from ear to ear. "Die, you alien pig, die!"

Rivulets of blood dripped down Ethan's neck from the thin red line across his throat. His eyes first went wide in surprise, and then less than a second later, his lids slid down over his sightless eyes as he lost consciousness. Before Ethan's body could slump completely to the ground, Kurt yanked Ethan's shirt up to help catch the blood spilling from his neck and then singlehandedly shoved him through the still-open portal into the DeBeers vault. Ethan crumpled into a heap on the floor of the vault.

"Close the portal, quick," Kurt said.

Alex hurriedly closed the portal and then turned on Kurt. "Why did you have to kill him? You could have just knocked him out."

"And then what? Whatever we did to him, he would have ultimately awakened and immediately used some sort of telepathy to alert Sam about what we have done." As Kurt spoke, he grabbed a tissue from a box on the table and began cleaning up Ethan's blood that had dripped on the carpeted floor.

"Yeah, but how do you know that they don't have some sort of system to tell Sam when one of his workers dies and their brain waves go offline?"

"Since the station's crew is not flooding in here with drawn laser weapons, then we have to assume that they don't know when one of their crew dies." Kurt stood up and stuck the bloodstained tissues in his pocket. "I bet they don't even miss him until its way too late."

"I hope that you're right. We still have two long hours until the station blows, and we finally get our chance to get out of here."

CHAPTER 43

"RICK," MARK'S VOICE said softly in Rick's bedroom where Rick was sleeping. Aided by alien technology, Mark's voice drilled deeply into Rick sleeping brain, waking him with a jolt.

"What?" Rick said as he sat bolt upright, eyes wide open. "What's wrong? Did someone else die?"

"No one has died. Sam has requested your presence at a meeting in thirty minutes in the special dining room."

"Is that the same place where we usually eat?" Rick's voice was still thick with sleep, and he blinked his eyes to try to wake himself.

"No. I will take you there when you're ready."

"Are the others going to be there?"

"All of the other survivors have been requested to be in attendance."

Rick hopped out of bed and dressed quickly. He ran a comb through his bed hair, but then he scowled at his lack of success at taming his mane. Water from the sink and additional combing finally achieved the result he was after.

"Okay. I'm ready."

"Take a left down the hall, and I will deliver you to your destination in a jiff."

"A jiff?" Rick asked as he left his room and headed down the hall. "Since when did the most powerful computer in the universe stoop to using contemporary North American slang?"

"I'm trying to make you feel at home in this very foreign place."

Mark opened a portal right in front of Rick. As Rick passed through the portal, he saw that Amanda was standing right in front of him by a set of open double doors. She turned to greet him.

"Good morning, Rick." She gave him a quick hug and then continued, "What took you so long? I've been waiting for at least… twenty seconds."

Rick gave her a quick kiss. It was still like a dream come true that such a wonderful and beautiful woman actually liked him. "If I'd known you were waiting for me, I'd have been here sooner. And, by the way, you look nice this morning."

She smiled. "And you look pretty awesome yourself. However, you didn't come here just to see me. Let's see what Sam wants."

Together they entered through the double doors. The room beyond was a little larger than a basketball court. Intricately-carved, wood, dining-room tables with accompanying chairs were scattered around the room. They were interspersed with separate sitting areas with couches with a central ottoman. The upholstery of the couches appeared to be made of leather. Large green and flowering plants that Rick didn't quite recognize were scattered amongst the dining tables and sitting areas. The room's high walls were finished in what appeared to be cherry wood. Large and stunning oil on canvas landscapes were spaced around the room's walls and were lit by unseen light sources. Some of the landscapes were of places on Earth that Rick had either visited or had seen in pictures. The other landscapes were clearly not from Earth since they displayed more than one sun or moon, or alien plants and animals.

Connie and Margie were already seated at a dining table in the center of the room, along with Sam, Michaela, and a few others that Rick didn't recognize.

"Welcome," Sam greeted Amanda and Rick as they arrived at the table. He motioned for them to sit in empty chairs to his side. "Kurt and Alex should be here in a moment."

Almost on cue, Kurt and Alex entered the room. They hesitated at the door.

"Please join us." Sam gestured for them to take a seat at the table.

After looking at each other for a moment, Kurt and Alex took the offered seats. Rick tried to catch their eyes to say good morning, but they avoided eye contact with the others at the table.

Sam stood. "I have called you here to meet a special guest. We are very lucky to have Simon Peter, one of the apostles from the Bible, visiting us." As Sam gestured toward a twenty-something handsome white-haired man to his left, the man leaned his head slightly forward and smiled.

Sam continued, "He just arrived a few minutes ago and is very eager to meet you."

Margie leaned over to Rick and whispered, "Wow. How do we rate? This is really rolling out the red carpet."

Kurt spoke up from the other side of the table as he addressed Peter. "You were crucified. It's not possible for you to be here in the flesh."

"But here I am just the same, Kurt," Peter said. "I assure you that I am very much made of flesh and bones. My wife and I were resurrected soon after my death. To be sure you understand, at the resurrection, my spirit was again placed in a body of flesh and bone, only this time the body was perfect. A resurrected body doesn't suffer disease or injury and can never die."

"You don't look any different from anyone else at this table," Kurt said. "How can we know that you're who and what you say you are?"

"Kurt, you have always questioned whether there is a God, a

heaven, and even whether there is life after death. I would hope that the things that you have seen on this station have helped you to realize that there is so much more to your existence than just your short time on Earth."

"Prove to me that you are resurrected being. Otherwise, I will just have to assume that you are another alien that is part of a race of aliens that aims to enslave me and my fellow humans for your nefarious purposes."

"Kurt, I don't need to prove myself to you," Peter said.

There was a quiet power in Peter's voice that made Rick's whole body tingle.

Peter continued, "It is you that needs to prove yourself to God. It is you that is still being tested to see what your spirit will do when it is far from its God and housed in a less than perfect body that feels anguish, pain, lust, and greed so powerfully."

Kurt glared at Peter without attempting to refute his words.

Amanda broke the silence at the table. "So, you really were with Jesus in Jerusalem?"

"I was. And what an opportunity it was. I can still feel the peaceful power in his voice as he taught my fellow Judeans."

Amanda said, "And you saw him heal people."

"I did. It was the most amazing thing I had ever seen. I never got tired of seeing the amazement and gratitude in the faces of those that he healed."

"And he really did instantly heal the blind, severely crippled, and mentally ill?"

"I would expect that question from the physician in the group. Luke the apostle was just like you, always asking questions about the body and how it worked. In answer to your question, yes, Jesus really did almost instantly heal even the worst of human maladies and deformities. I saw it happen with my own eyes hundreds of times."

"But, respectfully, that can't be true. How can trillions of cells that are defective from birth, such as in child with Down's syndrome, be instantly genetically altered just by the touch of a man's hand? It's just not possible."

Peter said, "There are scientific explanations for every miracle that Jesus and the prophets throughout the ages have ever performed. However, the science behind miracles is quite advanced, and for those that don't yet possess the knowledge behind miracles, then miracles seem to be accomplished by magic. But we deviate from the reason that I am here." Peter looked at Sam for a moment and then looked back at the rest of the group. "Throughout the galaxy, this is the first time that God's living children from a test planet have entered one of the many stations like this one. I am here to investigate how this could have happened and how it can be prevented in the future. To begin, I want to ask the survivors how they are doing. Have you all been treated well here on the station?"

Margie was the first to answer, "Sam and his staff have been most helpful, and the amenities the station offers are simply amazing."

Kurt said, "That doesn't change the fact that we are prisoners here, held against our will by an alien race."

Rick attempted to soften Kurt's words, "While I'm sure that I can speak for most of us that we wish that we could return to Earth, at the same time, we can't be critical of all of the hospitality that has been offered us here."

Peter said, "I'm glad that Sam and his staff are taking good care of you. And I'm glad that each of you survived the horrible plane crash. However, you weren't supposed to survive the plane crash, and you definitely weren't supposed to end up here on this station. The station has many built in failsafe mechanisms to prevent this very thing from ever happening. Do any of you have any idea of how this occurred against all odds?"

Silence reigned for a few moments as Peter looked around the table. Suddenly, Connie blurted out, "I do," at exactly the same time that Sam stated, "Yes."

"Go ahead, Connie," Peter said. "Tell me what you know."

Connie turned to Sam. "I think that Sam should tell you what happened, if that is okay with Sam."

Peter nodded.

Sam took a deep breath and then said, "Completely on my own, I disarmed the failsafe mechanisms and then maneuvered the station to be precisely in position for the plane to safely crash-land on top of the station."

Peter asked, "And why did chose to go against your mandates as the station supervisor?"

"I did it because I am in love with Connie." Gasps of surprise were heard from around the table. Sam said, "I didn't want her die before I had the chance to get to know her."

Peter said, "Sam, you were fully aware of the rules concerning fraternization with the people on Earth, and still you did this?"

"In my defense, I never traveled to Earth to meet her even once, even though I did think about doing it many times. I didn't meet her until she arrived on the station and was no longer on Earth."

"It is true that there isn't a rule that directly states that there can't be fraternization with people from Earth that are on the station," Peter said. "That's because there never have been people from test planets on stations. You didn't break the letter of the law, but without question, you broke the spirit of the law."

"And for that, I'm sorry."

"Connie," Peter said. "Are you okay knowing that Sam's affection for you led to all of this?"

"Yes, I am."

"Would you care to elaborate?"

"As years have gone by and I haven't been able to find a lifetime companion, I have often remarked that the guy I was supposed to marry didn't exist on Earth. I never knew just how right I was. Sam has become very deer to me."

"How sweet," Margie said.

"Sweet, my foot," Alex said. "Look what we had to go through just because Sam had the hots for Connie."

"True, but we'd all be dead if Sam hadn't moved the station," Rick said.

"I'd rather be dead than be an alien prisoner on this station," Kurt said.

"Okay," Peter said. "I think the situation is pretty clear. I'm glad to learn that the station is functioning properly, and the occurrence was due to operator error. So now that we have established that, why don't you all join me for breakfast?"

"Are you going to show us how you turned that loaf of bread and the fish into enough food for everyone?" Alex asked with a wry smile.

"Not unless you would like to eat two-thousand-year-old fish," Peter responded and then roared in laughter.

"Alex and I have already eaten," Kurt said. "You guys go ahead and have breakfast. We'll catch up with you later." Kurt rose.

Alex followed, and they left the room.

CHAPTER 44

ALEX WAS FRUSTRATED that again he had been forced to leave with Kurt when he really hadn't wanted to. Once they were in the hallway outside the room, Alex said, "Why couldn't we have stayed for a few minutes? I was hungry. Plus, I wanted to see if he was going to do any of his miracles."

As Kurt called up a portal to their staging room, he said. "I couldn't stand to be in the same room with those lying aliens for another second. Peter and the rest of them are pretending that they are powerful beings that can't die in order to maintain their control over us. Just wait. Peter will die with the rest of them when this station is obliterated."

Arriving at their staging room, Alex said, "You might think that you've got them fooled, but I suspect that they are a lot smarter than they let on. I'm worried that Mark or someone else might have discovered our bombs in the engine room and disabled them."

Kurt stopped. "I thought that they would all explode if someone tried to disarm even one of them?"

"Who knows what tricks these aliens have up their sleeves? Just to be sure, let's go back to the engine room and check on the Semtex to make sure it's still ready to detonate as planned."

"You worry too much. Let's go our rooms first, pack the diamonds, and then be sure to leave the rooms looking like we are still living there and are planning to come back. Leave all your personal items. Let's meet back here in about sixty minutes."

"Fine, leave me on pins and needles. You promise that we can check out the Semtex as soon as we get back here?"

Kurt was already stepping through a new portal to his living room as he called back, "Sure thing."

CHAPTER 45

"**P**ETER, I HAVE an important topic to broach with you," Margie said between bites of her breakfast.

"Go ahead," Peter said.

"While using the computer system, we have discovered that the Eastern Seaboard of the US is going to be hit by a sixty-foot tsunami in just under two days. There will be little time for an advance warning. The expected death rates are massive. New York City is directly in the bull's eye. Amanda has a brother that lives there, and I have a couple of friends that live there. Is there any way that we can convince you to pull off a miracle and stop the tsunami from occurring?"

"Your request is valid," Peter said. "It is so hard to watch so many suffer and die. Unfortunately, I can't do anything to stop the tsunami."

Amanda said, "But, if you are who you say you are, then you could stop the tsunami if you wanted to. The Bible contains many examples of huge miracles, such as the parting of the Dead Sea, the destruction of Sodom and Gomorrah by fire from the heavens, and the day the sun stood still for the Israelites during battle with the Amorites."

"For someone that professes not to believe in the Bible, you know it quite well," Peter said with a smile.

"Just because I don't accept the teachings of the Bible as being completely true doesn't mean that I don't remember what my parents and teachers taught me as a child," Amanda said.

Peter said, "Hopefully, your time here on this station has served to increase your belief in the teachings of the Bible. You and your companions have had a unique opportunity to see God's work in action on a scale that Earth's inhabitants were never supposed to see."

Margie said, "But, can't you at least warn the people in New York to get to higher ground? My friends have children, and it kills me to know that they're going to die."

"I'm so sorry, Margie, but it is not God's will that the tsunami be stopped."

Amanda asked, "Is God causing the tsunami to happen to punish the people of New York? Sure, there are some pretty evil people that live there, but it's unfair to all of the innocent children and good people that will die at the same time."

"God is not sending this tsunami as a punishment," Peter said. "The impending tsunami is just a chance occurrence in a world that was created to be a difficult proving ground for his children. Most bad things that happen to people on Earth, either individually or collectively, are just bad things happening by chance to good people. Don't think for a minute that it doesn't grieve God to see his children fall sick or be injured. No matter how many years you live, it never gets easier to see a child suffer and die."

Margie asked, "I understand what you're saying, but, please, just this once, can't you intercede and prevent this disaster? What would it hurt?"

"The degree of concern you have for the lives of your fellow human beings is wonderful," Peter said. "However, just like God doesn't often purposely send diseases and disasters to the earth, he also rarely intervenes in the random catastrophes that occur on

Earth. He only intervenes in the catastrophes of the physical world when it's needed to further his work. On the other hand, when disasters of a spiritual nature occur in his children's lives, he does readily and frequently intervene."

Amanda said, "It's easy to see where Kurt is coming from when he says that you are just a highly-advanced alien race that for some reason delights in creating and then observing human suffering. Even though I've heard both your and Sam's explanations, I'm still struggling with this whole thing."

"Just give it some time, Amanda," Rick said. "Look into your heart, and God's spirit will be there to help you to accept it."

Amanda looked hard at Rick. "You really believe that there is a loving God behind all of this?"

"I have always believed in God since before I can remember," Rick said. "Nothing that I have seen on this station has changed that belief. Instead, like Peter said, what I have seen here has strengthened my belief."

"And, you're okay with the tsunami killing millions of people while the station and its crew stand idly by, doing nothing to help because God said so?" Amanda asked.

"No, how could I be?" Rick said. "I grieve for days when I read in the news about the death of even one child. Without question, the tsunami will be horrible. As painful as it will be for all those people to die, I will cope with the pain by knowing that those that die will be in God's hands. We have seen firsthand that they go on to a wonderful place after death, where there is only joy and peace in the company of loved ones that have already passed on before them."

"I just wish that I had your faith, Rick," Amanda said. "Then, maybe this whole thing wouldn't hurt so badly."

"You really do believe in all this religion stuff?" Amanda asked. She and Rick had left Peter and Sam in the special dining room and had been making their way back to Rick's staging room. They were holding hands as they strolled along.

"I really do," Rick replied.

"So you believe that there is a heaven for the righteous, a hell for the wicked, and that our sins really do matter to God?"

"Like I said, I've believed in those things my whole life. It sounds like you did too when you were a child."

"I did, Rick, but then God didn't cure my grandmother when I prayed really hard for him to do so. As the years went by, he didn't answer my questions when I asked. He was like an absent father to me. So science became my stepfather. Science answered my questions. Through the study of the science of medicine, I was able to provide cures to people that they could never have provided for themselves through prayer. Somewhere along the way, I just stopped believing in God."

Rick was silent for a moment. "How's the not believing in God going now that you've been on the station for a while?"

"This place would make even an atheist question themself. At the same time, I can't shake the uncomfortable feeling I have about the motives of Sam, Peter, and all the rest of the staff here. How do we know for sure that they aren't just cold-hearted aliens?"

"Amanda, you've been listening to Kurt too much."

"I have not. The last thing I want to do is listen to anything he has to say. I can't believe that I was even remotely interested in him when we first got here."

"You were more than remotely interested in him. I saw you two in the dining room that—"

"Just a minute. You left me alone to fend him off."

"Sorry about that. I am glad that you picked me over him."

"I would pick you a million times over him."

"You like me that much?"

"I do, Rick. I haven't felt this way about anyone my whole life."

"Me too. When I'm with you, I feel like my life is complete, like

I've finally found something that I've been searching for my whole life but could never find." They stopped, and Rick took Amanda in his arms. He kissed her tenderly on the lips. "I really am falling in love with you, Amanda."

"What? You haven't already fallen in love with me? What's there not to love?

"Okay, if you put it that way, then I do love you."

"I knew you did. I just wanted to hear you say it."

"You're such a tease. Who raised you anyway? I need to have a talk with your mother."

"Like that's going to happen any time soon," Amanda said. She grabbed Rick's arm. "Come on, let's get out of the hall and back to your staging room. We don't want the public display of affection police showing up and embarrassing us out here in the open."

"But..."

Amanda stopped and looked at him. "You want me to say the 'l' word to you, don't you?" She smiled hugely. "Well, if you don't already know how I feel about you, then you are just going to have to figure it out for yourself. That's part of the mystery of Amanda." She laughed, poked him in the side playfully, and then ran down the hall toward Rick's staging room. "Last one to the room's a rotten egg."

CHAPTER 46

"I HATE THAT WINDOW," Alex complained as he glanced at the tall, narrow window next to the door to the engine room. "I feel like a naked fish in a fishbowl."

"Fish are naked anyway, and they don't care who sees them," Kurt called out from behind the side extension of the plasma sphere. "Plus, the window you are referring to is called a sidelight." Kurt paused for a few moments and then continued, "The Semtex hasn't been touched, and the detonators are all in place. I checked them all." As he finished speaking, he ducked under the side extension of the plasma sphere and joined Alex in front of the sphere.

"That's a relief," Alex said.

"You're just a worrywart. Security is so lax here that I had no doubt that the Semtex hadn't been discovered."

"We're down to thirty minutes. We'll have to be in the angel's staging room with a portal open to El Agua beach in Venezuela so that we can hop through a few seconds before the detonation. If we try to pass through the portal after the explosion, then Mark might not be able to keep the portal open due to the loss of power from the engine room."

"Sounds like a plan. I'll meet you... Crap!" Kurt lowered his voice to a loud whisper. "Peter just walked past the sidelight. I'm sure he saw me."

"Great. I knew that the sidelight would be our undoing."

"If he comes in, just act like we're here sightseeing. Turn around and look at the plasma sphere."

The two men quickly pivoted to the plasma sphere, staring at it raptly. Moments later, they heard the door to the engine room open. Pretending to be intent on observing the swirling colors in the sphere, they both ignored the sound of the opening door.

"Hello, gentlemen," Peter said.

Kurt turned to Peter's voice. "Hello, Peter."

Peter said, "We missed you for the rest of our breakfast meeting. The food was excellent."

"As I mentioned, we had already had breakfast," Kurt said.

Peter moved forward to stand next to Alex, facing the sphere. "The sphere is fascinating, isn't it? I remember the first time I saw one. I couldn't stop staring at the vibrant shifting colors. Its beauty still astounds me."

"Me, too," Alex said. "That's why we're here. It was pretty painful to learn that our plane crash-landed on the station just because Sam was in love with Connie. We came here, hoping that watching the colors in the sphere would help us to relax." Alex stopped as he saw a brief flicker of disapproval on Kurt's face at his feeble attempt to cover up their real reason for being in the engine room.

"We hadn't really had a chance to check out the sphere adequately the first time we saw it," Kurt said too cheerfully in Alex's opinion. "Well, we'd better get going. I have a few things I need to check on in our staging room."

"Not so fast, please," Peter said calmly. "I've been concerned about the two of you. You don't seem to be adjusting to being on the station as well as the others. Since you're going to be here for such a long time, I was wondering if there was something that I could do to help you feel more comfortable."

Kurt said quickly, "Oh, we're fine. I'm sure that as time goes on, we'll get more accustomed to being on the station."

"I just want to be sure that you're happy here," Peter said. "Say, I have always wanted to see the back side of the sphere. I heard that there are some interesting attachments there that power the ship." As he spoke, Peter moved forward toward the left side of the sphere, away from Kurt and Alex. He paused, looked back at the two men, and said, "You're welcome to join me, if you would like." He then turned back to the sphere. Raising his right arm to steady himself against the sphere, he went to crouch down to scoot under the side arm.

Kurt sprang past Alex toward Peter, his stiletto already extending menacingly from his right hand. Before Peter even had time to react, Kurt plunged his knife deep into the right side of Peter's exposed ribcage.

Eyes wide with surprise, Peter turned to Kurt.

Kurt's response was to grab Peter's extended arm and use it as leverage as he quickly withdrew the blade and then plunged it into Peter's chest again and again. Blood dripped from Kurt's knife to the floor each time he withdrew it from Peter's chest. Peter feebly tried to push back at Kurt's madly slashing arm, but within moments, his efforts became progressively weaker, and he slumped to the floor with his eyes closed.

Breathing heavily, Kurt said, "See? I told you that I could kill him. So much for their pack of lies about being God's immortal messengers. They're really just a bunch of worthless aliens." Kurt wiped his knife blade on Peter's shirt until it was clean.

"We've got to get his body out of here," Alex said.

"I know already, stupid," Kurt said. "It's because of your diarrhea of the mouth that I had to kill him in the first place. You had better hope that no one misses him in the next half an hour before the Semtex explodes and calls an alarm, or you're a dead man, just like Peter."

Alex's eyes widened in fear. "But we're partners, aren't we?"

"I've never been your partner." Kurt yelled as his eyes flashed with menace. He suddenly reared back and threw his knife at Alex's head.

At the last second, Alex was able to move his head just a few inches to one side as the blade went whistling past his right ear. The knife buried its tip in the control panel on the wall behind Alex. As Kurt stormed over to the wall to retrieve his knife, Alex slunk out of his path.

While Kurt struggled to extract his knife from the control panel without breaking the blade, he said, "You've always just been my gopher. In the future, you'll keep your mouth shut, or I will shut it for you permanently." The blade of the knife finally came free from the control panel.

As Kurt had been struggling with the knife, Alex had shrunk back against the opposite wall of the engine room.

After looking back and forth between Alex cowering across the room and the tip of the blade of the stiletto for a few moments, Kurt pocketed the knife. "I might need your computer skills, so I'll let you live for now. Help me get Peter's body behind the sphere before someone else walks by, or we'll have to kill them, too."

Alex sprang into action. In just a few seconds, the body was hidden behind the sphere. Looking down at the drops of Peter's blood on the floor, Alex said, "He didn't bleed much."

"I made sure to slice through to his heart on the first thrust. He didn't bleed much because his heart stopped beating almost immediately. I'm good at what I do. Go back to your room and grab a towel to clean up this blood."

Alex rushed out of the engine room to get the towel.

While Kurt waited for Alex's return, he milled around the side-light to block any passerby's view of the blood on the floor while pretending again to be looking at the plasma sphere. Moments later,

Alex returned; the blood was removed from the floor, and the towel was chucked on top of Peter's body behind the sphere.

"Let's get out of here," Kurt said.

As they left the engine room, Alex couldn't help but glance back to be sure that no one could see Peter's body behind the sphere. Outside the door, he bent over by the sidelight. Only when his head was within one foot from the floor could he tell that something was behind the sphere. That would have to do.

"Quit dawdling," Kurt said.

"Okay. I was just making sure the body wasn't visible from the hallway." As the men headed for their angel's staging room, Alex's heart was filled with dread. Kurt had tried to kill him. But how could he ditch Kurt without Kurt suspecting something and going psycho on him again with his knife? Alex tried to push the images of Kurt's savage attack on Peter from his mind but couldn't. Was that what Kurt had in store for him, too?

CHAPTER 47

"**T**HEY'RE UP TO something," Margie said.

"Tell again me what you heard," Rick said.

Rick and Amanda had been returning to Rick's staging room to do some surfing of the station's database when they had run into Margie. She had been rushing down the hall in the opposite direction.

"I had just left my staging room and was walking back to my bedroom the long way," Margie said. The survivors had started calling getting around the station without using portals "going the long way." "I was about to walk past the short hall that led to Rick and Kurt's angel's staging room when I heard them arguing through the open door of their staging room. Kurt was saying that he had to get something from his room before they left. Then Alex told him that there was no time since something that sounded like cement was going to explode in just ten minutes. Kurt yelled at him that he didn't have any right to tell him what to do. As Kurt was yelling, his voice seemed to be getting closer to the main hallway and so I opened a portal to the hallway outside the cafeteria so I could disappear quickly in case Kurt came bursting out into the hallway. Alex then yelled back that he didn't want to see Kurt get back too late and go down with the ship. I was too afraid to stay any longer, so I dashed though the portal and had Mark close it behind me as soon as I went through. I've been trying to find Sam and tell him about what I just heard. Maybe he can find out what they're up to."

"Kurt's going to blow up the engine room," Rick said. "I'm sure of it. There's no time to waste. Margie and Amanda, you go and find Sam as fast as you can and send him to the engine room. I'm going to hustle up there and see if I can find and disarm the bomb."

"Who died and made you boss?" Amanda asked. "I'm going with you, and there is nothing you can do about it."

One look at the expression of determination on her face and Rick knew that it would take longer than they had to talk her out of joining him. "Okay. Margie, you go and find Sam. Tell him to hurry."

Rick called up a portal to the engine room, and he and Amanda rushed through it.

CHAPTER 48

RICK TORE OPEN the door to the engine room and hurried inside. Amanda had to catch the door as it swung shut behind him and then open it again so she could enter the engine room.

"I guess chivalry died as soon as you knew that you had me," Amanda said.

Rick searched the room desperately for any sign of a bomb as he answered haltingly, "Sorry about that. I'll make it up to you later."

"Kurt isn't stupid. He would have hidden the bomb behind that huge sphere."

"You're right." Rick ducked under the right-side arm of the sphere. He almost immediately let out a cry. "Amanda, come here. Peter's dead."

"What?" Amanda said as she joined Rick. Seeing Peter's still form on the floor with numerous bloody stab wounds through his shirt, the doctor in her sprang to life. She rushed to Peter's side and shook him. He didn't respond. She put her ear by his partly-opened mouth as she observed his chest for movement. There was none. She tilted his head back with one hand and pinched his nose shut with the other. Then she gave him two breaths through his mouth, being sure to see his chest rise with each breath. As soon as she gave the two breaths, she placed the tips of her index and middle fingers on the front side of Peter's neck, feeling for a pulse.

As Amanda worked on Peter's still form, Rick alternated between observing her and looking around for a bomb. As his brain finally registered what his eyes were seeing, he realized that there were two detonators stuck into the white molding where the side arms of the plasma sphere entered the walls and four detonators stuck into four white cubes attached to the back of the sphere. Instead of white plastic, he realized that the white material had to be plastic explosive. His eyes widened as he gasped. "Amanda."

Amanda was pushing deeply and rhythmically against Peter's chest, a little faster than once per second, as she counted softly upward from the number one.

"Amanda, this place is wired to explode. We have to get out of here now!"

Interrupting her counting, but not her rhythmic compressions, she stated, "I... can't... I... have... to... try... to... save... Peter." She quickly stopped her compressions, gave Peter two quick breaths, and then resumed the rhythmic compressions, again counting upward from the number one.

"Amanda, Peter's dead. And we're going to die with him if we don't get out of here now." Rick placed his hand on her shoulder and tried to coax her to leave Peter's side.

Amanda shrugged his hand off her shoulder as she continued her compressions. "Fifteen... sixteen... go... get... help... twenty... twenty-one."

Mark's voice suddenly rang in their ears. "I have detected a highly explosive device in this room that is going to detonate in one minute and fifteen seconds. Blast door is closing in fifteen seconds, fourteen, thirteen..."

Amanda stopped CPR and jumped up. She grabbed Peter by one arm and yelled, "Grab his other arm, and let's get him out of here."

"Nine, eight, seven..."

Rick quickly grabbed Peter's other arm, and together they desperately pulled Peter under the right-side arm of the sphere and toward the door of the engine room.

"Three, two, one."

Rick was just starting to reach out for the door control panel when a featureless gray wall suddenly appeared where the door to the engine room had stood beckoning just a moment before. "Darn it! What do we do now?"

"Mark, we are in the engine room," Amanda called out. "Open the door."

A second of silence passed. "I don't think he can hear us," Rick said as he dropped Peter's lifeless arm on the floor.

Amanda wasn't about to give up. She began pounding on the blast door. "Mark, open the door." Tears began streaming down her face. "I just found the love of my life and now we're going to…"

Mark finally said, "I can't open the door. Kurt damaged the remote-control circuit in the panel for the door, and I am unable to reroute a signal. There is a red manual-override button on the panel to your left."

Amanda beat Rick to the control panel that stood to the left of the door. She stabbed the red button, and the blast door instantly disappeared into the ceiling. She took her finger off the button and ran toward the engine room door. "Come on!" she yelled, but before she and Rick had taken one step, the blast door slid back into place.

This time, Rick beat Amanda to the panel. He pushed the button, and the blast door opened again. "Go," he said. "Grab Peter and get him out of the room before the bombs explode. I'm sure that you have less than thirty seconds to get out."

"I'm not leaving you."

"Yes, you are. You need to save Peter. Hurry. Go now."

Amanda looked at Rick, tears streaming down her face, unable to force herself to leave Rick's side.

The engine room door opened, and Margie poked her head in

the door, which gave Rick an idea. Before she could speak, Rick commanded, "Margie, open the door all the way and then jump back out into the hallway."

Margie obeyed. A split second later, Rick took his finger off the button; the blast door reappeared, smashing the exit door into a thousand pieces. That hadn't worked. Discouraged, Rick pushed the manual override button again, and the blast door disappeared again.

Margie appeared at the open doorframe. Seeing Peter lying still on the floor, she sprang to his side. "We have to get him out of here now. Amanda, help me with him."

Amanda tore herself from Rick's side and rushed to grab Peter's other arm. Together, she and Margie pulled Peter out of the engine room. Rick instantly took his finger off the button. The blast door slammed back into place. He hurried to the sidelight to be sure that Amanda and Peter were okay. Tears filled his eyes as Amanda rushed to the sidelight, her eyes searching for his through the glass.

She suddenly realized what he had done. "Open the door," she yelled.

He could read her lips. There was no way he was going to let her die with him. He had searched for her his whole life, and now he was going to lose her by make sure she survived the explosion.

"No," he said as he shook his head. He put his hand to the glass and spread out his fingers.

Amanda did the same on the other side.

Rick smiled sadly and said, "I love you."

Amanda's face was twisted in agony as she said, "I love you, too."

CHAPTER 49

"**F**IFTEEN SECONDS," ALEX said from where he stood at the workstation in his staging room. The portal to El Agua beach was open behind him. He already had his canvas sack containing half of the diamonds and his gold bar slung over his shoulder. Of course, he had also stuffed the cash in the sack that he had secretly stolen. He closed all the windows there were open on his desktop and turned toward the portal.

"Let's go then," Kurt said. He walked calmly through the portal to the sun-drenched beach beyond.

Alex followed right behind him. A new life beckoned him, a life where he would never want for money again, where he could get any woman he wanted. Alex had taken just two steps past the portal when suddenly Kurt wheeled around and plunged his knife deeply into Alex's upper abdomen.

As he held his knife in Alex's abdomen, Kurt leaned forward and said, "Time to get rid of dead wood. Goodbye, partner." Kurt pulled the knife back out of Alex's abdomen.

Strangely, Alex didn't feel much pain from the knife wound, but he did feel his legs getting weak and unable to support his weight. He dropped to his knees and moved both hands to his upper abdomen. Almost immediately, his hands felt wet. He looked at his hands; they were dripping blood. He returned his hands back to his upper abdomen to try to stop the flow of blood. He was too weak to fight back as Kurt cut the strings of his canvas sack and removed it from his back. Feeling light headed, Alex fell to the sand. He barely registered the back of Kurt's legs as he walked away. Alex had known all along this was going to happen. *Why didn't I try harder to get away from him.* Alex knew he was dying and that there was nothing he could do about it. He didn't fight the gray as it filled his vision, and he was gone.

CHAPTER 50

MANDA'S BODY SHOOK with sobs. Rick's hand was just millimeters away through the glass of the sidelight to the engine room, so close and yet so far away. "Don't go, Rick," she cried in agony. "I love you. Don't leave me." Why hadn't he opened the door so they could have died together? To have the love of her life wrenched from her like this while she remained behind was so cruel. Even though her chest hurt so badly that it felt like a vise was squeezing it, there was no way she was going to leave the window. She barely noticed Margie as she was trying unsuccessfully to pull her away from the sidelight. She needed every last second with Rick.

Suddenly, a bright light filled the room beyond Rick, and an instant later, he was gone, wrenched away from the glass by a tremendous explosion. As the light generated by the blast faded to black less than a second later, Amanda collapsed in a heap on the floor, the enormity of her loss too great for her to withstand. Miraculously, the force of the blast didn't break the glass, send a shock wave through the walls of the engine room, or even make a sound. Amanda was completely uninjured. A fraction of a second later, the floor of the station dropped out from under Amanda and she was floating above the floor.

The moment of free-fall ended abruptly after less than a second. The floor of the hallway outside the station's engine room came to a sudden stop. Amanda landed unceremoniously on the floor. Margie lost her balance and fell over Amanda's still-prone form.

"What was that?" Margie asked in alarm as she righted herself. "It seemed like we were falling out of the sky for a second."

Amanda suddenly sat bolt upright; her cheeks were still wet from her tears. Ignoring Margie, she said in a rush, "He's going to go through a portal. I have to meet him there. I can convince him not to go." Amanda sprang to her feet and immediately requested a portal to the room where Rick was going to pass through to the world of spirits.

As Amanda rushed through the portal, Marge called after her, "Rick can't stay here because he doesn't have a body to come back to."

Amanda stopped and turned back to the still open portal. Margie was still in the hallway by the engine room, but Peter's body was gone. That was crazy, but Amanda didn't have time to deal with that right now. Amanda saw Margie look behind where she was standing. She was probably just as surprised to discover that Peter's body was gone. As Amanda turned away from the portal and headed for the nearest observation room, she saw that Margie had followed her through the portal.

As soon as Margie caught up with Amanda, she said, "You won't be able to talk to him, and he won't be able to see you."

Amanda ran into the room and rushed to the observation wall just as the light in the portal room beyond was increasing in intensity. The light rapidly coalesced into a scene of a beach in the Pacific Northwest. Amanda recognized it. It was Ruby Beach, one of her favorites. It must have been one of Rick's as well. It was just one more reason why she loved him and one more reason why she could never let him go. A moment later, the portal to the world of spirits opened, and a woman that Amanda instantly recognized as Janice,

Rick's deceased mother, stepped into view. She was accompanied by Rick's father, Walt, who Amanda had also seen just short time ago when Rick's mother has passed through the portal. Amanda turned to the other end of the portal room, waiting for Rick to appear.

"Mark," Amanda called out. "Open a portal for me next to the spot where Rick is going to appear."

"I can't do that," Mark said pleasantly.

"But you did it for Zach. Why can't you do it for me?"

"When I allowed Zach to enter the portal room, I knew that Tye had already passed through the portal to the world of spirits and that he was too late to confront her in the portal chamber. Little did I know that he would make a beeline for the portal to the world of spirits in an attempt to follow Tye. After Zach's unfortunate demise, Sam asked me to deny all requests by the survivors to enter a portal room while the portal to the world of spirits is open."

"I promise that I won't go through the portal into the world of spirits. Just let me into the portal room so that I can ask Rick to stay here with me."

"I am sorry, but I am not able to comply with your request."

"Then get Sam in here right now. I'm sure that he'll let me do it."

"Sam is very busy at the moment; he's trying to rectify the damage done by the explosion in the engine room."

"Tell him that this can't wait. He has to get here right now before Rick passes through the portal to the world of spirits."

"I will notify him of your request."

"Computers." Amanda threw her hands up in exasperation. "Even in the most advanced society in the galaxy, you still can't get computers to do what you want them to do." Light was beginning to build up on the opposite end of the portal room. Rick was about to appear.

"Amanda," Marge said softly at Amanda's side. "Sam is not going to let you into the portal room while Rick is in there, even if Sam does show up before Rick is gone."

"I just have to get into the portal chamber," Amanda nearly shouted. "Living on this station forever without Rick is not an option."

Rick appeared at the right side of the portal chamber. Amanda immediately shouted out to him, "Rick. Rick. Can you hear me?"

Rick didn't look over in her direction at the sound of her voice. He did, however, instantly recognize his mother and father. With a look of joy on his face, Rick rushed to his parents and hugged them both for a long time. "I missed you guys so much," Rick said. "Thanks for coming to be with me as I pass through the portal to the world of spirits."

Amanda started beating on the wall as hard as she could with her fists. "Rick, it's me. I'm right here!" Still, Rick didn't notice her.

As Rick and his parents stepped back from their embrace, Rick's father asked, "How do you know about the portal to the world of spirits?"

"Oh, you'd be surprised at how much I know. In fact, I want you to meet someone."

Ricks parents looked at each other quizzically and then back at Rick. Walt said, "Son, what do you mean that you want us to meet someone?" Walt gestured back and forth to both sides of the room with his upturned palm as he spoke. "No one else is here."

"Don't worry. I'm not seeing ghosts, besides the three of us." Rick grinned at his own joke. "I take it you guys don't know anything about what has happened to me during the last few weeks?"

Janice answered, "No, we don't. You were supposed to have died the day before me in a plane crash. Walt was waiting to greet you, but your portal session was cancelled at the last second with no explanation. As days went by with no word on your status, we both assumed that you were still somewhere in the Seattle area, lost in the confusion of the eruption. Then, only moments ago, we were notified that you were coming. We got here just in time."

"Well, you might say that I've been way off the grid for a while."

"What does that mean, son?" Walt asked.

"I was flying into Seattle on the day of the eruption and was supposed to have died when my plane crashed."

"Yes, that is what we were told was going to happen," Walt said.

"But, instead of dying in the plane crash, a few others on the plane and I survived the crash and ended up on this very portal station. In fact, I was watching in the portal observation room when you came to accompany Mom through the portal chamber. I have seen so many amazing things during my time on the station. I'll tell you about them later. More importantly, I met and fell in love with one of my fellow survivors while I was on the station. Her name is Amanda Thomas. I think that she has fallen in love with me, too."

"That is wonderful, Rick," Janice said.

"Except that she's still alive on the station, and he's not, dear," Walt said. "Kind of puts a damper on their romance, doesn't it?"

"Yes, Dad, it does, to say the least. The last thing I wanted to do was to leave Amanda. But when given the choice of either dying together in an explosion in the station's engine room or saving her by sacrificing myself, something inside of me told me that it wasn't her time to die. That split-second decision separated us for the rest of her life. So before I go through the portal with you, I want to introduce you to her, even though we can't see her. I'm sure that she's watching us from the portal observation room."

Rick led his parents in the direction of where he knew the observation room wall had to be, his hand outstretched to keep from running into it. Within just ten steps, he reached an invisible barrier in the middle of the image of Ruby Beach. Using both hands, he showed his parents how the barrier stretched in both directions from where they stood.

"Amanda is on the other side of this wall. Even though we are spirits, the wall is showing Amanda our images. She can also hear everything we are saying."

"Hello, Amanda," Walt said, facing the wall. "I'm sorry that I can't meet you in person. But if Rick has fallen in love with you, then you must be quite the woman."

"It's good to meet you, too," Janice said. "I was always hoping that Rick would meet a wonderful young lady that he could fall in love with. At the same time, I'm so sorry for your loss. One of the darkest days of my life was the day that Walt died."

"That's all past us now, dear," Walt said. "Nothing will ever separate us again."

"Margie," Amanda said through her tears. "She's right. Losing Rick is the worst thing that has ever happened to me. It hurts so badly. That's why I can't bear to let him go. As long as there is a chance, I have to try to get him to stay."

Margie put her arm around Amanda and held her close.

"Amanda," Rick said on the other side of the wall. He was looking through the wall at a point a few feet away from Amanda, so Amanda moved down the wall until she was in his line of sight. "I want to tell you one last time before I go that I love you. I will always love you. You are the most wonderful thing that has ever happened to me. Leaving you is the hardest thing I can possibly imagine doing, but I know that we will be together again. I will wait for you for as long as it takes."

As he finished speaking, Rick held his hand up to the wall, his fingers spread apart. Amanda quickly put her hand up on the wall, exactly opposite Rick's.

"I love you, too, Rick," Amanda said.

"I know that your hand is just inches from mine," Rick said. "It's almost as good as holding hands one last time." After a moment of silence, Rick smiled and removed his hand from the wall. "Goodbye for now, Amanda. I'll be waiting for you."

"Rick don't go," Amanda said. "Please don't go. Stay with me."

Unable to hear or see Amanda, Rick turned away from the wall and walked with his parents back toward the center of the image of Ruby Beach.

"Where is Sam, Margie?" Amanda said. "I have to get in there."

"I'm here, Amanda," Sam stated as he walked briskly into the observation room. Connie was close behind him, tears streaking down her cheeks.

Amanda rushed to Sam. "You've got to stop Rick from going through the portal." She grabbed Sam by the arm and pulled him to the observation wall as she continued, "You've got to do it right now."

Rick and his parents were beginning to walk toward the portal.

Sam said, "Amanda, I just can't do what you ask. I am so sorry."

"I can't live here for the rest of my life without him. I just can't. Please stop him." Rick was at the entrance to the world of spirits. Trembling with emotion, Amanda stretched out her arms and said, "Rick don't go." As Rick and his parents passed through the portal and out of sight, Amanda fell to her knees. Her head was bowed, and her shoulders shuddered as she sobbed uncontrollably.

CHAPTER 51

ALEX WAS SUDDENLY standing in his favorite childhood park near the house where he had grown up in Central Illinois. It was midday, and the sun beamed down from a clear blue sky on beds of flowers that didn't have a single wilted petal. Birds were singing in the trees, and a gentle breeze was rustling the leaves. No question about it; he definitely wasn't on El Agua beach in Venezuela.

Nearer the middle of the park, by the slides that he had loved to slide down and run back up as a child, he saw his mother. As he approached her, she smiled at him, but it was a sad smile. He had seen that same smile on her lips so many times before. The disappointment he saw in her eyes kept him from running to her side. As he slowly approached her, he said, "Hi, Mom. I'm sorry—"

"You don't have to tell me you're sorry, Alex. I blame myself for not teaching you right from wrong well enough. Heaven knows that I wasn't such a great example."

"But at least you didn't—"

"Hush, my son. Time is short. Let's not waste it on regrets."

"What do you mean time is short?"

A portal began to open next to the slides in the center of the park. "It's already time for you to go."

"Aren't we going together?"

"I'm sorry, son. I wish we could be together in the world of spirits, but we can't." She reached out for him and held him close.

"Where am I going, Mama?"

"A place you never learned about in church, because I never took you. You're going to spirit prison."

"What? Prison? Is that another name for hell?"

"No, sweetie. It is a separate place God has prepared for those that have committed grievous sins while on Earth, away from those spirits that haven't, where you can await the day of resurrection."

"But isn't it an awful place, full of fire and brimstone?"

"It isn't any of those things from what I have been told. I've never been there, but I have spoken to others that have been there to visit their loved ones. They say it is a beautiful place, but that it's hard for the spirits to be incarcerated there, away from their loved ones and with only murderers and unrepentant criminals as company."

"Do I have a choice? Can't I choose to stay on Earth as a spirit and haunt something?"

"No, you don't have a choice. Only Satan and his followers are allowed to roam Earth, causing the mayhem and mischief that you are referring to. The spirits of the dead that have lived on Earth must go to either paradise in the world of spirits or to spirit prison."

Alex pulled away from his mother's arms. "You can't make me go there." He looked around the playground. "And there isn't anyone else here to make me go through the portal either."

"I wouldn't think of forcing you go, my dear Alex. However, if you don't choose to go peacefully, the angels will make you go."

Two males dressed in white appeared through the open portal and took up a position on each side of the portal. They weren't smiling. Alex stared at the portal for a few moments and then said, "Fine. I'll go through the portal."

As Alex began moving toward the portal, his mother caught him and hugged him one more time. "I love you, Alex. I always will. I'll come and visit you in spirit prison."

Alex smiled sadly as he left his mother's embrace. "I will always love you too, Mom."

Without hesitating and without a glance at the angels, Alex walked through the portal and out of sight. The angels followed at his heels, and the portal to spirit prison winked closed a moment later.

CHAPTER 52

IN THE OBSERVATION room to the side of the portal where Alex had just passed, Margie and Amanda had sat silently with Sam and Connie, observing the proceedings. As Alex passed through the portal to spirit prison and was gone, Margie said, "My heart breaks for his mother."

Moments after the portal to spirit prison closed, another portal opened right next to it. It was the same portal through which Alex's mother had arrived from the world of spirits to prepare the portal room for Alex's arrival. As soon as the portal to the world of spirits opened, Alex's mother passed through the portal and was gone.

"She had to leave him once on Earth, and now she has to leave him again," Connie observed as the image of the park winked out of existence on the other side of the observation wall. Connie turned to Sam. "How long does Alex have to be in spirit prison?"

"Until he accepts God and repents of his sins. Then he can join his mother in the paradise."

"Well, that sounds easy enough," Margie said. "If I know Alex, he'll get that figured out in no time and he'll be out of spirit prison."

"I am sad to inform you that only a few spirits ever make that transition," Sam said. "Maybe Alex will be different than the rest.

Now, if you will excuse Connie and me, we have another matter to attend to."

Sam and Connie left the room.

"Well, it's just the two of us girls now," Margie said brightly, trying to cheer up Amanda. "Of course, unless you want to count Connie. To me, she doesn't count anymore because she wants to be here with Sam."

"I still can't believe Rick is gone," Amanda said. "I know that you want to cheer me up, but I just can't be happy without Rick. In just a matter of a few short weeks, he became everything to me. I don't think I can ever be happy again."

CHAPTER 53

"RICK, HOW ARE you this morning?" It was Rick's mother, and she sounded so close that she had to be right next to him. He looked all around where he was sitting on the shore of a lake where he had sat down on a rock to enjoy the beauty of the day, but his mother was nowhere in sight. All he could see were a magnificent young cougar and its mate resting in the grass not far from where he was sitting. The cougar raised its head to inspect Rick, but then a moment later lowered its head to its paws and closed its eyes. Rick should have felt abject terror at the cougar's close proximity, but he only felt peace.

"Mom, where are you?" Being a spirit was bringing so many new and wonderful surprises. Was this another one?

"I'm far from where you are."

"Then how are you talking to me? Are spirits telepathic?"

"Yes. I didn't want to surprise you too much. Learning that we can talk to each other from a distance is unsettling for new arrivals."

"So why isn't anyone else talking to me the same way?"

"They're being polite. They all remember how frightening it was for them when they first realized that we're all connected here."

"What do you mean by connected? Like we're all cell phones, and we can call each other?"

"No, it is much more than that. You can let people know where you are at, what you're doing, how you're feeling, and how you feel about them. It's all instantaneous."

"Wow. It's like social media on the internet, right?"

"You know I've never used social media. The recently deceased that have died young are taking to this connected thing like fish to water. They say that what we have here is like social media on steroids. It is different for me. I am still getting used to it."

"Okay. Then let me try it out. Dad, are you there?"

Rick's dad replied immediately, "I'm here."

Even before Rick's dad had finished speaking, Rick had felt a peaceful feeling of love and acceptance.

"I love you, too, Dad. Where are you right now?" And instantly he knew. His dad was playing tennis with his mother. How amazing was this? Wondering just how far the technology would go, he asked, "How about video? Can I see what you're doing?"

"Of course you can." Instantly, Rick was able to see their game of tennis simultaneously through each of their own eyes. It should have confused the heck out of him, but it felt so easy and natural. At the same time, the image of the lake where he was sitting was still just as visible. Rick lifted up his hand and looked at it while his dad served the ball to his mother. *This is so cool.*

"Rick," his mother said as she smashed the ball back over the net. Rick wondered where she had learned to play like that. His mother continued, "My parents, your grandparents, would like to say good morning. Can you give them permission to do so?"

"Sure, why not."

"Hi, Ricky," Rick's grandmother's voice spoke into his head. Almost simultaneously, Rick's grandfather's voice spoke to him. "Hello, Tricky Ricky. How've you been?"

Up to this point, Rick had been speaking out loud to the unseen voices of his loved ones in his head. But faced with the need to address his grandparents without ignoring his parents, he simultaneously greeted his grandparents in his mind without speaking aloud. At the same moment, he congratulated his mom on a great kill shot and chided his dad on letting his wife get the better of him in tennis. Carrying on all four conversations simultaneously took no effort at all. Even more amazing, he could feel their love for him without them even telling him.

"I had no idea that spirit brains could multitask like this," Rick said. "How many interactions can I carry on like these at once?"

His mother said, "As many as you want, as far as we know. It's nice to always be able to reach someone when you need to without getting a busy signal."

"So what's the point of ever getting together when we can always be in touch like this?" Rick asked.

Rick's grandmother answered, "In his infinite wisdom, God placed a dampening mechanism on the feelings of love, companionship, and friendship that we feel for each other while communicating this way. Those feelings are felt more strongly and more enjoyably when they are experienced in direct face-to-face communication. At the same time, it sure is nice to send a message of love to all the people you care about without having to talk to them all face-to-face multiple times every day."

"If the people that run Facebook, Instagram and Twitter on Earth could only see this. They would die to get this technology."

All four laughed at Rick's joke.

Rick said, "So why didn't God let us have this degree of interconnectedness on Earth? Relationships would have been so much easier."

"Our experience on Earth was really meant to be an individual test," Rick's father said. "With such close connection to each other, individual faith would have been much harder to develop, and it would have been hard to choose to disobey God when so many friends and family were watching from afar."

"And the lack of privacy doesn't bother you guys?"

Rick's grandfather said, "You can share as much or as little as you want of what you're experiencing with each person you are connected to. In fact, if you want to, you can choose to stop all communication with one or more individuals or with everyone."

"But, none of us do that," Rick's mother said. "We have nothing to hide and everything to gain. In the cases of undressing to change clothes or for intimate moments," his mother giggled, "No one watches. We just don't want to, now that we're spirits."

"With no rich or poor, no currency, no government, no military, and no enemies of any kind," Rick's dad said, "There is no reason not to leave the channels of communication open for everyone."

Rick asked, "But, aren't there some people here that are hard to get along with that you don't really want to know what you're doing? On social media, we call that blocking someone."

Rick's grandmother said, "Once we leave our bodies, we leave behind all the psychological and physical disorders that might have been burdening us on Earth.

Spirits don't have mental or physical diseases. There are no inappropriate or disagreeable people in the world of spirits. Any spirits like that are instead in spirit prison."

"What a rush," Rick said. "So I wonder who else wants to friend me out there?"

A man's voice spoke into his head, "Hello, Rick. Did you miss me?"

Risk asked, "Who is this?"

"This is Zach. After all we've been through, you've forgotten me already."

"I haven't forgotten you. How are you doing here in the world of spirits?"

"Wonderfully," Zach said. "I found the love of my life here and I couldn't be more happy."

"You're with Tye?"

"Oh, no. Tye was so yesterday. When I came through the portal and left my body behind, I suddenly realized that everything that I had felt for Tye was just an obsession stemming from my physical body. I didn't know her at all and suddenly wasn't interested in getting to know her in the least. And, I completely forgot about Tye when Paige showed up."

"Who's Paige?" Rick asked.

"I'll show you," Zach said.

Instantly, Rick could see in his mind Zach standing next to a woman with raven dark hair that cascaded below her shoulders. The woman smiled and said, "Hello, Rick. Zach has told me so much about you."

As she spoke, Rick could feel the love that they had for each other.

"Nice to meet you, Paige. I'm so happy for the two of you. How did you meet and fall in love so fast?"

Zach said, "Paige was my best friend in grade school and my girlfriend in junior high. Even though it was puppy love, it was real enough for us and we had made plans to marry once we were old enough. Unfortunately, Paige died of leukemia when we were in the eighth grade. I was confused about how to live alone on the earth without Paige for the rest of my life, so I started dating other women."

"You're such a lady's man," Paige said.

"I am not," Zach said. "I only have eyes for you, forever."

"Well, I'm glad that you're happy, Zach," Rick said. "We were sad when we learned that you had died and then we were even more sad not to see you go through a portal to meet your family."

A women's voice spoke into Rick's head, "Rick, I'd like to talk to you."

While he continued the conversation with Zach and Paige in one corner of his mind, Rick asked the woman in another part of his mind, "Who do I have the pleasure of speaking with?"

Even before she said her name out loud, Rick knew who it was.

The woman said, "It's me, Sally McBride."

Multiprocessing or not, Rick instantly ignored every other conversation in his head and focused on the voice of the girl of his high school dreams.

CHAPTER 54

AMANDA AND MARGIE stepped into one of the station's conference rooms where Mark had called them to a meeting with Sam. The room seated over a thousand. Most of the seats were taken. They hesitated just inside the door, not sure of where they should sit.

"Margie. Amanda," Sam said as he hurried toward them. "Thanks for coming. Let me show you to your seats."

The two women followed Sam down the aisle in the center of the room toward a table with a podium at its center at one end of the room. The closer that they approached the podium, the more self-conscious they became.

"Sam, we hadn't planned on sitting in the very front," Margie said quietly.

"There is someone that I want you to see," Sam said. As they arrived at the front of the room, Sam said, "He's right over here."

Peter stood up from where he had been sitting as soon as he heard Sam's voice. Seeing the women, a big smile broke out on his face.

"Peter," Amanda said. "You're alive!" She ran to him and hugged him tight.

He in turn enclosed her in his arms. "It takes a little more than a few stab wounds to kill me." Peter chuckled.

"But seriously," Amanda said to him as she stepped back. "I saw the stab wounds in your chest. I checked your pulse. There wasn't one. You really were dead. So how are you standing here in front of me?"

"Amanda, I'm a resurrected being. Like I told you, resurrected beings can't be killed. I played along with the whole thing to see just how far Kurt would carry out his evil designs."

Amanda was shocked. "You weren't really dead when I was doing CPR?"

"I held my breath whenever you were watching me, and when you took my pulse, I forced my heart to stop beating for a few moments. Pretty good acting, huh?"

"I am so sorry that I did CPR on you while you were still awake," Amanda said. "Did I break any of your ribs?"

"You couldn't break one of my ribs even if you hit it with a freight train. On top of that, resurrected beings don't feel pain. There's no need for us to feel pain since we can't be injured in any way."

"But what about the blood on your clothes?" Margie asked. "Where did that come from?"

"I'm really proud of myself on that one. I—"

"Peter," Sam interrupted at Peter's side. "Everyone is here."

"Amanda," Peter said apologetically as he lowered his voice conspiratorially. "I'll have to tell you later about how I faked the blood."

Sam directed Margie and Amanda to seats in the front row and then joined Peter at the front of the room. Peter sat at the table, and Sam took the podium.

"We are honored to have Peter, the apostle, visiting us at the station. It is a rare occasion for us to entertain a visit from any of Christ's original apostles. It is even more of a rare honor to have the leader of the original apostles with us. I will turn the rest of this meeting over to him."

Peter took the podium. "It has come to my attention that senior citizens on Earth have become major carriers of AIDS on Earth." More than a few of the staff looked at each other in surprise. "Really, they have." Sam's usually calm face even looked a little concerned. Peter paused for effect and then continued, "They are the most likely carriers of hearing aids."

"A smattering of laughter trickled through the crowd. "What?" Peter asked with a big grin. "Resurrected beings aren't supposed to tell jokes?" More laughter filled the room.

"It's true, however, that I didn't come here to tell jokes. We have a few serious matters to clear up. Mark, please retrieve Kurt Rollins from his hotel on Isla Margarita."

Suddenly, Kurt was lying on the carpet in front of the table where Peter and Sam were sitting. Kurt's eyes flew open and he quickly looked around in confusion. His eyes locked on Peter as he sat up, and his brows knit in anger. "You're supposed to be dead," Kurt snarled as he sprang to his feet. "I guess I'll have to finish the job right now." Instantly, Kurt lunged toward the podium, looking like he was ready to tear Peter apart with his bare hands.

Kurt never made it to the table. Peter raised his hand, and Kurt's hurtling body came to an abrupt stop in mid-leap.

Kurt's legs were peddling uselessly and his hands balling into fists vainly since nothing was close enough to strike, Kurt screamed, "Put me down you—"

With a wave of Peter's other hand, Kurt instantly lost his voice. He was still yelling, but not a sound could be heard.

"That's much better," Peter said calmly. With a slight bend of his wrist, Peter moved Kurt's body back until it was six feet away from the table. Kurt was still struggling against the force that was holding his torso in place. Peter said, "If you stop struggling and yelling, I'll release the protective hold I have on you, as well as on your voice." A few seconds later, Kurt stopped struggling, although he continued glaring murderously at Peter.

Peter lowered Kurt's body until his feet touched the floor. Then, with a twist of his hand, he released the hold he had on Kurt. As Kurt regained his balance a split second later, he snarled and attempted to spring at Peter again. Peter simply held up the same hand that had so easily controlled Kurt movements before and put a stop to Kurt's forward motion. Peter once again returned Kurt to a standing position six feet in front of the table as he stated, "I guess I can't trust you to stay put. And please hold your tongue. Only speak when I ask you a question." Kurt opened his mouth and began speaking, but no sound came out. He closed his mouth. However, he continued to glare at Peter. His muscles were tense and ready for action.

"You were the cutest little child," Peter said. "We had such high hopes for you. But things didn't turn out like we planned. Initially, you were not to blame. You had a terrible childhood, and you were born with genetic tendencies toward impulsiveness, aggressiveness, and risk-taking. But, on the other hand, you were given a wonderful mind, excellent social skills, and a handsome and strong body. You should have risen above your negative tendencies, like so many others have on Earth, and then used your talents to make the world a better place and to bless the lives of others. Instead, you have become completely focused on destroying people that don't live up to your false idea of perfection." Peter shook his head sadly. Kurt continued glaring at him like a feral animal, clearly just waiting to get free of the force that was holding him and to tear Peter apart, piece by bloody piece.

"Now, for even weightier matters. Kurt, you stand accused of murdering Ethan, attempting to murder me, and then attempting to crash this station into downtown Chicago, which, if it had succeeded, would have killed five hundred of us on the station and over two-million people on the ground. In addition, you have murdered thirty-eight others during your life on Earth, including Alex. Finally, you have assisted various others as they have murdered hundreds more. How do you plead to these charges?" With a wave of his hand, Peter released the hold on Kurt's voice.

"I'd do it all again in a heartbeat." Kurt said. His veins bulged in his neck, his eyes was mere slits, and his jaw was clenched. "You're just a bunch of freakin' aliens. I'll kill you all!"

"Enough." Peter signaled with his hand. Kurt lost his voice again, although his mouth continued to move as he yelled unintelligibly at Peter. "You leave me no choice. You are condemned to an immediate death for your grievous sins, for the good of humanity and for the safety of the workers on this station."

Instantly, Kurt's body began to fall backward. Amanda was aghast as she watched his body accelerate toward the floor until the back of his head struck the carpet with a dull and sickening thud. He lay still and wasn't breathing. In spite of her loathing for Kurt, Amanda could barely resist the urge to rush to his side to see if she could resuscitate him. A split second later she realized that Kurt's spirit was still standing upright in the same place it had been standing, like nothing had happened. How could she see him if he were a spirit?

Kurt spoke, although much more softly and with much less emotion, "So when are you going to kill me, Peter? I'm still standing right here in front of you. That only goes to prove that you're just a humanoid alien. You don't have the power to kill me from across the table with just your words."

Peter said quietly, "Look behind you."

Kurt wheeled around and startled at the sight of his body lying on the floor behind him, still and unmoving. His body's eyes were open and seeing nothing. Moments passed as Kurt stood looking silently at his tattoo-covered body.

"Kurt, turn around please so I can finish," Peter said.

Kurt turned back toward Peter; Kurt's face was expressionless. "You might have killed my body, you stinking alien, but I'll kill you with my spirit instead." Kurt leapt across the table at Peter again, hands reaching for Peter's throat.

As Amanda watched in horror, Kurt's hands reached Peter's neck. However, Kurt's spirit body kept going and passed through Peter's body like it wasn't even there. Kurt crashed headlong into the wall behind Peter and crumpled to the floor.

"Mark, open a portal to spirit prison," Peter said.

A glow began to appear in the wall behind Peter and next to where Kurt lay. The light quickly increased in intensity, and as it did so, Kurt sprang away from the portal, and sprinted right through the table where Peter was seated. He stopped in front of the table where he had started. Looking around wildly, he said, "You're not going to get me. If I can't kill you directly, then I'll have to use someone else to do it." He immediately launched himself at Amanda. Shocked and unable to get out of the way, Amanda froze and screamed as Kurt threw his arms around her like he wanted to cut her in half with a wicked football tackle. However, Kurt's spirit body flew through Amanda's body, as well as through the bodies of a few of the staff that were sitting in the rows behind Amanda. He instantly rose and walked through the rows of staff straight back to where Amanda was sitting. Without hesitation, he sat on her lap and sank through her body until he was sitting in the same chair with her, occupying the same physical space. Horror could be seen on Amanda's face in spite of her face being partially obscured by Kurt's. Kurt announced loudly, "I possess Amanda's body for my own."

"No you're not!" Amanda screamed as she sprang from her chair to get away from him. As Kurt stood to follow her, she turned to run.

"Secure him," Peter boomed. Immediately, two angels appeared through the portal, raised their right hands, and shot glittering beams of fire from their palms. As fast as lightening, the beams sped toward Kurt, each splitting at the last moment into two beams, like the forked tongue of a snake. The split beams wrapped around Kurt's wrists and ankles. A split second later, Kurt was lifted off the floor a few feet and held completely still by the flaming ropes.

Peter said, "Amanda, I am so sorry about that. You were never in danger. No spirit can have any power over any living being without their permission."

With her heart still in her throat and barely able to catch her breath, the best Amanda could do was nod. She took her seat by Margie.

"Kurt, God is not done with you, yet. Being away from the strongly negative emotions that you experienced in your body on Earth should help you make better choices. Use your time in spirit prison wisely."

"How did you do it?" Kurt asked.

"How did we keep the station from plummeting into the heart of Chicago and how did I survive your savage attack in the engine room? As for the station, see for yourself." Instantly a three-dimensional image of the station over downtown Chicago appeared in front of the room to the side of the table. "The station dropped about a foot after the engine was destroyed before two additional stations were able to secure it from falling further." Two identical black rectangles appeared at each side of the original station, and then the whole image winked out of existence. "We knew exactly what you were doing every step of the way. The other stations were already in position when the explosion occurred. As for me surviving your murderous intent, let's just say that when I told you that you can't kill a resurrected being, I was not lying. I faked the whole dying thing."

"You set me up. You have no right to send me to spirit prison."

"I'm sorry Kurt, but the justice of God must be carried out." As Peter finished, he turned to the two angels and nodded.

The angels at the portal pulled Kurt toward them by the flaming ropes quickly and effortlessly. He barely had time to struggle before he was through the portal and gone.

Margie leaned over to Amanda. "Whew. That was intense. You okay?"

"I think so. Thank goodness he's finally gone."

Peter said, "There is another important matter that I need to resolve while I am here. Sam, please stand."

Sam stood as Peter said, "Sam, you permitted a plane to crash land on this station, affording some of the plane's passengers the unprecedented opportunity to be rescued and to enter the station. This extremely unusual action was motivated by your unwillingness to allow a woman from Earth that you had affection for to die in the plane crash. Are these allegations true?"

"Yes, they are," Sam answered without hesitating.

Peter said, "And you did all this, aware of the absolute restriction throughout the galaxy against interaction between translated beings on our stations and God's children on the test planets?"

"Yes," Sam answered quietly.

"Once she was here on this station, you have interacted with and fallen in love with this woman from Earth, isn't that correct?"

Sam didn't answer immediately, but instead glanced at Connie in the front row. A hint of a smile stole across his face. "Yes, I have."

Some whispering was heard from the members of his staff.

Peter smiled knowingly and then said, "Connie, please stand." Connie stood up by her chair. Peter said, "Connie, do you share the same feelings for Sam? Do you love him?"

Connie blushed. Looking up at Sam, she stated, "I do love him." Sam beamed back at her.

"Then, please join him at his side at the table." Peter waited until Connie joined Sam and then continued. "Sam, do you have anything to say in your defense?"

"I never made contact with Connie while she was on the earth. Of course, I dreamed about doing it, but I was faithful to the rules of the station. Since she was supposed to die in the plane crash and never return to Earth again, then my interaction with her here on the station didn't violate the rules since she is no longer able to return to Earth."

Peter paused, looked directly at Sam, and then continued, "You knew that what you were doing was wrong." Sam nodded in affirmation. "What has happened here between you and Connie cannot happen again anywhere throughout the galaxy. A severe enough consequence needs to be meted out so that no one will consider allowing this to happen again. I have no choice but to remove you as station leader. I really should release you from your designation as a translated being and send you to your world of spirits to await the resurrection."

"Peter," Connie quickly said. "I want to be with Sam for the rest of my life and even longer. I feel in my heart that we're supposed to be together. Please don't send him to his world of spirits."

Peter looked at Connie and then Sam. He sighed. "I didn't say I was going to send Sam to his planet's world of spirits, just that I should do it. So I need to know, Connie: Are you willing to accompany Sam to his new assignment more than ten thousand light years from Earth on the Rutetope station?"

Connie looked at Sam to see his reaction.

Sam looked Connie in the eyes. "Rutetope is a hard planet. But there are worse. If you're willing to accompany me, we can make it through as long as we have each other."

Connie turned to Peter. "Yes, I'm willing to accompany him."

"Are you willing to marry him pretty much right now since I have to leave in a few minutes, and I can't send you together unless you are married?"

"He hasn't asked me yet," Connie said.

"Sam, what's taking you so long?" Peter asked.

Sam turned to Connie. "I'm sorry for the less than ideal setting for a proposal, but here goes. Connie, will you marry me?"

Without hesitation, Connie replied, "Yes, I will, Sam. But I have one big concern. You're nearly immortal, and I'm not. I will die on this planet Rutetope, and you will be left alone for centuries, still looking not a day over twenty-five."

Beaming, Peter said, "I hadn't gotten to that part yet. Connie, are you willing to be translated and serve God's children on Rutetope?"

"Are you serious? I get to be a young-looking angel and help people? Of course! Zap me right now. I'm ready." She held out her hands, looked up to the ceiling, and closed her eyes with a smile on her face. Light laughter filled the room.

"Open your eyes, Connie. Now take each other by both hands. You've already told me you want to marry. So by the power of the Priesthood of God that I hold, I pronounce you husband and wife. You may now kiss the bride, Sam."

Sam kissed Connie softly on the lips. As they finished, Connie said, "Who knew that I would hold the record for the shortest engagement and the fastest wedding on Earth?"

"You're not on Earth anymore, sweetheart," Sam said with a smile. "Things are a lot different here."

"You can say that again," Connie said.

Peter said. "I'm glad that is taken care of. We can take care of the translation part after this meeting. Since I am due on another station, I'll need to leave immediately afterward." Addressing the rest of the staff in the room, he said, "I call this meeting to a close."

"Peter," Amanda exclaimed from the front row as the other meeting attendees arose and moved toward the doors. She hurriedly approached the table. With tears filling her eyes, Amanda said, "I just can't live on the station for fifty or sixty more years without Rick. Please send me to the world of spirits right now. I know you can do it because you just did it to Kurt."

"That would be taking the life of an innocent person. You know I can't do that."

"You aren't being fair. You gave Connie what she wanted, and Margie is as happy as a clam with her work here. But, there's nothing for me here on the station. My life's work on Earth was being a doctor, but no one here needs me because no one gets sick." Her shoulders slumped dejectedly as she bowed her head, tears falling from her eyes.

"I'm sorry, Amanda," Peter said with care and concern, like a father worried about his daughter. "I'm sure that you'll find something on the station into which you can put your heart. The next station leader will be able to help you. Maybe you could do your family's genealogy. A lot of people find that to be quite fulfilling."

Amanda shook her head side to side without looking up. Suddenly she bolted for the door, yanked it open, and then slammed it behind her.

CHAPTER 55

"IS AMANDA GOING to be alright?" Peter asked Sam.

"I'm not so sure. I knew that she and Rick were falling in love, but I had no idea that his death would hit her so hard."

Peter said, "I'll have to tell the next station leader to watch her closely. But since the new station leader won't be arriving for a few days, maybe we can ask Margie to keep an eye on her for us until then."

Sam called Margie over from where she was still sitting in the front row.

"Margie," Peter said as she arrived at the table. "I'm worried that Amanda might try to end her life in a misguided effort to join Rick in the spirit world."

"I'd say that's an understatement," Margie said. "I was already planning to hang around her a little more in case she started leaning in that direction."

"That will help a lot. Would you let either Sam or the new station leader know if she says anything worrisome? Sam is going to be here for two more days while he packs and gets things in order. The new station leader will be arriving in two days."

"I'll let Sam know if she says anything."

"Thanks, Margie."

Margie said, "You said that you were going to explain how you faked your death in the engine room. I saw the bloody holes in your shirt."

Peter smiled. "It was really quite simple. I opened a tiny portal right against my skin wherever Kurt stabbed me. Instead of plunging into my chest, his blade cut through my shirt and then went through the tiny portals into a bag of fake blood that I had Mark make up for me. Not bad for an amateur, huh?"

"You had me fooled, for sure." She paused for a moment. "Ethan wasn't a resurrected being, so that was why Kurt was able to kill him. But, why didn't you and Sam intervene to save Ethan? He was one of your own people."

"It was Ethan's time to die," Peter said. "He has been a working as a translated being on stations around the galaxy for almost a thousand years. He is now with his family in the world of spirits that is associated with his home world. Ethan is very happy."

Peter turned to Sam and said, "Since I need to leave within thirty minutes, I need to meet with you and Connie in your office as soon as possible."

"May I ask one more question?" Margie said. "Would you please reconsider preventing the tsunami from devastating New York? The west wall of the Hudson canyon is going to collapse in just thirty minutes and trigger the tsunami. I know I've already asked, but I really love my nephews, and the thought of losing them in the next few hours is torturing me."

With a distressed look on his face, Peter said, "I have asked God myself to allow us to intercede, but he hasn't answered. Without his approval, I can't do anything to stop the tsunami."

"Then five-million people will die in two hours, just like that," Margie said as shook her head sadly.

CHAPTER 56

A MANDA SAT MOTIONLESS and alone in the portal observation room. Only her tear-filled eyes moved as she watched the spirits beyond the transparent observation wall.

"Grandma," a beautiful young woman with flowing auburn hair and sparkling green eyes exclaimed that had just appeared on the left side of the portal room. A look of sheer joy filled her face as she quickly closed the distance between her and her grandmother. The young woman continued, "I can walk."

"I can see that, Elle," the grandmother said as the young woman rushed into her arms. "I'm so happy for you."

"I knew that you would be here waiting for me, Grandma," Elle said. "Just like you said you would." Elle released her grandmother and then twirled away from her grandmother across a grassy meadow with her arms outstretched. "I always believed you when you told me about how I would someday be able to walk. And now it has come true." The young woman stopped twirling on the other side of the observation wall, just in front of Amanda, and then turned back to her grandmother.

"You were always so positive, Elle, even through all the pain and suffering from the surgeries, the bedsores, and the seizures. Your cerebral palsy was…"

Elle walked back to her grandmother. "It's all over now, grandmother. It's just a memory. More important are the memories of the happy times, especially the ones I had with you. You always cheered me up with your stories and your songs. You made life bearable when it was unbearable. Knowing that you would be back the next day was all that kept me going most of the time. I have missed you so much." Elle embraced her grandmother again.

"We'll never be apart, again, sweetheart. And you'll never be crippled or in pain again."

"Sounds awesome," Elle said as she smiled widely. A bright light rapidly increased in intensity in front of her in the meadow. Elle said, "It's the light you told me about. The way to the world of spirits."

"Are you ready to go through the light?"

"You bet. I've been ready for this moment all of my life."

Elle took her beloved grandmother by the hand and the two women walked through the portal and were gone.

Amanda sat stone still, tears streaming down her face, her chest tight with longing. It wasn't fair. These people were all so happy as they were reunited with their loved ones. It hurt terribly to know that Rick was alive and well just fifty feet away at the other end of one of the portal to the world of spirits, but he had just as well be light years away for all the good that it did her. Sam would never let her into the portal room while one of the portals to the world of spirits was open.

Her chest hurt so badly that she couldn't help but hope that she would have a heart attack right at that moment and die. If she died, Sam wouldn't be able to keep her out of the portal rooms. She was sure Rick would be there to greet her at her passing, and they would be so happy to be together again.

The scene in the portal room beyond the observation wall changed to a view of a picturesque log cabin at the base of a snow-covered mountainside. Groomed ski runs stretched up the mountainside, and a lone chairlift lofted over the top of the trees and out of sight into the distance. The sun sparkled on the snow invitingly. But, for Amanda, the scene held no joy. Another recently deceased person was about to be reunited with their loved ones, but she wouldn't be able to be reunited with Rick for over fifty years. She sobbed even harder. How she wished she could die right that instant and be the one that would appear in the portal room in the mountain scene in front of her. She looked down at her wrists, and a thought sprang into her mind that had she never entertained before. While she couldn't get sick and die of anything but old age while she was on the station, that didn't mean that she couldn't slit her wrists in a warm tub of water and take her own life. Fred Porter had successfully taken his life when he had jumped off the top of the station, and Sam hadn't stopped him. Quickly she looked away from her wrists, fearful of where that train of thought could easily take her. At the same time, she wanted to keep Mark from finding out what she had been thinking and alerting Sam, so that he wouldn't try to stop her if she ever decided to follow through.

A pretty redhead entered the scene in front of her from the world of spirits and moved into the center of the portal room, just in front of the cabin. Moments later, a handsome young man appeared at the other end of the portal room. Upon seeing the women by the cabin, his face lit up with a thousand-watt smile. "Trudy. It's you."

Here we go again. If she kept watching much longer, she was going to get seriously dehydrated from crying so hard. Tears had flowed freely for two long lost sisters that had been reunited in death after having not seen each other for fifty years and for a woman that had jumped into a flood-swollen river to save her child, only to end up being swept away herself and drown. She had really been hit hard by the unwanted baby that had lived only minutes after birth because its unwed teenage mother had strangled it. Why did there have to be so much sadness on this Earth? Sam and his people had the power to prevent most human suffering. Yet they remained quietly in their station, most often doing nothing to prevent that suffering. And that was exactly what they were doing to her, letting her suffer without Rick. They could help her if they wanted to. They could let her into the portal room and let her go through a portal to the world of spirits, like they let Zach. It wouldn't be suicide. It would just be moving onto a new life with Rick in a new place. But no. They wanted to see her suffer alone on the station for fifty years.

The young man beyond the observation wall spoke, interrupting Amanda's thoughts. "Sweetheart, our honeymoon cabin was the perfect choice. It makes me feel like the wonderful week we had after our wedding six months ago never ended."

"Easy for you to say, my love," his wife replied. "You were in a coma after the car accident. For you, it does seem like just yesterday that we were at the cabin. But for me, since I died instantly in the wreck, it has been six long months in the world of spirits without you, not knowing if you were going to join me or not. I'm sorry that you didn't survive the accident, but I am so happy now that you're here with me." The portal to the world of spirits reopened behind her. "The portal to the world of spirits is open. Are you ready to pass through it?"

"Where is it going to take us?"

"Sweetie, the world of spirits is a wonderful place. I know that neither of us believed in life after death when we were alive on Earth, but trust me, we should have. It's beautiful, wonderful, happy, peaceful, and even lots of fun. All that has been missing is you."

"Okay. I'm good. You have never led me wrong before."

"There is another reason that I'm glad you're here."

"And what is that?"

"An old boyfriend from high school that died in a diving accident our senior year has been hitting on me in the world of spirits. His line has been that you were going to be on Earth for years and would probably remarry, leaving me without a husband. He proposed that we become a couple in the world of spirits so that I wouldn't be lonely. He has been having a hard time taking no for an answer."

"Then he's going to be sorely disappointed. I'm back, and I'm not going anywhere." He smiled, put his arm around her waist, and together they disappeared into the portal.

That is the last straw. Rick was a great catch, and she was sure that every woman in the world of spirits that had died single was going to be after him. He would never survive single for the fifty or so years until she finally died of old age on the station. If that couple could have a happy ending together in the world of spirits, then so could she and Rick. Her mind was made up. No one was going to stop her.

CHAPTER 57

CONNIE HURRIED AFTER Sam. "Where are we going in such a rush?" Moments after Peter had said goodbye and had stepped through a portal to his next assignment, Sam had whispered in her ear to follow him. Taking his hand, she had barely been able to keep up with Sam as he brought up a portal and hurried through it to a hallway that she didn't recognize.

"Right here, my love," Sam said. Opening a door that was only feet from where they had exited the portal, Sam led the way into the room.

The lighting in the room was low, and it was hard to make out anything. Moments later, as her eyes became accustomed to the low level of light in the room, she made out a table against the wall. The table was completely covered by a white sheet. A number of irregular objects lay under the white sheet, but their exact nature was hidden by the sheet.

Sam turned up the lights in the room and then said, "It's Rick, Connie. Or at least what is left of him."

Connie stifled a gasp. She stood staring at the table. "Why are you keeping his remains? Shouldn't you have buried him?"

"I owe it to Rick to bring him back," Sam said. "He gave his life saving all of us on the station."

"You can bring him back from the dead? I figured that would be impossible, especially with the way he was blown..." She hesitated, unable to continue.

"If it's God's will, then God will allow me to use the power he has bestowed on me to bring Rick back from the dead. I didn't dare try when Peter was here since he would have probably told me no. But I can't shake the feeling that God wants me to bring Rick back."

"Well, then get on with it before God changes his mind. Amanda's happiness probably depends on Rick's return."

Sam smiled. "Okay, then. Here goes." Sam placed his hands on top of what looked like Rick's head under the sheet. Closing his eyes, he stated, "Rick Jones, by authority from God, I command you to rise from the dead." Rick's scattered body parts under the sheet remained motionless. Sam took his hands off of Rick's head and lowered them to his side.

"Nothing is happening," Connie said. "How long is it going to take?"

"I don't know, to be honest."

"What do you mean? Haven't you done this before?"

"I haven't. In fact, I don't even know if God will honor my request that Rick be brought back to life. Even though I feel like he wants me to use his power to bring Rick back to life, it will only happen if it is his will."

"Well, for Amanda's sake, I hope it happens soon."

CHAPTER 58

"**R**ICK." RICK'S MOTHER'S voice entered his conscious mind along with a sweet sense of her love for him. Even though he carrying on a conversation with his mother in his mind, his eyes never even blinked as he continued listening to Sally McBride. Sally had joined him for dinner and was telling him about what had happened to the people that they had known in high school that had died since graduation.

Rick said to his mother, "What is it, Mom?"

"You have to go back, Rick."

"What do you mean by go back?" Rick sensed a feeling of longing from his mother. He hadn't felt that from her since he had arrived.

"You're being called back from the dead. I've never heard of this happening so long after death, at least since Christ raised Lazarus two thousand years ago. I have been asked to see if you're willing and ready to return."

He was so riveted by what his mother had just said that he totally stopped listening to Sally. Of course he would go back. He wanted nothing more than to spend the rest of his life with Amanda.

Without further hesitation, he said to his mother, "Yes, I am ready right now."

Simultaneously, he interrupted Sally, "I have to go, Sally. I am being called back to Earth."

"Oh," Sally said. "You barely got here. I was hoping to spend more time with you."

Rick smiled. "I thoroughly enjoyed our time together, Sally. It was so good to see you again. However, I have to return to the woman that I love."

A portal opened to the side of the table where they were seated. Rick stood and Sally rose to join him.

"Goodbye, Rick." She hugged him close. "Amanda must be pretty special to have earned your love."

"She is more than special," Rick said.

Rick's mother spoke into his head, "Go through the portal, my son. I love you, and I'll miss you."

"Goodbye, Mother," Rick said. He simultaneously sent a good-bye message and his love to all of his relatives and friends in the world of spirits. Out loud he said, "Goodbye, Sally." Still smiling at Sally, he walked through the portal.

CHAPTER 59

AMANDA STOOD ON the edge of the portal platform, looking down thousands of feet to the islands dotting the ocean below. A life with Rick in the world of spirits was just one tiny step away, and yet she hesitated. Was she afraid of the fall, or was she still not completely willing to give up her human body to be with Rick? She didn't fear death. Just weeks before, she hadn't believed that there was life after death. Now, thanks to her time on the station, there was no doubt in her mind that she would continue living after her death, with all of her memories and her love for Rick intact. Jumping to her death wouldn't really be a suicide but just moving on to life in a different plane of existence. *Why does everyone on Earth fear death so much?*

She had tried to get to the roof of the station like Fred Porter. That hadn't worked since the door had been locked. She had asked Mark to open it, but he had declined. Frustrated, she had gone to her angel's staging room and had sat at the table, her head in her hands, too sad to cry. And then, the thought had hit her. She could open a portal high in Earth's atmosphere and jump out of the portal. Hoping to complete the task before Mark could stop her, she had opened a view on her desktop to the Bora Bora Pearl Beach Resort in Tahiti where she had spent a wonderful week three years previously.

She had pretended to be enjoying the views of the resort for a few minutes and then had abruptly moved the view to five thousand feet above the resort. She had held her breath for a moment as she had opened a portal at that location on the wall behind her, and had turned to see if Mark would really allow her to open the portal, but he had. Without hesitating, she had hurried to the portal and then had come to a screeching halt at the precipice.

The Pearl Beach Resort looked so small from five thousand feet. She wondered if it would hurt when she hit the ground. Her mind dismissed that notion with the cold fact that she would die instantly upon hitting the ground at terminal velocity, feeling nothing. Looking behind her to be sure that no one was going to try to stop her, she found that the angel's staging room was still empty. She knew that she didn't have long though. By now, Mark had certainly alerted Sam to her intent, and he was rushing to save her. Even worse, Sam would bring Margie and Connie with him. They would cry and beg her not to jump. She couldn't put them through that. She had to jump now.

Still, she couldn't bring herself to jump. "You aren't doing it to die," she reminded herself out loud. "You are going to still be alive. You're not committing suicide."

The sound of the door of her angel's staging room opening from beyond the portal galvanized her into action. Instantly, she leapt away from the platform, out of reach of even the fastest person that might try to reach out and save her. As she accelerated toward the Earth, she rotated a little, looked back up at the portal, and saw a tiny figure in white standing in the portal. Whoever it was, they had been too late to stop her. And now there was no going back. Wrapping her arms around her chest to keep warm, she fell even faster toward the beautiful aquamarine water just off the shore of the resort. The wind whipped her eyes and made them tear up so much she finally just closed them. She smiled as she tried to guess what scene Rick would call up for her in the portal room back on the station when it was her time to pass on.

CHAPTER 60

"**S**AM, IT'S MOVING!" Connie said with her eyes riveted on the sheet that still covered Rick's body parts on the table. Sam turned to the table and within moments was rewarded by seeing parts of Rick's body aligning themselves anatomically under the sheet.

Connie said, "It's so eerie. It's like watching a horror movie."

"To me, it's the power of God at work."

Sam walked over to the table and pulled back the sheet, revealing Rick's head and upper torso. His right eye was closed, but his left eyelids were missing. The left side of his face was crushed in and bits of skull were showing through where the flesh had been torn away from the bone by the force of the explosion. His whole chest was crumpled in; torn muscle and bone were showing here and there, and he wasn't breathing.

"Oh, Sam. He looks terrible."

"Just watch." Sam stepped back from the table and slipped his arm around her waist.

Moments later, Rick began breathing on his own. As Connie watched, the bones of his face and chest audibly ground back to their correct anatomical locations, and just moments later, muscle and then skin began growing over the previously denuded areas. As soon as the scalp reformed over the now-healed skull, hair began to grow on his head at a rapid rate. His lips became pink again and his cheeks rosy, like he was only asleep and had never died. Rick's eyes popped open. He looked around for just a moment and then sat upright abruptly, the sheet falling to his lap.

"Connie. Sam," Rick spoke, his voice clear.

"It's good to see you again," Sam spoke in his usual calm voice.

Connie was not as reserved. "Rick. You're alive." With tears in her eyes, she flew to him and gave him a massive hug.

Rick laughed. "It's good to see you again, too, Connie. And I have to say that your time on the station has been very kind to you. You don't look a day over twenty-five. Is there something that you aren't telling me, or is it just makeup?"

"Always the funny guy, aren't you? Sam and I got married while you were in the world of spirits."

"Congratulations. That would make anyone look younger." Rick turned to address Sam. "I'm feeling pretty bare here with just this sheet around me."

"Hang on while I explain," Sam said. "I know this is really bad timing, what with you just being brought back from the dead and everything, but Amanda just jumped out of a portal over Tahiti. I rushed to save her but arrived too late. I guess after spending hours watching people being reunited with their departed love ones in a portal room, she decided that she wanted to die so that she could join you in the world of spirits."

"What?" Rick said. "I'm back here now, and she's headed for the world of spirits? Am I too late to save her?"

"Yes and no," Sam said.

"What do you mean?" Rick said.

"You'll need to jump after her to save her. It needs to appear to be as natural of a rescue as possible."

"You want me to jump off of the station just like her? Won't that kill me?"

"If you died on impact, then that wouldn't be much of a rescue, would it?"

"Okay. I'll trust you. I just need a swim suit, and I'm ready. Amanda needs me, and Tahiti sounds nice."

"I just happened to bring along a pair of swim trunks right here in my pocket," Sam said. He pulled out a pair of navy-blue swim trunks, handed them to Rick, and directed him to change in a nearby closet.

Once Rick was in the closet, Connie said, "Sam, you knew Amanda was going to jump, didn't you? You knew that Rick was going to die and that you were going to bring him back alive. You even knew that Kurt was going to try to blow up the station. You knew all those things, and yet you let them happen. It is a strange way of getting things done."

"I had to let Kurt prove to us that he was evil. I couldn't condemn him before he acted because intent is not a sin. If we were all judged by the fleeting intents of our hearts that we quickly chose to ignore, then we would all be condemned to hell. Once Kurt finished doing all that he did, then I had to get busy putting everything back together again, as best as I could."

"I wish you could have just sent him to spirit prison in the beginning. Then we wouldn't have had to go through all this suffering. But how did you know what he was going to do before he did it?"

"The more perfected a person becomes, the more they are allowed to see into the future. Don't worry. I know what you're thinking. We can't travel in time. However, as a translated being, I can see dimly around the corners of life ahead, allowing me to keep myself and those that I care for safe. In contrast, God, as perfected as he is, can see clearly far into the future."

"That is so fascinating. You'll definitely have to tell me more about that later."

The closet door burst open, and Rick joined them in the center of the room in his new swimsuit. Connie couldn't help but notice his nice physique. His skin was flawless and golden brown, making him look a lot younger.

Rick said, "I'm ready. But, Sam, you said 'yes and no' to my question about whether I was too late to save Amanda. What is the 'yes' part?"

"Let's just say that you're going to have some convincing to do," Sam said. "There's no time to explain. You don't have a moment to lose if you're going to save her." A portal opened just to Sam's left. "Your portal is waiting, sir." Sam gestured to the portal with his head tilted forward and a smile on his face.

"Some ride you're giving me. It's straight down!" As Rick was speaking, he quickly passed through the portal and jumped without hesitation, even before he finished his sentence.

CHAPTER 61

MARGIE WAS SEARCHING the information in the computer system for news of the tsunami. Strangely, there had been no mention of the tsunami by the media outlets on Earth. Puzzled, she asked the system to display the tsunami that was supposed to kill five-million people in New York City. Sure enough, the massive tsunami had occurred and had been traveling toward the eastern seaboard at a hundred miles an hour. On the other hand, the news media outlets on Earth were all abuzz about the once in a lifetime appearance of seven bow echoes all along the New England coast. A bow echo was a massive half-circle of thunderstorms with a tremendous downdraft of wind in the center of the half-circle that then shot away from the half circle like an arrow from a bow. Margie instructed the system to bring up an image of the seven bow echos on top of the image of the approaching tsunami and had been amazed to see that each of the seven bow echos was aimed right at the leading edge of the tsunami. The bow echos had been whipping up tremendous waves that had been slamming into the tsunami. As a result, the tsunami had progressively diminished in intensity. In the end, the tsunami that was supposed to have decimated New York City had ended up just flooding some of the lower-lying city streets.

It had to have been Peter. "Peter, you are such a little devil," Marge said out loud. Immediately feeling a little guilty for referring to Peter in a less than a reverent way, she quickly looked around her staging room to be sure that no one was there to have heard her. She was still alone. That resolved, she returned to the images in front of her.

Peter must have gotten through to God. The tsunami had been all too real and could have only been stopped by a miracle. Margie quickly had the system check on her nephews. They in their homes riding out the remnants of the storms left by the bow echos. They were safe.

She was grateful that at least one of Earth's major disasters had been miraculously averted. At the same time, she was frustrated that other disasters, including the eruption of Mount Rainier, had been allowed to proceed without divine intervention. There just weren't satisfactory answers as to why God saved people from some disasters and not from others. She gladly put those frustrating thoughts aside and resumed writing her novel that she was going to title *The World's Greatest Love Stories*.

CHAPTER 62

RICK HIT THE water hard, but it didn't hurt. The velocity of his fall drove him fifteen feet under the water amidst a bloom of bubbles. As the bubbles cleared, Rick looked up at the surface of the ocean all around him, trying to find Amanda. The water was bathtub warm, and visibility was excellent. Amanda was nowhere in sight. He was a little confused because he pretty sure that Sam would have had him jump close to where Amanda had landed. Before shooting to the surface to look for her there, he checked around below him. Still nothing. As he turned his face upward to the surface, a distant flash of white caught his eye. He looked again and saw a dim form far below him, sinking out of sight. He swam hard toward what had to be Amanda. Her arms and legs were outstretched and weren't moving, and her hair was billowing around her face. He grabbed her in his arms and shot upward as fast as he could go. The shimmering surface was so far away. He became worried that he would run out of air before he made it to the surface, but he pushed that thought from his mind and kicked even harder. Sam wouldn't have had them go through all that they had been through just for Amanda to die in the end.

Rick broke the surface like a dolphin. Instantly, he positioned

Amanda in front of him with her face out of the water. Then, while treading water as hard as he could to keep them both on the surface, he pinched her nose and breathed into her mouth. The air went in easily, and he saw her chest rise. He gave her another breath and then looked at her face. Her eyes were still closed. She still wasn't breathing. He gave her two more quick breaths and then grabbed her around the chest with one arm, securing her back to his hip. He began side kicking for the shore. The shore was only one hundred yards away, but it took five minutes to traverse the distance because he had to stop every ten seconds and give Amanda two quick rescue breaths. He had no idea if she were alive or dead, and he couldn't check for a pulse while he was treading water.

Finally, he felt sand under his feet. Quickly rising, he plucked Amanda from the water and carried her to a dry area above the reach of the waves. Putting her on the sand, he went to resume rescue breathing when she suddenly coughed up a ton of sea water and opened her eyes. She was alive! He rolled her on her side as she continued coughing.

"Amanda. You're alive." It felt so good to see her again, even though they had only been apart for a few days.

Amanda's coughing slowed, and she opened her eyes, trying to focus on Rick's face. Finally she spoke in a hoarse voice, "Where am I? What am I doing on this beach?"

"Amanda, you jumped off the station. Don't you remember?"

She blinked and looked hard at his face. "I don't remember jumping off anything at all." She paused and struggled to get up on her elbows. "Do I know you?"

"Of course you do, Amanda. It's me, Rick."

Amanda sat up and pulled her wet shirt down over her partly exposed abdomen. "I have never seen you in my life. You must be mistaken."

Dumbfounded, Rick opened his mouth to speak, but he couldn't think of anything to say. Had she suffered amnesia from a head injury from hitting the water? If that wasn't the cause, then had Sam done something to her memory? What would have been his purpose in doing that?

Looking around, Amanda said, "How am I on this beach? How did I end up wearing this outfit that I don't recognize. And, why am I soaking wet? The last thing I remember was being on a plane that was preparing for landing in Seattle."

Rick was totally confused. "I jumped off of the station and rescued you just a few minutes ago. You were unconscious when I found you, and you were sinking like a rock. A few seconds more and you would have been fish food."

Amanda struggled to her feet. "Thank you for rescuing me, if it really was a rescue. How do I know that you aren't a trafficker in human slaves and that I nearly drowned trying to escape from your ship? How else do you explain how I was preparing to land in Seattle one second and then I wake up on a tropical island?" She paused and looked down the beach for a moment. "I recognize this place. I stayed on this very beach two years ago. The hotel that I stayed at is just a few hundred yards away." She turned and began walking purposefully down the beach, away from Rick.

"Wait, Amanda," Rick called out as her followed after her.

Amanda turned. "Hey, I'm grateful that you rescued me, if what you say is true. For that you are a hero. But now, unless you want to creep me out and ruin your moment of glory, let me go." Amanda continued walking up the beach.

"But…" Rick stopped. Amanda clearly didn't want him around. *What choice do I have but to stop following her? How could this have happened? It has to be Sam's doing. But, if that's the case, then why didn't Sam erase my memory also? At least then it wouldn't be hurting so bad to stand here and watch as the girl of my dreams walks away from me without looking back.* Memory of their time together on the station flooded his mind. He just couldn't let her go. Running after her, he yelled out, "If I am just a stranger on the beach, then how do I know that you're an internist at the University of Washington Medical Center? I know that you were born in Concord, New Hampshire and that you went to Penn State in biochemistry. You fell in love with Seattle after you did your internal medicine residency at the University of Washington Medical Center and decided to stay in Seattle."

Amanda stopped dead in her tracks. She turned slowly toward Rick as he approached. "Anyone could have looked that stuff up on the internet."

"Okay, how about when you were six years old and you thought your puppy was stuck outside in the middle of a winter night, but when you went to check on your puppy, you got locked outside? No one heard you knocking. You were freezing to death. You prayed for help, and an angel whispered in your ear that the basement window…"

"Stop," Amanda said softly. She wiped away a tear that had formed in the corner of her eye.

Rick ignored her and finished, "… was open, so you were able to get back inside to safety. The next day, your parents told you it was your guardian angel that had saved you." He came to a stop six feet in front of her.

"That's not fair to use that story." She blinked back her tears. "It's way too personal. At the same time, there's no way you could have known about that. I've never told anyone besides my parents, and that was thirty years ago." She blinked back more tears as she retraced her steps until she was just in front of Rick.

"There's more. If hearing more will keep you from walking away again."

"You've got my attention. How do you know so much about me? Who are you again?"

"My name is Rick Jones. I'm from a small town just south of Seattle."

"That doesn't ring a bell. But we obviously know each other, or you would never have known that story from my childhood. How did we meet?"

"Oh, Amanda. That would take a whole book. And, even if I did try to tell you how we met, you wouldn't believe me. Especially since you don't believe in angels, even though you were raised Catholic."

Amanda smiled. "Wow. This is so freaky. It's like you've known me for years, but I don't remember a thing about you. Did I have a head injury or something? Like the girl in that movie *50 First Dates*?"

"No, it isn't quite like that."

"I'm sorry, but I just have to ask. Were we romantically... linked... in this life I don't remember?"

Rick blushed. "We liked each other a lot."

"Hum. I can't believe I went for a younger man. I usually date older men. How old are you?"

"Thank you for the compliment. I'm thirty-seven. You're the first person that has ever thought that I looked younger than my age."

"You don't look a day over twenty-five. I bet you get carded at bars all the time."

Rick laughed. "I never have before, although I don't usually have a lot of time to hang out at bars to find out."

"Well, then that makes you the youngest looking guy that I have ever dated. So if you know me so well, then what kind of tattoo do I have on my left lower abdominal area?"

"We were pretty close, but I never had the chance to see that part of your..."

"Then we must not have been very close because when I really like a guy, I am known for not holding anything back."

"Maybe I'm just old-fashioned about that kind of stuff. Maybe I wanted to wait until marriage or something like that."

Amanda laughed. "Okay, okay. You seem to have the right answers to all of my questions. You're still going to have to tell me how we met, even if it does take all day. I promise to have an open mind, even though I don't believe in angels. In the meantime, tell me about yourself. What do you do?"

"I'm an auto mechanic. I own my own shop in Kent."

"You're a what?" Amanda asked with her eyes wide and her mouth slightly agape.

Recoiling from the look of shock on her face, Rick instantly figured that she must consider uneducated auto mechanics to be the last people on Earth that she would be interested in. His old insecurities screamed at him to cut his losses and just let her go. Then he remembered that on the station Amanda had said that she didn't care that he was just an auto mechanic and that she liked him just for who he was. In spite of his raging insecurities, he knew he had to believe that she would still end up liking him again for who he was, just like she had before on the station.

"I said I'm an auto mechanic," he replied courageously.

"It was you that was in the dream that I had last night. Although, come to think of it, I'm not sure when the dream was. That's funny. Anyway, I dreamt that I met the man of my dreams and that he was an auto mechanic from Seattle. I don't remember anything else about the dream. Just that."

"Amanda, I am the man of your dreams. I'm in love with you, and you were once in love with me. I'll wait as long as it takes until you fall in love with me again."

"Oh, you will, will you?" Amanda said with a smile. "I've never been one to trust dreams, but in this case, I just might make an exception."

ABOUT THE AUTHOR

Derek Muse is married and has seven children and two grandchildren. He spends most of his free time with his family, but during the remaining moments left each week, he enjoys baking, ballroom dancing, walking with his wife, and throwing pottery.